Strange Fates

Also by Marlene Perez

Dead Is the New Black
Dead Is a State of Mind
Dead Is So Last Year
Dead Is Just a Rumor
Dead Is Not an Option
Dead Is a Battlefield
Dead Is a Killer Tune

The Comeback
Love in the Corner Pocket

Strange Fates

Nyx Fortuna: Book One

MARLENE PEREZ

www.orbitbooks.net

Copyright © 2013 by Marlene Perez
Excerpt from *Dark Descent* copyright © 2013 by Marlene Perez
Cover design by Lauren Panepinto, cover images by Shutterstock.
Cover copyright © 2013 by Orbit Books.

Orbit
Hachette Book Group
237 Park Avenue
New York, NY 10017
www.orbitbooks.net

Originally published as an e-book by Orbit Books
First print on demand edition: March 2013

Orbit is an imprint of Hachette Book Group. The Orbit name and logo are trademarks of Little, Brown Book Group Limited.

The publisher is not responsible for websites (or their content) that are not owned by the publisher.

ISBN: 978-0-316-25156-3

Printed in the United States of America

Contents

For my mother. I miss you every day.

Fortuna audax iuvat—Fortune favors the bold

Chapter One

The dank bathroom smelled, the stench thinly disguised by a lonely pine-scented air freshener that had probably been there since the club first opened.

I'd been at the bar nursing a beer since six, waiting for somebody who had information I needed. After I figured out my guy wasn't going to show, I'd drowned my disappointment with several shots of the Red Dragon's cheap whiskey, and now I was paying for it.

I started to push open the stall door, but a couple stumbled in, obviously looking for more privacy. The Red Dragon men's loo wasn't my idea of a romantic interlude, but whatever rocked their boats. I peered through the crack in the door to make sure they were decent.

The guy, a hipster-looking dude with a supercilious attitude, said something I didn't catch, but I heard the girl loud and clear.

She was tall and curvy, with ice-blond hair, the rare shade of white blond that nowadays almost always came out of a bottle. Her eyes were probably blue, I speculated.

A glimpse of her heart-shaped face propelled me forward,

but I forgot the door in front of me and banged my shin in the process.

"There's someone in here," she said.

I took another peek. God, she was gorgeous, but I'd met plenty of gorgeous girls. The spark of mischief in her eyes called to me. I'd bet the last hundred in my wallet that trouble followed her like a cat after cream. I wanted to get to know a girl like that.

Apparently, so did her date. "It's just some drunk," the guy said. "He won't even know we're here."

"I changed my mind," she said. "Let me go."

The guy smacked his lips a couple of times, which grossed me out no end. It was a good thing my stomach was empty, especially when I heard his sales pitch.

"C'mon, baby," he said. "You know you want to." Charming.

The girl pushed him away. "I said no, Brad."

"And I said yes," Brad replied.

I stepped out of the stall, unwilling to be witness to Brad's borderline attempted date rape any longer. Besides, I kind of liked the idea of playing knight errant for a change.

"She's not interested," I said. I crossed to the sink, washed my hands, and splashed cold water on my face. There was something about the girl that bothered me, but I couldn't get a fix on it.

When Brad looked away, the girl kneed him in the groin so hard he fell on the floor, gasping.

Evidently, no knight in shining armor was needed. I liked her even more. I stepped over Brad's prone form and extended my hand to the girl. "Hi, I'm Nyx."

She took it and a tingle went through my hand and a few other places. I was wrong. Her eyes were green, not blue. Even better.

"I'm Meadow," she said. The lilting sound of her voice sent the vibrations through me again.

"Hippie mom?" I asked.

"No, lunatic," she told me.

It must have been clear I wasn't following, so she elaborated. "Lunatic mom, not hippie mom. My mom's way too young to be part of the peace generation. She did go through a grunge phase, though."

I ignored Brad's bitching and moaning and concentrated on Meadow. "Wanna get out of here?"

You'd be surprised how many times that line actually has worked, but I wasn't really counting on it to work on Meadow. Despite the fact that she'd been playing grab-ass with a creep like Brad, she seemed intelligent enough.

She smiled at me. "I don't think so."

"Listen, Nyx," Brad blustered from the floor. "Meadow is mine."

I raised an eyebrow. "She doesn't seem to think so."

"Wanna dance?" She gave me a smile so dazzling that my head spun.

I nodded and grabbed her hand and we exited the bathroom, ignoring Brad as we went.

The music hit my bloodstream as potently as any alcohol. I lost myself to the rhythm as Meadow swayed in front of me. Heads turned to enjoy the view. I couldn't blame them.

The tap on my shoulder wasn't completely unexpected. I knew Brad would come looking for us eventually. His hurt pride wouldn't allow him to slink off, no matter how much the kick to the balls had made him want to.

I took my time turning around. Brad would probably take a swing the minute I did and he didn't disappoint me. Mortals were so predictable.

I ducked and his fist slammed into the dancer behind me.

Dancer-dude shoved a burly-looking guy, who flew into a couple making out. That guy moved his girlfriend out of the way and shoved the burly guy. Burly guy flew into a group of girls and they shoved him back into the crowd. Burly guy bounced around like the ball in a giant pinball machine. Pretty soon there were punches being thrown wherever I looked. Two girls rolled around on the floor, pulling each other's hair. That's when it became a serious bar fight.

I looked around for Meadow but couldn't see her in the brawling crowd. I finally spotted her as she made her way to the bar, but then I lost sight of her when Brad took another swing at me. That punch connected to my jaw. I bit my tongue hard, and blood spurted into my mouth.

I grinned at him and hit him in the gut. I was no longer a tearstained child, drenched in my mother's blood. Blood didn't frighten me any longer. Time had hardened me. I wasn't just a survivor. I was a fighter. There was a knife hidden in my boot, but I didn't need it to fight a mortal.

Someone slammed into me and I lost my balance, but I was holding my own. I'd learned to fight a long time ago and I'd learned to fight dirty. Things were going well, too well, it turned out. Someone behind me hit me over the head with what felt like an anvil, but was probably just a barstool. I went limp as the world exploded behind my eyes. I shook it off and tried to stand, but that douche bag Brad put a knife in my heart.

And I'm not exaggerating the excellence of his aim. His blow went straight to my heart. It should have been a killing blow, but instead it felt like my heart was being squeezed by a giant fist. I stood there staring at him like an idiot as my blood dripped onto the floor. My aunts always said that I'd come to a bad end, but that was more of a promise than a prophecy.

"Was she worth dying over?" Brad stood over me. "I guess you'll never know." Ah, there it was. Although luck was always on my left shoulder, calamity kept her company on the right.

The world wasn't any better or any worse today than it was two hundred years ago. Mortals still killed each other in the name of their god, money, or sex.

Some things never changed.

"That hurt," I finally said, right before I passed out.

I bet you're wondering what kind of phony asshole I was or if I was crazy or high or both. I have been those things at one time or another, but that was the old me. The new me was one thing and that is truthful. I couldn't die, no matter how much I wanted to.

When I came to, I heard Meadow and Brad talking—arguing actually. I opened my eyes and saw two of everything, so I closed my eyes while I listened to their conversation.

"We can't just leave him," Meadow protested.

"I'm outta here," Brad said. "My dad will kill me if this hits the papers."

"I'm staying," Meadow said.

"Suit yourself," Brad said. "It's your life, what you have left of it."

If I ever saw that Brad guy again, I was going to curse him with an STD he'd never forget. I passed out again.

When I came to again, I was on the floor, but there was a guy taking my pulse.

"I'm an EMT," he said. I detected a slight slur to his words. He'd been drinking.

"Sure you are," I said.

"I'm off-duty," he said. Like I'd let a drunk corpse chaser work on me.

Meadow was kneeling there beside me, but there was only one of her this time. She was holding my other hand.

I sat up and almost gave the EMT a coronary. Brad was gone, which wasn't surprising. There were a bunch of people standing around me, but they didn't concern me. Meadow and the EMT had hopefully blocked me from the crowd's curious eyes—and if not, the dark bar and substantial amounts of alcohol that had been consumed would do the rest.

My jacket was on but my shirt had been ripped open, probably to get to the wound, but I didn't care about that. My rib cage ached and my jeans were smeared with blood. I touched a hand to my chest to make sure my mother's chain was there. It was made of such fine silver that most of the time I forgot I even had it on. I relaxed a fraction when I felt its weight, like a breath, light and warm, at the back of my neck.

"Your wound," the EMT said. "It's gone." I'd been skewered like a pig and would have another scar to add to my collection, but he didn't see that. I'd used a little magic to convince him otherwise.

"My jacket must have taken the worst of it," I lied quickly.

"Yeah, his motorcycle jacket is practically in tatters," Meadow said. "But he's barely scratched." It hurt to look into her green eyes. I realized what was familiar about her. She looked just like Amalie, but Amalie had been dead for a hundred years. I shook off the feeling of déjà vu.

I liked a girl who knew how to ad-lib. She had to see the gaping hole in my chest. I didn't have the strength to glamour both of them. I was intrigued by the matter-of-fact way she was handling my near-death. If I were a normal guy, that is. There was no way she could have known about me.

"It's not a motorcycle jacket," I replied. "It's a World War

Two fighter pilot jacket." There were healing amulets sewn into it. I needed the amulets before I passed out from the pain.

"I'll take him home," she said. "He'll be fine."

"Meadow's right," I said. Her momentary lack of recognition of the name confirmed what I'd already suspected. Meadow was definitely not her real name. Probably something she told losers like Brad.

"A scratch?" The EMT was dumbfounded. "But there's blood all over the floor, all over him, all over everything."

"Yeah, I bleed a lot," I said.

"He's a hemophiliac," Meadow said. For a minute, I thought she'd oversold it, but the EMT bought it. The crowd dispersed after they all realized there was nothing exciting to see.

I scrambled to my feet and grabbed my jacket. "It's been fun, but I've gotta go." The sharp pain to my heart reminded me how stupid it had been to make a sudden movement, but I needed to make my exit before the cops got there. Or someone much much worse.

On the way out, I didn't see any surveillance cameras, which was a relief and another reason I gave holes like the Red Dragon my business.

The street was deserted, but it wouldn't stay that way long. Bar fights brought the cops, usually with sirens blaring, so I took it as a good sign that it was quiet.

I looked younger than my driver's license indicated, but that was to throw off the Wyrd Sisters or anyone else they sent looking for me. They'd managed to garner quite a bit of information about me, including the fact that I liked a lager now and then. My current driver's license said I was twenty-five, but I wasn't sure it would stand up to official scrutiny.

I'd grabbed a handful of cocktail napkins, but I had a feeling they wouldn't be nearly enough to stem the blood flowing down my chest. Though I'd made it out of the bar without any problems, the girl caught up with me two blocks away.

"Wait up," she called out. I kept walking, hunched over from the pain.

The original goal of the night was to meet my contact and get wasted, but now I just wanted to get the hell out of Dodge. Or Minneapolis. At least long enough to lick my wounds. I'd need every bit of strength for what I had planned. Meadow, or whatever her real name was, stayed close on my heels.

"I don't know how to say this politely," I said. "But get lost." A strange girl who looked like my dead ex? That smelled like trouble.

I kept one hand firmly on my wound and tried not to think about how my blood was slowly soaking a cheap bar napkin. It had started to snow and I blew on my other hand to try to warm it. Minneapolis was cold as Hades, but I didn't think my aunts would expect me here.

"I know a safe place," she said, panting a little as she caught up with me. "You're fast. It took me a few blocks to find you."

I swayed and stumbled and she grabbed me to help me stay upright. I moved away from her. "I can walk on my own," I croaked.

"Suit yourself."

We walked in silence for a moment.

She was so close that our arms brushed and I could smell her fresh citrusy scent. It didn't seem like her. I had expected her perfume to be something that suggested smooth whiskey and rumpled sheets.

"My car's this way," she said.

I wasn't sure I could trust her, but I was definitely attracted to her. It had been a long time since I'd felt anything that strongly. I shook my head to clear it.

It was the floral barrette that decided it for me. It looked like it belonged on a third-grader. I went along with her, even though my instinct warned me against it. I could pick up my Caddy in the morning. I'd made sure no one would spot it and if anyone tried to touch it, they'd regret it.

"What makes you think I need a safe place to stay?"

"The fact that you only had fifty dollars, no credit card, fake ID," she replied. She handed me my worn leather wallet.

I shot her a look. "I had a hundred in my wallet, not fifty."

"I wasn't going to keep it," she said, offended. "I wanted to see if Nyx was your real name."

I hesitated. She was cute, more than cute really, and I barely had enough money on me for a bus ticket out of there.

"So what's your real name?" I asked.

"What gave it away?"

I'd surprised her. Good. "You aren't as clever as you think you are," I said. What gave it away was that she waited a beat too long before she answered to Meadow. "What's the con?"

"It's not a con," she replied. "I'll explain in the car."

The distant wail of sirens made my decision easy. The scenery would be better with Meadow than where the cops would take me. I seriously doubted I'd find out her real name. I didn't really blame her. Names had power.

For instance, Nyx wasn't my real name, either, but I had taken it after the last time Gaston had found me, and I'd grown fond of it. I'd found myself reaching for that name more than any other, giving it out as easily as normal people did their given names. Regular Joes handed out their true names like verbal party favors instead of what they really were, secrets they should guard with their lives.

We came alongside a cherry-red Lexus with a license plate that read ZOOM-ZMM.

Meadow opened the passenger door and gestured for me to get in. I slid in cautiously.

"*I* don't give people phony names," I told her. A lie, but she didn't have to know that. "You were Meadow earlier. What's your story?"

She shrugged. "My name is Elizabeth. My real name." She looked me up and down. "You should see a doctor."

"No doctors," I said. She didn't seem surprised. Was she a poor little rich girl who picked up criminals for kicks? Not that I was a criminal, but I wasn't the kind of boy you brought home to meet the folks, either.

"I'll take you to the cottage." She started the car and pulled out without bothering to look in the mirror. I winced, but it didn't slow her down. She gripped the wheel tightly, and I noticed her long slender fingers had nails that were bitten to the quick.

She drove without fear, taking the turns on the icy road with cavalier abandon. I didn't find it appealing, especially after she took a speed bump at fifty and my head went all fuzzy.

"Elizabeth, do you mind slowing down?" I said. I didn't believe that she'd given me her real name this time, either, but I liked the name Elizabeth.

She didn't answer, but she did slow down. When she turned a corner, though, jarring pain radiated out from my heart to my head. That was the last thing I remembered before I passed out.

Chapter Two

When I woke up, the car had stopped. Elizabeth was on the phone arguing with someone. I hadn't known her long, but I could already tell arguing was a habit. She saw I was awake and hung up with an angry snap.

"Let's go," she said.

I moved too quickly and got a sharp reminder I'd recently been stabbed. "I'll be fine in the car."

"It's twenty below," Elizabeth replied. "You'll freeze to death."

She opened the car door for me and slipped an arm around my shoulders.

I shrugged it off. "I can walk." I lifted my shirt and examined the wound. The amulets had done their job: The bleeding had turned to an ooze.

I climbed out slowly, stiff from being all scrunched up in the seat. I stood there on shaky legs and blinked in the cold moonlight.

The enormous three-story house in front of me must be the "cottage" she had mentioned. It was a mansion really. Only the wealthy would have the nerve to call it a cottage. Just beyond, a lake gleamed a silvery blue in the moonlight.

"Where are we?"

For a tiny second, it seemed as though she wasn't going to answer me. Wild thoughts of abduction and murder flashed through my mind. I knew I was being paranoid, but with relatives like mine, who could blame me?

"Lake Harriet," Elizabeth said, and when there wasn't a hint of recognition on my face she added, "Where we live. In Minneapolis. Minnesota." The sarcasm in her voice was hard to miss.

I shot her a dirty look. "I know where I am. I just didn't recognize this part of the city." Besides, I hadn't been out that long, not long enough to leave Minneapolis completely.

I wondered what I was getting myself into. I was pretty sure it wasn't going to play out like my new favorite fantasy, which involved Elizabeth, a bed, and a bottle of tequila.

I managed to walk inside without assistance, although it hurt to breathe if I moved too quickly.

The place was posh, with white marble in the entryway and long curvy staircases leading to what I assumed were equally luxurious bedrooms. I wondered briefly which one was Elizabeth's, but turned my attention to my host.

"Let's get you cleaned up," she said. I followed her to the kitchen. She gestured to a bar stool. "Sit down and take off your shirt."

"Why?"

"So I can ravage you," she said sarcastically. "Why do you think? So I can clean your stab wound."

I took off my jacket and shirt carefully, but a piece of my shirt got stuck on a bit of dried blood and Red Dragon cocktail napkin and I winced.

She grabbed a clean dish towel and ran it under the hot water.

"This is going to hurt," she warned.

"You don't have to sound so happy about it," I replied. She placed the towel on my chest gently, but I let out a whimper anyway. Not very manly of me. I couldn't be killed, but I could feel vast amounts of pain.

She escorted me to the great room, which looked like it was decorated by someone's rich old grandmother, but featured an outrageously expensive sound system and carpet so thick it felt like I was walking on pillows. I usually avoided places that smelled of money and smugness, and this place reeked of both.

I wandered over to the bookshelf and eyed the photos. Elizabeth as a debutante in a white gown, posed with a laughing older man and woman. Another one of a handsome young man with curly blond hair and brown eyes.

I picked up the photo of the young man to examine it more closely. "Attractive-looking guy," I commented.

She took the frame out of my hands and stared down at it, her expression unreadable. "Yes, he is," she finally said. She put it back on the shelf, clearly trying to tell me the subject was closed.

But I didn't listen. "Who is he?"

"It's my brother," she said.

"Your brother?" I wasn't going to get any more information from her, so I let the subject drop.

She was cute and I was definitely attracted to her, but a few hours earlier she'd been making out with the guy who stabbed me. It should have been a turnoff, but my libido didn't seem to realize that. I was reacting to the resemblance to Amalie.

"Nice place," I commented. "Is it just you here?"

Elizabeth hesitated. She took a seat on the comfy-looking sofa and I did the same. "No," she said. But she didn't elaborate.

I sat next to her, close enough that our legs bumped.

She changed the subject. "Would you like a shower? Something to eat?"

One of the rules of living on your own was to never turn down free food. The other was to watch your back. I had a feeling there was nothing free about my supper or this situation. She wanted something from me, but what? I decided to play along, for now.

My stomach growled and Elizabeth giggled. "I'll take that as a yes. I know a place that makes a mean burger."

She ordered the food and then said, "I'll show you where you can clean up before you eat."

The guest room was as luxurious as the rest of the house and had a killer view of the lake. The landscape hanging on the wall looked like an original Turner, and the four-poster bed had to be a couple of hundred years old. She handed me a towel and a robe and left.

I hung my jacket on the back of the chair—within easy reach—stripped off my jeans and shirt and threw them on the floor, and took a shower to get some of the crusted blood off me. I mumbled a quick little spell to further assist in the healing process.

Magic is hereditary. All the books in the world can't teach you magic if it's not in your blood. There was magic in my blood, strong magic. The magic of the great and powerful Wyrd family. My family's thing was that there were no boys born into the Wyrd line, only girls. Strictly matriarchal. Until me.

People in my family lived longer than most. And I would live longer than anybody. Whether I wanted to or not.

I was toweling off when there was a knock on the door. Elizabeth entered without waiting for a response. I grabbed a robe and put it on. I wasn't a prude, but I didn't want any questions about the scars that studded my body.

"Dinner's here," she said. "But I thought you might appreciate something clean to wear." She handed me some sweats and a T-shirt.

"I guess you can order anything for delivery these days," I joked, but I was wondering where they'd come from. They were well used but clean.

She cleared her throat. "They belong to my brother. He's…out of town."

"That's very hospitable of you." Very hospitable. Suspiciously so. Why would a young woman invite a total stranger home?

She seemed to read my mind. "I can take care of myself. Just because I'm friendly doesn't mean I'm stupid."

I nodded to let her know I understood. I waited, but she didn't show any signs of leaving, so I finally shrugged on the sweats and took off the robe.

She was staring. "Enjoying the view?" I asked.

"Yes," she breathed. "Yes, I am."

I felt too exposed, so I grabbed the tee and put it on. She was a complication I didn't need, but my body responded, even while my brain told me to run.

I needed to get out of that room and fast. "You mentioned food?" I said. "I'm starving."

I followed her down the stairs, enjoying the view the whole way. I finally remembered to check my libido at the door and make sure I wasn't walking into a trap.

"I thought we could eat in the family room," she said. "The dining room is so stuffy."

"Nice place," I commented. There were no signs of any magical allegiance. I had pegged Elizabeth as a mortal, but I'd been wrong before.

There were four Houses in the magical world, and all members were descended from a god. The old gods had faded away when Christianity took hold, but their progeny lived on, less than gods but more than mortals.

They eventually organized into the House of Fates, the House of Zeus, the House of Poseidon, and the House of Hades. Nobody knew where the old gods were now, but there were plenty of rumors. All that was left were the magical creatures, concealed from or ignored by the ordinary world.

There were bagfuls of delicious-smelling greasiness on the coffee table, but my gaze kept returning to Elizabeth.

She still wore that ridiculous floral barrette and I had to stop myself from unfastening it and running my fingers through her hair. She had a body it would take me a long time to get to know. She caught me staring at her.

"You look hungry," she said. "Eat. I ordered plenty."

If she only knew what I was really hungry for. I was instantly attracted to her, but I knew getting involved would be a bad idea. It wasn't love at first sight. I didn't believe in falling in love, especially not the first time you got a look at someone.

I mean, how could you see the sum of someone's soul by a quick glimpse into her eyes? I needed at least a dinner and a movie first. But lust at first sight? That I believed in.

She caught me staring and blushed. I was practically salivating over her, like a cartoon big bad wolf over a succulent little pork chop.

The burger was as good as promised, so juicy and tender I had to refrain from licking the plate. Once full, I realized I was incredibly weary. The knife wound throbbed, which reminded me how stupid I'd been. It had been nearly six months since the last contact from my aunts. It was almost like I wanted to be found, calling attention to myself that way.

Drifts almost covered the windows, which only added to the claustrophobic feeling. We were snowed in. I had to force myself not to think about how the white flakes slowly covering the windows made me feel like I was being buried alive.

I hated the damned snow and even more, I hated the feeling of being trapped. I was in Minneapolis to settle a score with my mother's killers and find my thread of fate. A thread of fate is your life force; when it's cut, you die. Problem was, mine was missing.

I was sure my thread of fate was hidden in one of my mother's charms. She never took that necklace off. It had disappeared after her death, when I hadn't been thinking clearly. I'd found the chain six months later, but the charms had already been sold several times over by then.

The silver chain was cold against my skin. I couldn't bring myself to touch the charm hanging on the end. It was the only charm I'd found. I'd been so sure that the diamond-studded key held the answer, but it wasn't the one I needed. The one hiding my fate.

"There are some board games in the game room," she said. "I'll go get them."

"I'll go with you," I said.

The game room contained a pool table and a bookshelf filled with the souvenirs of someone's childhood: Monopoly, Twister, worn baseball mitts, and a couple of adventure novels. There were several video game consoles and a television set up in front of an old couch. It was an adolescent boy's dream room.

"Did your family spend a lot of time in here?"

"We used to," she said. Her voice was clipped, signaling she didn't want to talk about it.

"What should we do to pass the time?" I asked.

She moved away from me every time I took a step closer to her. She didn't seem the nervous type. I was finally getting the idea that she didn't have the same activity in mind as I did.

"Video games?" she suggested. "I bet I can kick your ass in Zelda."

The game had barely booted up when the lights flickered and went out. I stubbed my toe on something and swore.

"Hang on a minute. There are some candles around here somewhere," she said. A match flared and her face came into view, looking ghostly by candlelight.

She handed me a candle and then lit a few more until the room was illuminated. She crossed the room and rummaged through the board games. "We can play until the lights come back on."

She set up the board on the coffee table and tossed me a couple of pillows. I knew she expected me to sit across from her, but I took a spot next to her on the floor.

I had thought of one way to forget all about my cabin fever. My rule was to never get involved, but I was a man, too, and it had been a long time since I'd touched a woman and even longer since I'd slept with one. One night with Elizabeth would be worth the risk. I'd leave in the morning before anyone could catch up to me.

I touched her face. "You have the softest skin."

She handed me the dice. "You go first."

I put the dice down, carefully. "I'm going to kiss you now," I told her.

"Nyx, this is a bad idea," she said in a small voice.

"You're not attracted to me?" I knew she was, but wanted to see if she'd deny it.

"It's not that. It's not a good idea to—"

"I think it's a very good idea." I bent and kissed her, maneuvering her toward the couch as I did. In the back of my mind, I wondered why my defenses were down, but the thought slipped away.

As I kissed her again, I heard eerie laughter. At first I thought it was just my imagination, but the sound came again.

"Did you hear that?" I asked.

"It was probably just the wind," she replied, but her voice was shaking.

"I don't think so." I went to the window and looked out, but the falling snow obscured my vision.

"There's no one out there, not in this storm," Elizabeth insisted.

"I heard something," I said stubbornly.

I listened again, but there was only the sound of the wind roaring through the trees. By the expression on Elizabeth's face, the mood was ruined.

"I think you should go."

What had her so spooked?

"There's a storm raging outside," I said. "Where would I go?"

She relented. "Okay, but you need to leave in the morning. Early." She kept glancing at the door when she said it. Was she expecting a boyfriend to come home soon?

A door slammed and a young woman walked into the room.

"Sorry, I didn't know you had company," she said. She was an attractive brunette with razor-sharp cheeks and fey eyes to match her pixie haircut. She had a drop of magic running through her veins, but so little that she probably wasn't even aware of it.

Elizabeth glared at her. "Well, I do."

I gave her an inquiring look and she made introductions. "Nyx, this is my roommate, Jenny. Jenny, Nyx."

I cleared my throat. "Nice to meet you, Jenny."

She ignored me and turned to Elizabeth. "If you're okay, I'm going to bed."

"We're fine, Jenny," Elizabeth said.

"Don't stay up too late," Jenny told her sweetly. But before Jenny left, she glared at me. I glared right back.

"You didn't mention you had a roommate," I said, after I was sure Jenny wasn't eavesdropping in the hallway.

Elizabeth shrugged. "I didn't think it was important." She grabbed a deck of cards. "Want to play?"

"Why not?" I grabbed the deck, cut the cards, and shuffled.

"Where did you learn to do that?" she asked.

"I lived in Monte Carlo for a couple of years."

"Where else have you lived?"

"We moved around a lot when I was a kid." Before she'd died, my mother and I had lived in too many cities to count. It wasn't safe to stay in one place for too long.

"We?"

"My mother and me." I studied my hand. I could have closed my eyes and told you what cards I had, but I didn't want Elizabeth to see my expression.

"What was she like?"

I cleared my throat, which had grown closed. "Great."

I had a clear flash of my mother's face, glowing from the light of the paper lanterns lighting the evening sky. We celebrated the summer solstice in Poland with thousands of strangers, but I wasn't the only one watching my mother's face instead of the sky lanterns.

I kept a suitable poker face and changed the subject. "Are we playing or what?"

We played several games, but she showed no sign of tiring. She didn't show signs of anything really. Most people had a tell, something that gave them away when they had a good hand. They tugged on their ears or leaned back in their chairs, something.

I regretted mentioning my mother, even briefly. The memories would be hard to keep at bay.

I stood and stretched. "I need some air."

"I'll go with you," she said quickly.

Outside, the freezing air cleared my head of things I was better off not remembering. There was a swing on the front porch and Elizabeth sat there. It looked way too inviting, so I took a backless stool across from her. A luminous moon hung low in the sky, but was slowly being blotted out by delicate flakes of snow.

I nudged the swing with my foot and set it to rocking. I touched her shoulder and brushed away a clump of snow. I was making excuses to touch her. "We should go inside," I said. "It's getting cold."

"I thought you wanted some fresh air," she said, exasperated.

I was twitchy. It was hard to stay in the same room with her and not get ideas I shouldn't have, even with a throbbing headache. I was in Minneapolis for one thing and it wasn't a girl, even one as beautiful as Elizabeth.

I suppressed a yawn. She took that as a hint and stood. "I'll see you in the morning."

Once in my room, I couldn't sleep. I crossed to the window

and stared out at the frozen water below before I finally crawled into bed and collapsed.

When I woke, the sun shone through the slats in the closed blinds. I looked around, disoriented, until I remembered the previous night's events and why I wasn't in my less-than-luxurious room at the Drake. My freshly laundered clothes were neatly folded at the foot of the bed. It bothered me that someone had been in and out of the room without waking me.

I got dressed and wandered into the kitchen, drawn there by the smell of frying bacon.

Jenny was standing in front of the stove. I could feel her scowling, even though her back remained firmly turned.

"Smells good," I offered tentatively. "I guess the power's back on."

She ignored my attempt at small talk. "There's juice and coffee in the dining room," she said. "I'll bring you in a plate." There were bar stools tucked neatly under the countertop in the kitchen, but I didn't press my luck and obediently went into the dining room.

I poured a cup of coffee and sat. When I spied a folded-up newspaper on the table, I grabbed it and scanned it for any description of last night's escapade. There was a small entry in the police blotter about the bar fight, but no mention of a stabbing.

From Jenny's reaction, I wasn't the first freeloader to stay the night. I wondered exactly how many moochers had crossed the threshold. My curiosity was soon satisfied.

Jenny handed me a plate with such force that my scrambled eggs nearly slid off.

I righted the plate and saved my eggs. "Where's Elizabeth?" I wanted to say good-bye before I left.

She paused. "Elizabeth is out shopping."

She wasn't going to tell me anything. The name did fall smoothly off Jenny's tongue, though. Maybe Elizabeth *was* her real name.

"I have my eye on you," Jenny said. She shot me a squinty look. "I know your type."

I looked up from my paper. "Exactly how many of my type have there been?" Her hostility didn't bother me. Compared with my aunt Morta, she was a walk in the park.

She gave me another look. "Six," she said. "There have been six others in as many weeks. All sponges. Out for what they could get."

I was lucky number seven. Interesting. Elizabeth had been here at least six weeks and had brought home six stray puppies. Who or what was she looking for?

"What does Elizabeth get out of it? Besides the obvious."

That stumped her for a minute. "She's kindhearted. Like me."

I nearly snorted coffee through my nose. Jenny seemed about as charitable as a cobra, but it was Elizabeth who really intrigued me. She was a strange mixture of street and sweet. You always had to watch the sweet ones.

Chapter Three

Elizabeth was back before I'd finished my scrambled eggs.

"No luck?" I asked as I scooped up the last bit of egg with my buttery toast. Crabby or not, Jenny was an excellent cook.

I looked up from my food just in time to catch the look the two of them exchanged. Elizabeth was tight-lipped and unsmiling.

She wasn't carrying any bags. I'd never met a girl yet who came back from a mall empty-handed, at least not the ones with money to burn.

When she shrugged off her coat, I could see she wore a low-cut top and a tight skirt. Her hair was slicked back, and the floral barrette had disappeared. It was the little things that changed her into a completely different person. Actors often had that same ability to transform into someone else at the drop of a hat.

Mom and I had spent the summer I was twelve working for a traveling theater troupe that, ironically enough, was performing "the Scottish play." Mom always said Shakespeare hadn't gotten much right, except that they were witches. She'd also hinted that Shakespeare had had a crush on my aunt Nona.

When we were on the run, my mother would only use magic as a last resort, for fear her sisters would sense it and use it to track us down. I stuck to the same rules. No sense asking for trouble.

"No luck shopping, he means," Jenny said, breaking my reverie. Idle conversation, or was she letting Elizabeth know what alibi she'd given me?

I was a suspicious bastard the best of times. My gut told me to cut and run. "Thank you for the hospitality," I said. "But it's time I go."

"Do you have to leave?" Elizabeth fiddled with her purse strap.

"Why did you bring me here?" I asked.

She hesitated. "I felt responsible," she said. "I mean, because you got stabbed."

"You didn't do it," I said. "And I feel much better today."

Although I felt the same pain as anyone, I did mend quickly.

"We thought you could stay with us for a few days," Elizabeth said. "Just until you get on your feet. Unless there's somewhere else you have to go? Family or friends?"

"There's no one," I said. "But I can't stick around." She couldn't seem to make up her mind if she wanted me to stay or to go.

I'd learned a long time ago not to try to tell anyone the truth about myself. The one time I did, I'd ended up involuntarily committed to a mental health facility. But back then, there was nothing healthy about the place I'd been. I shuddered at the memory. That was the last time I'd opened my mouth about living forever. Or close enough. I'd live until I found my thread of fate or my aunts did.

Being an immortal was like walking around talking in a language that nobody understood anymore. My aunts were the only other people I knew of who'd lived for centuries. My mother had been the only one in history who had been ballsy enough to try to outwit her sisters.

I had a plan when I came to Minneapolis. I'd been alive a long time and Minneapolis in winter seemed like the perfect place to die, but on my terms, not anybody else's.

Elizabeth was a complication. She intrigued me, which was an emotion I hadn't felt in a long time. But I didn't need complications. I needed revenge.

"Why not?"

"I need to find a job," I replied.

"We'll find something for you to do," Elizabeth promised.

"Like what?" I raised an eyebrow. I wasn't exactly employable, at least not doing anything legal.

She paused, a bit too theatrically.

"Why don't we have him sort through Mr. K's papers?" Elizabeth asked, too casually.

"That's a great idea!" Jenny replied without any hesitation.

It was tricky, practiced spontaneity, and she didn't quite pull it off.

"I haven't even said yes yet," I said. "And what kind of papers are we talking about?"

"Historical documents," she replied, like that cleared it up for me.

"I'll think about it," I replied. "In the meantime, I need to go out to pick up a few things."

They were both staring at me curiously, so I added, "Smokes, maybe a razor." I didn't smoke. They didn't need to know where I was really going, which was out the door as fast as I could.

Bolting was kind of a shitty thing to do, considering Elizabeth had given me a place to stay, but I didn't have the energy for a scene. She was clearly used to getting her own way.

"Why don't you stay here until you make up your mind?" Elizabeth said, "It's almost four. I need to make a call anyway."

Four P.M.? I'd slept most of the day away. It didn't give me much time. I was almost out of cash.

I went back to my room and took a long hot shower. The chest wound looked like it was healing pretty well, but it hurt when the water hit the crusted wound.

After I toweled off and dressed, I noticed that someone had placed a bouquet of hothouse flowers in a crystal vase on my nightstand. I plucked a rose and inhaled. It was one of the soulless new strains that didn't have any scent, but it would have to do. I shrugged on my jacket and placed the rose inside my jacket, where it would be safe.

I wondered if I could find a place to make an offering. A place of magic and luck would be preferable, but I would settle for an altar to Lady Fortuna.

Nobody believed in magic anymore, anyway, unless it happened in the pages of a book.

Some people still believed in Lady Luck, though. My mother had many names. The Greeks called her Tyche. The Romans called her Fortuna. She was the fourth Fate, the youngest Wyrd Sister, Lady Fortuna.

There were few reminders of my mother's power floating around. I'd found altars in Vegas, Atlantic City, and the back rooms of several restaurants in San Francisco's Chinatown. I left an offering in every city. It was my way of remembering her.

I took a bus from the posh suburb where Elizabeth lived and got out a few streets from where I'd parked the Caddy. It started up right away. The car was my prized possession, a purple 1956 Cadillac Eldorado convertible, so I was relieved no one had messed with it. The wards I'd put on it would have discouraged all but the most determined vandals.

I cruised around Minneapolis, but finally ended up wandering into a bingo game at the Uptown VFW. Not exactly high-stakes gambling, but there was a certain amount of luck involved, so it would have to do. It was twenty dollars for fifteen games, which depleted my cash considerably.

I played a couple of games and won a hundred bucks. I didn't always win, but I was my mother's son, after all. I left the rose next to my board and collected my winnings.

A chill wind hit me as soon as I stepped onto the street, and I turned my collar up against the falling snow. My ungloved hands were already freezing.

I found a grocery store and picked up a razor, some chocolate, and a cheap pair of gloves. The store was nearly deserted, except for a bored clerk at the front. I was walking down the neat rows of canned goods, heading for the refrigerated section, when the lights flickered.

I froze when I saw a familiar figure reflected in the glass of the display case. He was blond, with watery blue eyes and pale skin. His nose, pink from the cold, made him look like a cuddly rabbit. In reality, he was the farthest thing from cuddly that I could think of.

Gaston, my aunts' errand boy, was a general pain in the ass. He was also a Tracker, one of the best. He could sniff out his prey better than any hound dog. He had just enough magic in his blood to be dangerous.

He turned, stared straight at me, and took a swig out of a bottle of orange soda. Gaston had been drinking nectar of the gods since he'd started tracking for my aunts. It kept him alive, but it also kept him crazy.

He flipped the bottle top over and over and I noticed the Parsi logo, or Parcae—another word for the Fates. My aunts were nothing if not subtle.

I tensed, waiting to see if my disguise had held. I'd dyed my hair, turning its normal brown to the color of black licorice. Just to be certain, I'd paid a bloody king's ransom for an occulo spell, which would hide my identity from anyone looking for me. The essence of what made me *me* would be concealed. The medicine woman I'd bought it from was the last one in America who could work an occulo spell.

It was impossible to hide the magic coursing through my blood, but the medicine woman had assured me that a casual observer would see a low-level magician from the House of Zeus, nothing more. "But you must be careful of the eyes," she had warned me.

"You changed the color," I objected.

"The eyes hold the secrets of the soul," she replied. "That is something a spell cannot conceal."

Sunglasses helped to conceal my eyes. I wore them whenever possible, but it worried me that the spell wasn't foolproof. Would it hold or would I find myself running from the Fates' Tracker again?

The spell held and Gaston paid for his purchases and left without giving me a second glance.

I added a lottery scratcher to my purchases. I would need all the luck I could get. The ticket was a winner, so I turned it in and pocketed the cash.

I'd obtained the occulo spell after Gaston found me last time. Despite the frigid weather, I was sweating as I remembered our last little visit. He had hunted me down on the beach on a remote island in the South Pacific. It belonged to some celebrity who had probably forgotten he even owned it.

I had been following a lead about a coral fish that the celebrity was supposed to have at his house on the island. The lead didn't pan out, which meant I hadn't found my mother's charms. I was almost certain that my thread of fate was hidden in one of those charms.

I'd decided to take advantage of the celebrity's absence and take a little vacation on his deserted tropical island. I never knew when my aunts would lash out at the nearest innocent bystander.

I had three aunts, all of whom wanted to kill me, but Morta was the one who wanted to make me suffer first.

I'd been lying on the beach, watching the fish dart through the azure water, when a shadow fell over me. I'd thought I would be safe there. I was wrong.

"Son of Fortuna," Gaston said. "Time's up."

"How did you find me?" It was too late to run.

But Gaston didn't try to kill me that time. He'd learned it wouldn't work.

Instead, he just gave me a particularly nasty smile. "You know what I want. Just give it to me and your aunts will leave you alone."

"I don't have it. How many times do we have to go over this?"

"As many as it takes," Gaston replied. "Your aunts' patience is wearing thin."

"Tell the Wyrd Sisters that I don't have what they're looking for," I said. "And even if I did, I wouldn't tell those hell-ridden hags."

He shrugged. "Suit yourself. I'm just here to deliver the message." My aunts. The three Fates: famous meddlers, witches, and keepers of the threads of fate for the human and magical worlds alike. Nona spun the thread, Decima measured the thread, and Morta cut the thread of fate, which ended a life. Only the gods were more powerful than the Fates, and they'd faded away a long time ago.

What many people don't know was that there used to be a fourth Fate. Fortuna, the sister who added a bit of luck to the mix. Fortuna, the forgotten Fate.

The human world was bereft of luck. Fate had killed luck and I had watched it happen. Her sisters had made sure my mother's role as the fourth Fate had been obscured by time, wiped from history. They'd torn down her legacy as surely as the pharaohs of old Egypt had destroyed their predecessors' temples.

Morta was the one who really had it in for me. She probably sharpened those scissors of hers, just waiting for the day she finally found the silver thread my mother had stolen and hidden. The silver thread that Morta was supposed to have cut when I was a baby, but my mother stole it and hid it away. The three witches had been looking for it, and me, ever since.

Morta cut my mother's thread when I was twenty, which was also the year I'd stopped physically aging. I didn't know why. I just knew I was stuck unable to die, probably forever. Or at least until I found my thread.

Shakespeare had been alive when my mother was born. In fact, he knew my aunts, which explained a lot about *Macbeth*.

I didn't want to think about that right now. I didn't know what I was going to do when I found my thread, but I didn't want them to make that decision for me. I'd never feel safe, not with those three hags at my back at every turn.

My mother lost her job the day I was born. Her family, my

three aunts, took one look at me and the evidence of my gender and promptly fired her. In the history of our family, there had never been a male born to one of the Sisters of Fate. Until me.

My hands clenched, but I managed to remain calm. "Deliver the message and get out of my sight."

I realized that Gaston had been speaking for quite some time. I'd missed part of it, but it seemed to be running along the lines of how much he'd relish the day my time was up.

"So you don't have anything new to say?" I interrupted him.

He stared at me, nonplussed. "Did you not listen to anything I have said?"

"Not really," I replied.

"Morta wants your head on a platter," he summarized.

I shrugged. "She's wanted that since the day I was born."

"This is different," he said. "I think this time she means it."

"I'm alone," I said bitterly. "She murdered the only person I've ever loved. There's nothing left."

He just chuckled. "Poor dumb son of Fortuna. Didn't you know? Your mother's little stunt won't save you for much longer."

"What are you talking about?" I asked. Mom never told me who my father was, so the only family I had in the world wanted me dead. "It's not like my mom had the chance to give me all the deets on the crazy relatives," I continued. "Since they killed her."

They couldn't kill me, but they could make my life pretty miserable. My aunts' job, as far as I could tell, was to play one giant game of Red Light, Green Light with the world. Morta's job, which entailed lots of slicing and dicing with those enormous golden shears of hers, was to give someone a permanent red light. She wasn't Death exactly, but those scissors of hers gave Death the signal where and when to show up. Morta would snip a thread and Death would mosey on down to collect the soul.

Gaston grinned evilly. "There are ways to make an immortal less, well, immortal. Very unpleasant ways. Make it easy on yourself and give me the thread."

"You've got to be kidding me," I said. My disbelief had made him laugh harder. "For the millionth time. I. Don't. Have. It."

He'd left me bloody and beaten, but alive. The worst part was that I could tell he really enjoyed his work. Half of the scars on my body were courtesy of Gaston, my aunts' Tracker.

Why had he let me go? Experience told me that it was only because my aunts had something worse planned for me.

I knew I wouldn't be so lucky next time. I needed to face my aunts. I'd been on the run for two hundred years. I was tired of running.

I came back to the present and realized I'd gripped the chocolate bar so tightly, it had snapped in half.

I was in Minneapolis, my aunts' territory. The Fates could live anywhere. Why had they chosen Minnesota?

It was time to fight. But although I knew I'd be fighting a war I'd be sure to lose, I needed to arm myself for battle. Gaston had said it himself. The aunts had power and I needed it. I knew exactly where to start.

Chapter Four

Seeing Gaston had shaken me up more than I wanted to admit. It didn't help that the Minneapolis snowstorm had turned into a full-on blizzard.

I was a stain on the family honor. The Fates were so furious at their little sister's betrayal that they expunged her name from the family tree, but they didn't manage to stamp out her name from history completely. My continued existence served as a reminder of their failures.

My aunts had no compunction about using humans to hurt me, which is why I could never get close to anyone. I'd learned that lesson the hard way.

They couldn't kill me because my mother stole the silver thread, the one that her sister had woven so carefully before I was born. The silver thread they wanted to snip when they found out that they weren't so omniscient after all, since their sister had given birth to a boy, something that had never happened in the history of the Fates. At least not a boy who had survived Morta's sharp scissors.

I came to Minneapolis deliberately, after getting a tip that my aunts had set up shop there. I knew they were here, but they didn't know I was, at least not yet. But they would. The Fates weren't all-knowing, but they were powerful and they had spies everywhere.

The rest of the world may have forgotten my mother, but I hadn't. I would avenge her death, find my thread of fate, and call it a day.

At some point, the hunted get tired of being the ones running and decide to do a little chasing of their own. The Fates were not immortal. Every few hundred years, the old Fate would step down and her daughter would take her place. But my mother's sisters, her murderers, were the ones I sought.

Since my birth, my mother had trained me in magic to prepare me for the day she wouldn't be there to protect me. It wasn't that she wanted anything to happen to her sisters. Unbelievably, to me at least, she still loved them.

But when it was them or me, she'd chosen me every time.

"Don't you regret it?" I'd asked her once. We were hiding on a tiny island, Capri, I think, when I was about eleven. I swam with the naiads. I was brown and happy and had forgotten the threat of her sisters.

Her mind was on other things, perhaps how to shield me from the debauchery going on around us. "Regret what, my little minnow?"

"Me."

The charms on her necklace chimed like little bells as she swept me into her arms, ignoring my awkward attempt to fend her off. "Never."

I let her hug me for a few minutes before I wiggled out of her arms, aware that I was no longer a child. I didn't know then how powerless I was.

Gaston would find me eventually, but I hoped it wouldn't be before I was ready for him.

I had stashed the Caddy and decided to hoof it the rest of the way. It was touch and go trying to get back to my room, since the storm had moved in quickly and I was stupid enough to be out walking in it. I'd already spent way too much time. Elizabeth had been a delightful distraction, but she was a distraction I couldn't afford.

I hadn't even made it four blocks before it hurt to breathe. It was so cold that every breath I took was like inhaling icicles. I wasn't going to make it, not at the rate I was going.

The cold was hampering my ability to think, but not so much that I didn't notice that someone was behind me, walking fast.

"Hey, hey, mister, wanna party?" A street kid, dressed in a ripped parka with ratty fur lining the hood, came apace with me.

His triangular-shaped face had that chapped-skin look of someone who spent a lot of time outdoors. Despite the parka, he shivered as he put his hand on his hip.

"You're trying to hustle me in the middle of a blizzard? Beat it, kid," I said. "I've got my own problems."

He sized me up. "Need a place to stay?"

"I'm good, thanks," I said through chattering teeth.

"Where you going?" he asked. "The Amsterdam? The Drake?"

My face must have given me away. "You'll never make it," he said. "I know a place. It's close."

"I don't have any money," I said. "Or anything else for you."

"It's cool," he said. "You can crash there tonight. I'm Jasper, by the way."

I was freezing my balls off so I nodded. "I'm Nyx. Lead on."

He led me to a rusted-out fossil of a car, which might have been a Mustang in another life. The car skidded its way through the icy streets. The backseat was piled high with blankets, canned goods, and clothes.

He parked on the street and we walked to a deserted military fort, which was surrounded by a barbed-wire fence. NO TRES-PASSING signs were prominently posted, but Jasper ignored them and slipped through a hole in the fence.

"Right this way," he said. He led me to a boarded-up brick structure. Someone had written DEAD HOUSE in graffiti across the outside of the building.

"It used to be a morgue," Jasper explained.

I was walking into a setup. Jasper had a touch of magic, enough to beguile, to charm, or seduce weak-minded mortals, but not enough to affect me. His clothes were free of any symbol to indicate an allegiance to a certain House, which wasn't surprising. He probably didn't even know he had any magic in his blood.

But underneath the magic, I sensed fear.

He wasn't ready to let me know about whatever it was that he had planned for me, but it wasn't going to be good.

He moved a piece of plywood covering a window. It had been pried open before and simply hung by a single nail to give the illusion it was secure.

"After you," he said politely. I stuck my head in, expecting to find Jasper's partner in crime waiting for me, but the room was empty except for the stench of old urine and mold.

I crawled through the window. Jasper followed and looked around with an air of coming home.

"The gurneys they used to move the bodies are still here," he said. "C'mon, I'll show you."

He gave me a tour of the place. For a military morgue, the place was surprisingly clear of ghosts. I didn't pick up on one.

Everyone talks about how ghosts feel cold, but they don't mention that it's more like a bite of frost in the blood. I'd seen more than my fair share of ghosts. They were everywhere, except here, in the place I expected to find them.

There was something there, waiting, but whatever it was, it wasn't a ghost. Somehow, the thought was not comforting.

We reached the room I assumed was where Jasper spent most of his time. He'd furnished it in late Dumpster diving. There were no windows in the room. A curbside-find sofa leaned drunkenly against one wall, and a small pile of canned goods was stacked near a camping stove.

"Have a seat," Jasper said. He waved at the couch, but I chose the broken-down lawn chair instead. Less comfortable, but it had a view of the door.

"So, you don't know anyone in Minneapolis," Jasper said. "No friends or family."

It was a statement that felt like a question.

"No one here to care if I live or die," I replied. It wasn't exactly a lie. The Sisters of Fate would dance a jig if they heard of my demise, but I wasn't going to share my family problems with total strangers.

The thing waiting was getting impatient. I could feel it stir. It sent prickles down my spine, but as suddenly as it came the sensation was gone.

"I should be going," I said.

"No, don't go!" He sounded alarmed. Why would my departure warrant such panic? I gave him a questioning look.

"You can't go out in the middle of a storm," he added. "You'll freeze."

"My jacket's lined," I said.

His eyes gleamed with avarice when he looked at my leather jacket. He was mostly human, but I could sense his magical blood. His intentions were obvious. He would wait until I was sleeping and bash my brains in and steal the jacket. Or something like that.

There wasn't much I could do in weather like this, anyway. He was a scrawny human. I could take him in a fight.

"I'll stay," I said. "Thanks."

He heated up a can of soup on the camping stove and put two cups on the steel gurney he'd been using as a coffee table.

"We can eat on this," he said. He poured the soup into two chipped coffee mugs, and we ate in silence.

I fished in my pocket for the chocolate I'd bought earlier, unwrapped it, and handed him a piece. "It's not much of a dessert."

His face lit up. "Chocolate," he said. "I haven't had chocolate since last Christmas." He gobbled his piece down with enthusiasm.

"Here," I said. I handed him my half of the candy bar.

"Are you sure?" he asked.

His face had the radiant look of a child. It wouldn't have been difficult to get him to do my bidding. I wondered what his master had given him. I hoped it was more than a few pieces of candy.

It had grown dark while we ate. Jasper lit a candle with the flame on the camping stove and turned off the burner.

"I know something that will improve your mood," he said.

"What's wrong with my mood?" I wasn't used to anyone paying attention to my emotions.

"You seem tense," he commented. "Just relax. I'll make you something to drink. Then we can talk about what's bothering you."

I stifled a harsh laugh. Seeing Gaston had stirred up bitter memories, but it wasn't anything I wanted to share, especially with a pseudo-solicitous runaway.

He went into another room and came back with a bottle of cheap vodka and a liter of soda.

There was no way I was going to drink the roofie he had planned for me. Poor Jasper. He thought he was being so deviously clever, but his intentions were clear to anyone who had the brains to truly see him.

On the inside, he was a scared child, clearly being bullied into this by someone bigger and stronger. Changing what you looked like on the outside was easy. Changing the person on the inside was considerably more difficult.

I'd learned over time that what made Gaston such a great Tracker was his ability to see beyond someone's exterior. Instead, he hunted by spotting patterns in someone's behavior, learning to think like his prey, and striking.

My first attempt to alter my patterns of behavior didn't end well. No cities by the sea. No major metropolis. Instead I found a tiny landlocked town and rented a room above a butcher shop.

The smell of fresh blood was bad enough, but it was the sound of the butcher sharpening his knives that really got to me. There were nights that the sound of a blade striking against stone gave me nightmares. It reminded me of the sharp *scrick* of Morta's scissors as she cut my mother's thread of fate. I lasted three days there before I moved.

Jasper broke my reverie by handing me a drink in a jelly jar.

He took a seat on the sofa. "Cheers," he said. He drank his down in one gulp and waited expectantly for me to do the same. I didn't have to take a sniff to confirm that the drink was spiked. The interesting part was that it was a magical concoction, well beyond his limited talents.

"Sorry, I don't drink," I said. I handed him the doctored booze. "Have mine."

I wasn't surprised when he declined the offer.

"I think I'll call it a night," I said. I would leave in the morning, before he was up.

"But it's early," Jasper replied.

I yawned unconvincingly. "I'm beat."

He reached behind the sofa and came up with a couple of bedrolls. He handed me one.

I made a pallet and tried to ignore the dark stain on the sleeping bag. It could be coffee or vomit or any other bodily fluid, but I knew what it was. Blood. Scrawny little Jasper was into some nasty business, but I got the impression it wasn't altogether willingly.

I spent the next few hours staring at the ceiling, waiting. I took off my jacket and used it for a pillow. There was a spiderweb in the corner of the ceiling and a piece of peeling paint in the shape of a duck. I waited for something that never came.

At about three, I dropped off. I dreamed of drops of blood and the terrible sound of a golden knife cutting a silver thread.

I woke to the sound of my own scream. I sat straight up and then realized where I was.

Jasper was gone, but there was something else there. My skin did that itchy, twitchy thing it did when I came across another non-mortal. I fell back onto my pallet and feigned sleep.

At first, I couldn't identify the creature that stood in the shadows. I realized what it was from the smell of rotten cabbage and decaying flesh.

Chapter Five

A troll was in the room, watching me from the doorway. That explained why I hadn't identified it right away. Trolls were rare. I had seen one once before, in Norway, by a fjord. Judging from the stench, this one had probably come up through the sewers. Or maybe they all smelled like that.

It also explained the lack of ghosts. Most trolls didn't care what they ate. Lost souls were as good as a steak to them.

Mossy and green, his toad-like eyes gleamed through the darkness as he crossed to my pallet. His fat tongue came out as he held up my arm and pinched my bicep. Despite the pain, I stayed limp.

A troll with a taste for human flesh. Exactly the kind of bullshit I didn't have time for right now.

A gob of drool ran down my face, and I decided that it was time to make my move. I didn't anticipate how hungry the troll was. He chomped down on my arm, but I moved at the last second and his teeth scraped my arm. He didn't manage to get a good grip, though, and I wiggled away and rolled onto my feet.

Trolls have jaws like enormous pit bulls. It was all over if he managed to get his teeth into me.

I ran for the door and the troll followed at a leisurely pace. He was fat and lazy. He'd gotten used to Jasper fetching his supper and he wasn't expecting a fight, which told me that Jasper had been too cowardly to tell the troll I hadn't slurped down the cocktail like the rest of his victims.

My jacket! I'd forgotten to grab it in my haste, but I wasn't leaving without it. The troll blocked my way.

I desperately cast my eyes around the room, searching for anything to use as a weapon. I'd never win if it came to a show of strength. He was about a hundred times stronger than I was, but fortunately I was about a hundred times smarter.

Magic was a last resort. I didn't want to advertise that I was in town. Instead, I grabbed the gurney and wedged it into his stomach. I grabbed the lawn chair and beat him over the head with it, but trolls have extremely thick skulls, to protect their tiny brains. I broke his nose, but he just grinned at me before he tossed the lawn chair away and advanced.

He wrapped one fleshy hand around my neck and squeezed until I thought my windpipe would collapse.

In desperation, I rasped out a little sleep spell—*dormite, dormite, dormite*—and he dropped immediately. I always got the words for sleep and death mixed up. Had I remembered the right words?

Apparently, I had remembered. The troll was unconscious, but alive. For a brief second, I thought about leaving him there for Jasper to find, but decided against it. The troll would have him back in thrall and bringing him victims in no time.

"Is it over?" Jasper's voice came from the other side of the door. "May I leave now, master?"

"It's over," I said grimly. "Now get in here and help me."

There was a long pause and the sound of a choked-back sob. He came into the room with the look of someone who expected a beating. "He's really gone?"

"Not yet, but he will be," I replied. The only sure way to kill a troll was to expose it to sunlight. The sunlight would turn our nasty friend into stone. At least I hoped it would.

Jasper chewed his fingernails nervously, and for the first time I noticed the small trident inked on his ring finger.

Trolls belonged to the House of Poseidon. They preferred somewhere dark, but near water. They loved dank caves, but would settle for any underground water system, such as a sewer or swamp.

We loaded the troll onto the steel gurney they'd once used to carry in dead bodies and wheeled him outside.

"What now?" Jasper asked. Relieved tears slid down his face, but he shook them away.

"We wait until sunrise," I said. "Unless you'd like me to leave you and troll boy here to continue with your little arrangement?"

He shook his head. "God no." He tried to suppress his sobs, but they bubbled out of him. Finally, he regained his composure enough to say, "He made me do it."

"How many?" I asked.

"Three," he said. "The first one was…messy." His throat worked and he suddenly leaned over and heaved out last night's soup.

Trolls ate every bit of their victims, bones and all. I imagined the crunch my bones would have made. They also had enormous appetites. It was likely that the number was more like three dozen, but I wasn't going to argue with Jasper when he was in this condition.

We stayed there until the first rays of the sun touched the troll's prone form and he turned to stone.

"Let's get some breakfast," I said. No wonder the kid was so skinny. Being in the thrall of a troll wore you out.

Jasper approached the stone troll and spit a huge loogie. "He killed my best friend the first night. He would have killed me, too, but he needed me."

"To bring him his dinner," I said.

Something changed in his face. "You're him, aren't you?" Jasper asked.

"Him, who?"

"The guy everybody's looking for," he said. "Fortuna's son."

It was a shot in the dark. There was no way he could know that.

"Who is Fortuna's son?"

"Dunno," he replied. "But the Fates want him. Word is he's supposed to bring about their downfall. They pretty much rule Minneapolis."

He had no idea. "I'm a minor magician from the House of Zeus," I said. I motioned to his trident tattoo. "I don't even warrant an insignia. Why did you think I might be this guy?"

"You knew how to kill the troll," he said. "I didn't."

I shrugged. "I read a lot. It doesn't take a lot of magic to outwit a troll. But I'm not looking to get noticed, if you know what I mean."

"You freed me," he said. "I wouldn't want to have the Fates take notice of me. I won't say anything."

I relaxed a fraction. The ring of gratitude in his voice convinced me. "What have you heard about Fortuna's son?"

"There's a bounty on his head," he said.

Old news. "Anything else?"

"The Fates have a new manufacturing venture," he said. "Right here in Minneapolis."

"Why Minneapolis?" I asked.

"Something about the water being perfect for it," he said.

"Perfect for what?"

"Something in research," he said importantly.

"What kind of research?"

"Something about a new flavor of orange soda. They're calling it ambrosia."

Sounded oddly benign for my aunts, but hey, witches needed to make a living, too. Except that ambrosia was also known as nectar of the gods, something that any mortal would kill for. In theory, ambrosia could extend a mortal's life, maybe even make him live forever. But it had been banned by all the Houses years ago because it caused madness in mortals, followed by an agonizing death. Even the aunties wouldn't want to piss off the entire magical community in order to make money. Would they?

Money was power, and power was the one thing my aunts loved more than trying to kill me. "Where did you hear this?" I asked.

"Some guy who worked in their labs," he said. "Alex told me the water was perfect for it."

"Alex? Was he one of your marks?"

"No, Alex was my friend," Jasper insisted.

"Where did you meet him?" I asked.

"Around."

I frowned at his answer. "Be more specific. I just saved your life."

"He used to volunteer at this soup kitchen on Nicolett. I'd cruise by every few weeks to pick up a bag of groceries and we became friends," he said. "He was working on something special."

"Special how?"

He shrugged. "I didn't really understand it, but it had something to do with the water."

I processed the information. My aunts were gathering wealth. Either that, or they just enjoyed the power over humans. "Anybody else know about this?"

"Nobody," he replied.

"Make sure it stays that way," I warned. "The Fates make that troll look like a teddy bear." He gave me a sharp look and I added, "Or so I've heard."

"Anything for you," he said. His look of hero worship made me squirm. I'd only disappoint him, eventually. Or get him killed. Or both.

"What now?" I asked him.

"I want to go home," he whispered. "I want to forget it ever happened."

I gestured to the car. "What's stopping you?"

His face blanched. "It's not mine. I don't want it. I never want to see it again." He broke into noisy sobs and I realized that he was even younger than he had first appeared.

"C'mon, I'll buy you breakfast," I said. "And we'll figure out what to do next."

He drove us to a restaurant called Hell's Belles, which was a few blocks from the Greyhound station.

The place was crowded with mortals and mages alike. All the tables facing the door were already occupied, so we had to settle for the counter.

"Funny," I said. The fry cook was a demon, and so was the waitress serving coffee at the counter.

"What is?" Jasper asked.

"The name," I said. "Hell's Belles, get it?" It was the perfect name for a demon-owned establishment.

He shrugged. "Not really," he said. He turned his attention to the menu.

The prices were reasonable, though. Jasper ordered like he hadn't had a decent meal in years. "And a hot chocolate, with lots of whipped cream," he added.

"Just coffee for me," I said.

The food came and the smell of hot biscuits and bacon made me regret not ordering anything. Jasper handed me one of his biscuits and shoved the little bowl of gravy at me. "You've got to try these."

The biscuits had been beaten into submission until they were melt-in-your-mouth fluffy. Everything was hot and fresh.

The diner gradually emptied out until we were the only customers left.

The older demon came over to refill my coffee. She had the eyes of an old basset hound, but the nose of a young one. She sniffed the air delicately. I hoped my disguise would hold. The coffee spilled over into the saucer as she scanned the diner, but she finally retreated to the kitchen.

"How long have you been in Minneapolis?" I asked Jasper. It was a long shot, but maybe he had some useful information, besides the fairly old news that my aunts were looking for me.

"About a year," he said. He shuddered, remembering. "Tank and I ran away, but all our money was gone within two weeks. We thought we were so smart, breaking into the old fort."

He stared into his hot chocolate for a long time, but finally roused himself. "You know the rest. What about you?"

"Just got into town," I said.

He leaned in closer and asked in a whisper, "How did you know? About the troll?"

"I felt him," I explained. "Trolls are predators. I know that hunted feeling like the back of my hand."

I glanced around cautiously, but we were the only customers. I was probably telling him more than I should have, but didn't they say confession was good for the soul? Besides, Jasper would be on the next bus out of town. I'd make sure of it.

He wrapped a couple of the biscuits in a paper napkin and put it in his pocket.

I wasn't hungry anymore, but I did the same.

"You're on the run?" he asked.

I shook my head. "Not anymore. No more running. I'm going to kill the people who murdered my mother and then kill myself." He didn't need to know the specific details, which were a little more complex. "I'm probably doing the world a favor."

He'd obviously heard it all before because my cold-blooded statement didn't even faze him. He bit into his toast. "Sounds simple enough," he said, between bites.

"It won't be." Major understatement. "Now finish your breakfast."

I paid the check and put a healthy tip under my plate. It's not smart to piss off a demon, especially if she's stuck waiting tables.

In the end, we drove to the bus terminal on Hawthorne, where I bought him a ticket to some Podunk city in Iowa.

"Don't come back," I warned. "And if you say anything…" I left the threat unfinished.

"I won't," he promised feverishly. He tossed me the car keys. "The Mustang's yours if you want it. If not, leave it for the tow trucks to find."

He sounded sad and I wondered what waited for him at

home if he was reluctant to leave Minneapolis. "It's for your own good."

He stopped at the bus stairs. "Nyx, a lot of shitty stuff has been done in the name of good."

This from a guy who'd lured several people to their deaths. But he had a point.

He boarded the bus and took a window seat. I stayed where I was until the Greyhound disappeared from sight.

Chapter Six

I left Jasper's car at the bus station and picked up my Caddy. Something pulled me back to the lake I'd seen from Elizabeth's house. I got lost twice, but I finally found her neighborhood. I parked the car a few blocks away and walked toward the water.

The storm had died, but the drifts were up to my shoulders in spots. The snow crunched beneath my feet as I walked. The tree branches were heavy with snow. I brushed against a pine and got a bunch of snow down the back of my neck for my carelessness.

Each step became harder and harder as I waded through drift after drift. I was so cold it was as if my bones had frozen.

What was compelling me to the lake?

It was more than sheer curiosity. It was if someone had called to me and I had to answer the call.

Finally, I reached the water. The surface was smooth and serene to the naked eye, but there was something in the black depths. Something waited. The ice in the lake cracked and boomed and I jumped.

I heard a whisper. "Little minnow," it said.

The sound came from the water's edge. "Show yourself."

The face of a naiad appeared. She was a blue so pale she was almost translucent, and her dark hair tangled about her shoulder like weeds. She had full, slightly fishy-looking lips, but I had to resist the urge to step closer to her.

Rivulets of ice water dripped off her face, but she caught them with her long silvery tongue.

"Come closer," she beckoned. "I'm cold. Keep me warm."

I wanted to do a lot more than keep her warm, but naiads were dangerously sexy. I had enough magical blood to resist her blandishments, but mortals could not.

"Greetings, Poseidon's daughter," I said, finally remembering the traditional greeting to water-dwellers. "None of your tricks, nymph," I added. I wagged my finger at her but was careful to keep out of her reach.

"Willow," she said. "You may call me Willow."

"Nyx," I said. I hadn't conversed with a naiad for a long time, but that summer on the island of Capri, we'd lived with a colony of friendly naiads. They had tolerated a miniature male in their midst for my mother's sake.

"Your heart belongs to another," she said. She pouted, crossing her arms over her chest. When she did, the necklace of worn stones she wore rattled. At least I thought they were stones. Some naiads liked to wear necklaces made of men's teeth to show how many they'd seduced and killed.

The rivulets of water turned to icicles, and she shivered.

True love was often the only thing that kept a man from death by naiad. Or so I'd been told. "No, my heart is my own," I said. "But I'm wise to your wily ways."

She turned to go, perhaps off to seek easier prey, but I stopped her. "Wait!" I said. "Willow, what's down there?"

"I'll never tell," she said. She giggled and put her hand on mine before she dove into the icy water without a backward glance.

I heard someone walking through the snow, swearing, and then Elizabeth was standing behind me.

"Who were you talking to?" Elizabeth asked.

Had she sensed the nymph's presence? Most mortals were clueless about magical beings, even when they were right in front of them. "I was talking to myself," I said. "Bad habit, I'm afraid. How did you find me?"

"I've been looking all over for you."

"Why?" I asked. I sounded suspicious.

"I need your help," she said. "Rather desperately. I need you to find my brother Alex."

"I'm not a cop," I said. "Or a private detective."

"I've already tried the police department and a detective. They didn't find anything." She stood there shivering and turning blue. Her eyes were swollen and red from crying.

I knew then I would help her, even though it was against my better judgment. That name, though—I'd heard it recently.

"You're freezing," I said. "Let's find some place warm to talk."

"What were you doing out here?" Elizabeth scolded. "The lake's not safe."

"I wasn't planning on a dip," I said. "It seems safe enough." No matter what the naiad had tried to tempt me into, I wasn't stupid enough to swim in frigid water.

"Well, it's not," she snapped. "People die in weather like this. Get hurt, disoriented, lie down to sleep and freeze to death."

I was already lost, disoriented. "I'm touched by your concern," I said sarcastically.

Did Elizabeth have any idea of what kind of magic was

guarding the lake? There was more than a water nymph living there.

"Let's get back to my house," she said. She tugged on my hand to guide me away from the lake.

My anger left as quickly as it had come. Even with swollen eyes, she looked cute in her red knit cap and mittens.

She let out a hiccuping sob and I pulled her close, just to comfort her, but the embrace changed into something else. I had to kiss her. It was becoming a habit, this need to touch her.

"You taste like honey," I whispered.

"My lip balm," she replied.

She was wildflowers and thistles, guaranteed to sting eventually. I kissed her again and we bumped teeth.

She removed her lips from mine, too quickly. "Are you going to stick around?"

"I've thought about it," I said.

She must have heard a warning in my voice not to press the issue, because she dropped the subject. "Let's go back to the house. You must be hungry."

"I've already eaten," I said. I grabbed her hand and she let me keep it. We walked back to the house hand in hand.

Jenny was pacing on the front porch, a lit cigarette burning to ash in her hand. "I see you found him," she said.

Elizabeth dropped my hand. "I found him."

"Where did he wander off to?"

"I needed some air," I said.

"For two days?" Jenny asked.

Sarcasm was lost on her, so I tried the direct approach. "How about it's none of your business?"

I glanced at Elizabeth, but she didn't comment.

I felt uneasy in my own skin. It had been a long time since

I'd been around people for an extended time. I'd been around them, I guess, but often I hadn't actually interacted with them.

Jenny ground out her cigarette. "I'm going to hit the gym," she said and went inside.

"Are you sure you'll be okay?" Elizabeth said.

I nodded. "Don't worry. I won't wander off again. At least not until you tell me about your brother Alex." I realized where I'd heard the name. From Jasper. Someone once said there were no coincidences. "I'm not making any promises, you know."

"I know." She sat down next to me, but was careful to sit far enough away that we weren't touching.

"About six months ago, Alex got a new job," Elizabeth began. "He's in R and D, cutting-edge stuff. My brother is brilliant."

"What's the name of the company he works for?" I asked.

"Parsi Enterprises," she said.

"What do they do?" For one thing, they bottled that sugary orange soda that Gaston guzzled down. I was almost certain that Alex had worked for my aunts. He wasn't their first employee to disappear and he wouldn't be the last, but it sent my nerve endings screaming.

"He never told me," she admitted. "He was secretive about his work, but he was in research and development."

She was silent, and I realized she was getting to something she wasn't looking forward to telling me.

"And then?"

"He was gone. Without a word."

"What made you think it was something sinister?" I finally asked. "Maybe he's shacked up in the Bahamas with some girl."

It sounded like the story she was telling me was true, but I couldn't be sure.

"Alex would never leave without telling me first," she said. "Not unless someone forced him."

"Family money?" I asked. It was a reasonable question. In my experience, people did horrible things for cash.

"Some," she replied. "But it's not enough to kill him over."

She might be surprised what someone would do for a few bucks.

"Can you think of anybody who would have a grudge? Ex-girlfriend? Someone Alex used to be friends with?"

"Everyone likes Alex," she said.

"What did you do after you realized he disappeared?"

She sniffled and looked away in embarrassment. "The usual. I called the cops, hired a private investigator, but nothing helped."

"Whose house is it, really?" I asked. "And is Alex really your brother?"

For a second she looked like I'd punched her, but she recovered quickly. "I'm sorry for lying to you. Alex is my brother and the owner of the house."

"Do you trust him? Your brother?"

"He would do anything for me," she said quickly. "He would never leave without telling me. Alex has simply vanished."

"So why were you inviting strangers into your home?" I asked her. Something about her story didn't make sense, but maybe I was missing something.

"What do you mean? You were injured. I was trying to help you," she said. The hurt in her voice made me feel like a jerk.

Jenny had let me know I wasn't the first stray Elizabeth had brought home, but I didn't want to bring that up now, not when Elizabeth's tears still clung to her eyelashes.

"I came to Minneapolis for a reason," I said. I didn't want to tell her too much. The less she knew, the better. "And I haven't accomplished that goal yet."

"I understand," she said. "I'll just have to find Alex on my own."

I thought of how I'd met her, in the bathroom of the Red Dragon with that sketchy guy Brad. "I'm not saying I won't help you," I said. "But you have to be honest with me."

She nodded. "That's fair."

"Are you okay here by yourself?" I asked.

"I'm not alone," she said. "There's Jenny." She hesitated. "You could stay here, too."

"Not a good idea," I said. I didn't want her anywhere near the trouble that was bound to start once my aunts realized I was here. I'd crash at the Dead House until I figured out something else.

"The offer stands," she said.

"What about your parents?" I said.

"They're dead," she said baldly.

"I'm sorry."

"What about you?" she asked. "Where are your parents?"

"Both dead," I replied. I actually had no idea about my father, but I assumed that after all this time he was gone.

"Were you close to them?"

"To my mother," I said. "I never knew my father."

"Tough to lose your only parent," she said.

I put my arm around her. "We're both orphans."

"Not exactly the best thing to have in common," she commented wryly.

I dropped my arm. "It's something," I said.

"Yes, it is definitely something." She took my hand and held it tightly. I wanted to hang on, to pretend, just for a second, that something more was possible, but there wasn't going to be a happy ending to my story, just a blood-drenched one.

Chapter Seven

Elizabeth stared out the window at the snow falling. I'd never realized before that there could be so many different ways for it to snow. This time, the snow was well behaved, dropping from the sky in dainty swirls.

The view was gorgeous, but I don't think she really saw it.

"Are you guys hungry?" Jenny asked.

"It's really coming down out there," Elizabeth said.

I nodded. "Do you want to go out tonight?"

I wasn't keen on the idea of fighting the weather; from the looks of it, neither was Elizabeth.

"You can't go out in this," Jenny interjected. She acted more like Elizabeth's jailer than her roommate.

Contrarily, I said, "Why not? It's better than sitting around all night."

"I'd rather stay here," Elizabeth said. She shot me a pleading look out of those green eyes of hers and I was lost.

I smiled at her. "If that's what you want."

Jenny snorted in derision, but I pretended to ignore her.

"It's too cold anyway," I said.

"I'll build a fire," Elizabeth said.

"It's a gas fireplace," I pointed out.

"Exactly," she said.

I laughed and she grinned triumphantly. She flicked a button and a flame lit. Instant roaring fire.

I had to admit it was cozy, sitting snug in their living room as the storm raged outside.

I settled back into the sofa and watched the snow fall. Contentment made me nervous. Is this what it was like, not to have a sword dangling over your head all the time?

What prompted my aunts' rage? They would leave me alone for months, years sometimes, and then Gaston would appear. I didn't kid myself that it took him that long to find me. How could I finally get them out of my life?

I turned the questions over and over in my mind. Elizabeth's resemblance to my dead ex wasn't a coincidence, but what was it? A trap? Good fortune? Something somewhere in between?

I realized that Elizabeth was looking at me expectantly. She'd obviously said something I'd missed.

"You're staring."

"You remind me of someone I used to know."

"Is that a good thing?"

"I'm not sure."

Apparently, it was up to me to provide the entertainment. "Up for a game of poker?"

Jenny looked from Elizabeth to me. "I'm going to bed."

She was barely out of the room before Elizabeth jumped up and went into a discreetly concealed cabinet near the fireplace.

"Let's make this game interesting," she said. She handed me a bottle from the cabinet and sat next to me, so close that our legs were touching. She'd given me a bottle of

Mezzaluna Italian vodka, my favorite. Coincidence?

"This is my favorite," I said.

"Mine, too," she said.

"I have the devil's own luck," I warned her.

She grinned at me. "I'm willing to take the chance." She grabbed the bottle and poured healthy amounts into each glass. "What are the rules?"

"Lowest hand drinks?" I suggested.

We popped some microwave popcorn and used that to bet with.

I watched Elizabeth's face as we played. My gaze was drawn to her, despite my best efforts to keep my mind on my cards.

An hour later, I wished I had picked some other rules. Elizabeth had spectacularly bad luck and had lost the last five hands. I wasn't one of those guys who needed to get a girl wasted to get her to make out with me. At least my ego hoped I wasn't.

I'd won again, but this time I pretended I had the low cards. Elizabeth had somehow gotten closer to me. She'd inched closer, probably without realizing it, during every hand.

"You're cute," she slurred. Her pale skin was flushed, and my eyes traced the lines of her body as she stretched like a cat.

I couldn't do this. I couldn't let anything distract me from my plan, and Elizabeth could be much more than a distraction.

"I need a break," I said. I stood and went down the hall to the bathroom, where I splashed cold water on my face.

When I went back into the living room, Elizabeth was gone, so I headed for the guest room.

I bumped into someone standing in the hall and reached out to steady her. Elizabeth.

"I thought you went to bed," I said.

"I needed to check on something." She didn't move away

from me. We were so close I could smell the alcohol on her breath.

We stood there, in the dark, where it was quiet, except for the sound of our breath mingling. I wanted to kiss her more than anything. Instead, I realized I was holding her and took a step back.

"Good night," I said.

"Good night," she replied.

A pair of men's pajamas was folded neatly on the bed. I took off my jeans and slid into the cotton bottoms. A fellow could get used to this kind of life, but I needed to keep my distance from her. I needed to find my mother's charms, take care of the aunties, and get out of Minneapolis. I needed to get away from Elizabeth.

Chapter Eight

The next morning, the weather finally cleared up. When I came down to the kitchen, Jenny was drinking a Bloody Mary. The smell of vodka was strong so I sat at the opposite end of the counter in my borrowed pajama bottoms. The house was warm so I hadn't bothered with a T-shirt. Besides, I bet it pissed Jenny off that I was walking around shirtless. She'd taken an immediate dislike to me, which was more than reciprocated.

"A little early, isn't it?"

"That's rich coming from you," she snapped.

Elizabeth walked in wearing a maroon sweater and a plaid skirt. Complete posh schoolgirl outfit, even down to the pearls studs decorating her earlobes and the headband in her hair.

I poured a bowl of Wheaties and offered it to her, but she shook her head. "You look different," I said. "Like a schoolgirl."

"I *am* a schoolgirl," she said. She laughed at the look of horror on my face.

"Scared you, didn't I?" She chuckled. "I'm completely legal. I'm in college."

I was perplexed by the many faces she'd shown me. Who was the real Elizabeth?

"I have a class in approximately twenty minutes," she continued. "What are you going to do today?"

"I've got stuff to do," I said. I was going to hit the streets to look for my mother's charms. I needed to check my messages. I'd never heard from the guy I was supposed to meet at the Red Dragon. It worried me that someone else had bought the charm from him before I could. Or worse.

"You could come with me," she suggested.

I shook my head. "I'm done with school," I said.

"Dropout," I heard Jenny mutter.

I ignored her. "I could use a ride to my car."

I wouldn't be surprised if Gaston was already trolling the city looking for me. The guy had the nose of a bloodhound when it came to me. He'd sniffed out my hiding spot more times than I wanted to admit. He and my aunts would figure out I was here soon enough, but I wanted it to be a surprise. The kind they'd never forget.

I grabbed my stuff and walked out to Elizabeth's sports car. She slid into the driver's seat and started the car. "Where to?" she asked.

"It's just a couple of blocks away," I said.

"You promise you'll call me?" she asked.

She grabbed my phone and programmed her number into it. It was the kind of phone you could use a couple of times and toss, but it freaked me out to have her number stored there.

"Don't you have to get to class?"

She made a face at me but headed the car in the right direction.

She sang along with the radio as we drove. I didn't say anything, just watched her. Why was she so eager to keep me around? I didn't kid myself that it was my strong jaw. She wanted something from me, besides finding her brother, but I wasn't sure what it was. A competent private detective could find her brother before I could. There was more to the story than what she was telling me.

I hopped out while the light was red. "I'll see you later," I said.

"I hope so," she said. "You promise you'll be in touch?"

"I'll be in touch," I said. I watched her drive away.

I hit a couple of antiques stores, but I didn't have any luck. My source had been sure that the cat carved from ebony he had was the one I was looking for. He'd indicated that the other charms were in Minneapolis as well. I dialed his number, but it was disconnected. I slammed the phone down and swore.

My next stop was the manufacturing district. Jasper had mentioned my aunts were producing something the magical world had never seen before. But what could it be? And Elizabeth had said her brother was in research and development.

I headed back to the Drake, but as I walked along Fifth Avenue, a few blocks from the hotel, the wind kicked up, sounding like someone was howling in pain.

I glanced up at the graying sky and froze.

High in the sky, large birds circled lazily above the hotel. My skin felt too tight, and it got hard to breathe.

I squinted and took another look. Not birds, harpies. The bird-women were really my aunt Deci's favorites. She loved them like they were her own sisters. If the harpies were in town, my aunts had something horrible planned for somebody. I hoped it wasn't me.

I forced myself to turn and walk, not run, in the opposite direction. The Drake was out and I couldn't risk going back to Elizabeth's. I'd have to rough it for the night. I needed to test my disguise. Come face-to-face with my aunts and see if they recognized me. Infiltration. Retribution. Revenge. My plan in three easy steps, except there wasn't going to be anything easy about it.

It was a big leap of logic to assume that Elizabeth's brother Alex was the same Alex Jasper knew, but I did know that Alex had worked for my aunts. Maybe I'd be able to find out what happened to him and spy on my aunts at the same time. But none of it would work if the spell didn't hold and my aunts recognized me.

As much as the thought gave me the shakes, I knew I'd have to face them and soon, if I had any chance of my plan succeeding.

But first, I was going to reunite with the Caddy and head to the library, where it was warm. And more important, where they had computers.

The Internet was as almost as good as witchcraft and not nearly as detectable. It only took me an hour or two to find out enough about my aunts' new business to figure out my strategy. The company website indicated that Morta, Deci, Nona—and surprisingly, Nona's husband, Sawyer Polydoros—all worked at Parsi Enterprises. Since when did the Fates bother getting married?

Elizabeth's brother had worked at Parsi before his disappearance. Why was I not surprised? I printed out the address and stuffed it in my jacket pocket.

I found the address easily. Parsi Enterprises was in an old converted warehouse building in the North Loop neighborhood.

A security guard sat at a desk in the lobby, reading *Guns &
Ammo*. When I approached, he grabbed a clipboard. "Name?"

I wasn't on any list for the building. "Uh, I wanted to drop
off a résumé," I said.

His clipped "Name?" told me I wasn't going to be able to
breeze right on in.

I couldn't risk using magic to convince him, not so close to
where the Wyrd family made their fortune. I held out the sheet
of paper with the directions on it and hoped he wouldn't look
too closely. "I wanted to drop off a résumé," I repeated.

He sneered at my beat-up leather jacket and scruffy Docs.
"Twenty bucks," he said.

I handed over my last twenty and the guy pocketed it before
he returned to his magazine. I took that as my cue and rode the
elevator to the third floor.

Once there, I admired the limestone blocks and heavy
wooden beams. The building was built to withstand time. Or
a magical onslaught? A familiar sensation alerted me that the
third floor had been warded.

The elevator opened onto a suite. Everything was decorated
in soothing neutrals, but a pair of shears, the symbol of the
House of Fates, had been woven into the pattern of the carpet.
At least I knew I was in the right place.

I ignored the bored-looking girl who lounged in the waiting
area and approached the receptionist, who looked almost as
bored.

"May I help you?" he asked. He wore a suit and tie and a
tiepin with the House of Fates insignia, but I didn't feel any
magical ability coming from him at all.

"Are you hiring?" I asked.

An imposing-looking woman with high cheekbones and silver hair swept into the office and threw down her gloves. Morta. Would my disguise hold?

"Trevor, any messages?" she asked the receptionist.

I choked back the desire to reach out and squeeze her neck until she stopped talking.

He gestured to the girl. "Naomi's here."

Morta gave him a short nod and seemed to notice me for the first time. "What do you want?" she snapped. Her eyes were sharp as thorns.

"A j-job," I stuttered. I wiped my sweaty palms on my jeans.

She was used to intimidating mortals, so my bumbling response didn't even cause her to raise an eyebrow. "We're not hiring."

The girl had wandered over while we were speaking. "Is Aunt Deci coming, too? I'm starving." She pulled the hood of her jacket down, which revealed red hair and freckles.

"Aunt Deci isn't feeling well, I'm afraid," Morta replied. "Maybe next time."

My legs began to work again and I left. As I pushed the elevator button, I realized what the young woman had said. *Aunt* Deci. I'd just met my cousin. What had the receptionist said her name was? Naomi.

As I crossed the street, I spotted a crumbled five-dollar bill in the gutter and grabbed it before the wind could blow it away. I headed for the coffee shop directly opposite my aunts' office building.

I ordered a large coffee, took a seat near a front window, and waited. They were probably grabbing an early dinner. I didn't know what I was waiting for until they emerged from the building and got into a town car with Morta at the wheel.

It was after five. Their little desk jockey was probably gone by now and I could sneak by the security guard. Their office was warded, but not by anything I hadn't seen before.

The thought of going back there made my throat turn dry, but I crumbled my empty to-go cup and headed back to rifle through my aunts' office.

I made it to the third floor without any problem. I didn't expect to find anything at the reception desk and didn't. I froze. Someone was coming.

I moved away from the desk and was standing with my hands in my pockets when an older man with auburn hair came out of one of the offices.

"Can I help you with something?" He had a slight Southern drawl, but he hadn't lived there for a very long time. I wondered exactly how long it had been.

"I was looking for Alex," I said.

"I'm afraid he's not with us anymore," the man replied.

"But he loved this place," I ad-libbed.

"He quit about a month ago."

I tried to look more down on my luck than I usually did. "Damn," I said. "He said something about a part-time job. I could use the work."

He gave me a charming smile. "Sorry, I don't do the hiring," he said. "Why don't you leave your résumé and I'll give it to HR?"

His resemblance to Naomi convinced me to attempt to extend the conversation.

"I don't have a résumé," I said. "But I'm a hard worker."

I tried to look hungry and harmless at the same time.

It must have worked.

"There's a deli down the street," he said.

I shrugged. "I'm broke."

"My treat," he said. "I'm Sawyer Polydoros, by the way."

"Nyx Fortuna," I replied.

"Fortuna?" he asked. "That's unusual."

Had I just given myself away? I should have realized they would associate that name with my mother. "Family legend says that my grandfather was a hopeless gambler," I said. "He changed his last name, hoping it would be lucky."

"Well, Nyx Fortuna," Sawyer said, "are you hungry or not?"

"I could use a hot meal." And information from Nona's husband.

"After you," he said.

It wasn't until he reached for his coat and we left the third floor that I realized I'd just agreed to have dinner with a necromancer.

Sawyer Polydoros was unlike any other necromancer I'd met. Nona's husband was a handsome man with a booming voice and more than a little Southern charm. He smelled the same, though. Underneath his expensive cologne, the unmistakable odor of grave dirt, mummy dust, and old bones came off him in waves. What was different was the air of kindness and interest in the living world.

Necromancers were also known as bone-conjurers, and since one of their talents was summoning the dead they were on the top of the heap at the House of Hades. Sawyer didn't wear an insignia from the House of Hades or from the House of Fates, which intrigued me.

Necromancers were almost as rare as trolls. Most had spent so much time in the dark that they had forgotten how to smile, but Sawyer's smile lit up the tiny deli.

We ordered thick sandwiches piled high with pastrami and settled in at a corner table.

"Have you been with the company long?" I asked.

He nodded. "My wife and her sisters own it."

"Sisters?" I tried for a casual tone.

"Nona has two sisters who run the business with her," he replied.

"Only two?" My curiosity was showing, so I added, "I mean, it's a pretty large corporation and all."

"There was another sister," he said. "But she died long before I met Nona."

"Tragic," I managed to grit out.

He nodded. "Nona never talks about her, but I think they were close."

So close they murdered her. Sawyer was clueless. Did he even know his wife was a Fate? He was a necromancer, so he couldn't be completely clueless. I hoped the occulo spell concealed my magic.

He noticed my untouched sandwich. "Eat. You must be starving."

I bit into the sandwich and chewed thoughtfully. It was delicious, but my mind was on other things. My aunt was married to a necromancer.

"This is the best deli in the city," Sawyer proclaimed.

He was right.

"So how do you know Alex?" Sawyer asked.

"We're old friends," I lied. "Couldn't find a job back home and Alex convinced me to try my luck out here. I don't know a soul in Minneapolis."

We finished our meal, making inane small talk.

"I'd better go," I finally said. It was clear I wasn't going to find out anything else. "Thank you for dinner."

"It was my pleasure," Sawyer said.

"You sure there isn't any work for me?" I asked. The occulo spell had held. Now it was time to get close to my aunts. Close enough to stick in the knife.

He laughed. "You're persistent, I'll give you that. I'll see if I can get you an interview. No promises, though."

He took down the number of my brand-new burner phone. I switched numbers every few months. The not-so-anonymous death threats got old, and I figured why make it easier for Gaston to find me.

I could still feel Sawyer's eyes on me when I left the deli. As my mother always said, once a necromancer, always a necromancer. A bone-conjurer in the mix spelled danger, but I wasn't going to stop searching for Alex, especially now that I knew he was linked to my aunts.

Chapter Nine

That night, I camped out at the Dead House at the abandoned fort. The stone troll was right where I'd left him, which was comforting. There was no evidence that Jasper had been back. I parked the Caddy in the empty lot across from the Dead House and triple-warded it before I snuck inside.

I slept soundly for the first time in weeks.

The next morning, I stepped into a day that gleamed bright and clear. It was as if the storm hadn't even happened, if you ignored the snow crunching underfoot.

I needed to get my hands on a bloodstone, two if I could, but one was essential. I could protect myself from magic, but Elizabeth was defenseless. I'd give her the amulet and then dump her. I needed a clear head and no distractions.

I hopped into the Caddy and drove until I found Hennepin. I passed a Masonic temple, a comic-book store, and an Irish pub, before I finally found a bank. I needed to make a withdrawal. The amulet wouldn't be cheap. I had money stashed away, a lot of it. I relied on good luck—and if I had to, hard work—for money for my minimal day-to-day expenses. I liked knowing that if my luck ran out someday, I'd have something to fall back on.

I'd discovered a long time ago that the old saw was true: Money didn't buy happiness. On the other hand, poverty sucked. I'd discovered that, too.

I needed cash to buy what I needed. The kind of people who had what I needed didn't exactly take Visa.

I filled out a withdrawal slip and got in line for the teller. I sorted through my IDs to find the one I would need and handed it over with my slip when my turn came.

"How would you like this, Mr. Fortuna?" the teller asked.

"Hundreds, please," I replied.

I looked around nervously. I half expected my aunts to show up, hissing about ill-gotten gains, but the transaction went smoothly and I exited the bank without spotting them. It was pure stubbornness that made me cling to the name Fortuna. It was my mother's name and when I heard it, I thought of her.

I walked along Hennepin, trying to get a feel for any magic lurking inside the restaurants, bars, and clothing stores that lined the street.

I wandered for blocks without picking up anything, but finally caught a faint trace of magic.

I looked around and paid attention to my surroundings for the first time in hours. It had grown dark during my search and I was in the seedy part of town. But the trace of magic was coming from a pawnshop on the corner.

The sign read ETERNITY ROAD PAWNSHOP. There was the usual stuff in the windows, a brass trumpet, a couple of diamond rings, and an old moth-eaten fox stole that screamed to me of its death. There was no sign of the bloodstone I was seeking, but I didn't really expect it to be in a display window.

The bell over the door clanged when I entered, but the store was empty. The interior was crammed with floor-to-ceiling shelving and a stack of wooden chairs created a wobbly tower in one corner.

An enormous stuffed bear stood in the other, poised to strike, but there was a mischievous expression on its face. The shop reminded me of my mother's closet, safe and warm and stuffed full of fabulous trinkets.

"Hello?" I said. "Is anyone here?"

There was no answer, but I felt magic somewhere in the store. A jewelry case contained cut-rate diamonds. The bottom case held an emerald that sparkled with magic and two bloodstones, imbued with protective power.

A mannequin was dressed in a shimmering gown with a dusty feather boa around the neck. On her head was a cloche hat with one faded silk flower.

When I was fifteen, my mother's luck started to run out. She'd sold or traded magical items before, but they were mere trinkets. I was too stupid to know that what she'd done was something different, something drastic. She'd sold the diviner's ring, the pack of gilded tarot cards, and the pair of golden dice, but she held on to her necklace.

When I closed my eyes, I could see the charms: a black cat carved from Indian ebony, the little coral fish, an emerald frog, a diamond-studded key, a miniature book, an ivory wheel of fortune, and a horseshoe made of moonstones. The diamond-studded key hung on the chain around my neck. I was still looking for the rest. The charms held all of Lady Fortuna's luck and I was determined to find them.

As I examined the exotic and mundane items, something drew me to the display case behind the old-fashioned register. I knew I was in the right place when I saw the gleam of a dragon's scale, a lapis lazuli ring taken from the hand of a murdered king, and one perfect bloodstone.

"Can I help you?" When I turned around, a younger guy wearing designer jeans and a shirt with a unicorn on it stood there. His auburn hair was sculpted into place with a precision that revealed a fondness for hair products.

"How much for the bloodstone?" I asked. A bloodstone held strong protective magic. It would be my parting gift to Elizabeth. After that, I'd stay away from her until I found her brother.

"It's not for sale," he said flatly. That'd work for the tourists, but not for me.

He didn't look like he belonged in a musty old pawnshop, but it was clear this was not an ordinary shop and he was not an ordinary guy. His eyes gave him away. They were green, but shone with odd silvery specks. Silverlight.

When I was little, my mother had taken me to visit a very powerful sorcerer. The man was kind and had given me a tin bear, which he'd enchanted and made to dance. I was shy and hid in my mother's skirts, but not before I noticed the sorcerer's eyes, which had the same silvery gray specks as the man standing before me. I was almost sure he was a sorcerer from the House of Zeus. "How much for the bloodstone?" I asked again.

"What does a pretty boy like you want with something so powerful?"

The House of Zeus was the top dog, which may have accounted for his superior air. His eyes swept over me, searching for a marking that would announce my allegiance. He wouldn't find one.

His was easy to spot. He wore a silver ring with an oak leaf engraved on it. Their ceremonial robes used to be embroidered with a thunderbolt, but that caused a little confusion after a popular children's book featured a boy with a lightning-bolt scar. The House of Zeus then adopted a simple oak leaf as its symbol.

Everyone deferred to the House of Zeus, except the Fates. Even a sorcerer from the House of Zeus, the most powerful sorcerer's family there was, wouldn't take on a Fate.

"The unicorn tee's a nice touch," I said.

He blinked but didn't say a word.

"Cut the crap," I said.

"Who are you?" he asked.

"That's not important," I said impatiently. "How much?"

"I'm afraid your identity is essential," he responded. "I don't sell items of power to just anybody."

The gleam in his eyes told me he enjoyed messing with me.

"If you don't know who I am, you don't have the power I thought," I said. "And if you do, stop screwing with me and sell me the bloodstone."

He gave me a slow nod. "It'll cost you."

"I have plenty of cash," I said.

He raised an eyebrow. "I don't need money," he said.

"What do you want?"

A large man came out of the back. He bore a strong resemblance to the pain in the ass I was currently haggling with. "Talbot, quit annoying the customers," he said jovially. "I must apologize for my son."

As he drew nearer, his smile froze and he mumbled something under his breath.

Whatever it was, it was a doozy. "Pop!" Talbot said, shocked.

The big man ignored his son and trained his gimlet gaze on me. "What brings you to Eternity Road?"

"I need a bloodstone," I said. "Red jasper. You have one. Will you sell it to me?" A bloodstone of red jasper was the most powerful protective amulet I knew of.

He narrowed his eyes as he considered my question. "Only time will tell."

"I'm afraid all I have to offer is cold hard cash."

He stared at me, but I met his eyes and his frown finally disappeared. "Well, then, let's do business," he said.

"Thank you," I replied. "I'll take the bloodstone and that moonstone, too."

We settled on a price, which took a good portion of the wad of hundreds, and he handed me the stones.

I asked, "Can I see that ring?" I pointed to the lapis lazuli.

His smile told me that I was going to be paying through the nose for it.

"What does it do?" I feigned disinterest, but the ring had called to me from the moment I saw it.

His eyes didn't reveal what he was thinking, but I detected a tiny frown hovering around his lips. "I thought you might already be familiar with its finer points," he said.

I tried to keep my expression neutral, but he knew he had me. That ring could come in handy. Lapis lazuli was often used in divination, but that ring was exceptionally powerful.

"I have heard of it," I said evasively. "How much is it gonna cost me?"

He named a figure that made me quickly suppress a gasp. "That's serious money," I said. "I'll think about it. Can you hold it for me?" I hesitated and then added, "Or any similar items."

He nodded. "For you, I'll hold it for a week, but I can't promise anything longer than that."

He put my purchases in a cheap plastic bag and handed me a

business card. I glanced at it briefly. It read AMBROSE BARDOFF, PROPRIETOR, ETERNITY ROAD, in an elaborate Gothic script. There was additional wording beneath his name, in letters too small for me to decipher. I shoved it into my coat pocket and left the store.

I had the bloodstone, which would protect Elizabeth if I couldn't.

I didn't see how the Fates were connected to Alex's disappearance. Fear wasn't an emotion I associated with my aunts. Their policy was usually kill first and ask questions later.

Chapter Ten

I drove to Elizabeth's. I rubbed my temples, trying to stave off a headache, and gritted my teeth as I accelerated through yellow lights all the way there. What were my options? My plan for vengeance wasn't going exactly as planned.

One of the things I quickly realized was that finding a thread was not enough. I needed to cut it myself. I wasn't going to hand it over and give Morta the satisfaction of snipping it in two. After I found my thread of fate, I'd have to steal her golden scissors to cut it. I closed my eyes and pictured the charms dangling from my mother's silver chain, the chain I now wore around my neck.

I found Elizabeth and Jenny in the kitchen. "You were gone a long time," Elizabeth said.

"Afraid he stole the silver and left town?" Jenny asked baldly.

I'd thought about it. Not making off with the silver, but leaving Minneapolis.

"Did you find out anything?" Elizabeth asked.

"Not much," I replied. "I stopped by the company he worked at. They said he quit."

"That's not like Alex," Elizabeth said. "He never quits anything."

Jenny sighed, clearly no longer interested in our conversation. "I'm making Cornish game hen for dinner."

Elizabeth and I had plans, real plans. My original plan had been to take her out, give her the bloodstone, and end it. But now that I knew my aunts were involved, I needed Elizabeth for information. I'd get her drunk and see if anything slipped. I didn't want to do it in front of the ever-watchful Jenny.

"It's almost time to leave for the movie," I said. I ignored Jenny, who was, as usual, hovering within earshot.

"Why don't we just stay in?" Elizabeth suggested. "After all, Jenny went to the trouble of cooking."

I gave her a pleading look and she relented.

"We have plans," Elizabeth told Jenny. "I'm sorry we didn't tell you ahead of time."

"What plans?" Jenny pried.

"Just dinner and a movie," I said. Jenny smiled at her. "Have fun."

Elizabeth blushed and I leaned into her and said, "You're cute when you blush."

"Give us a minute, handsome," Jenny ordered.

"I'll wait by the car," I said. I put on all the layers necessary for a Minnesota winter and left the house. I half expected her to drag Jenny along with us, but Elizabeth was alone when she finally showed up fifteen minutes later.

It was just enough time for me to get nervous. It sounded too intimate, just the two of us on a real date, and I didn't do intimacy. Besides, I hadn't been on a date in what felt like a hundred years.

"C'mon, let's go somewhere," I said. "I have money burning a hole in my pocket."

She didn't answer me, but her expression was woeful.

"Look, I'm sorry," I said. "I'm an asshole to mention money to a rich girl like you. You're probably used to nicer places than I can afford. I was thinking an upscale pizza place."

"I'm not rich," she said. "Until a few years ago, when my mom married my stepdad, Mom and I sometimes had trouble paying the rent."

I felt like an ass for upsetting her. "I'm sorry I jumped to conclusions," I said.

"You're not the first person to think that I'm a spoiled little rich girl," she replied.

"I don't think you're spoiled," I said.

She gazed into my eyes for a long time, long enough that I was starting to feel nervous, with a somber expression. She finally said, "I thought you were taking me to dinner."

I felt the tension leave my shoulders. "That's the plan. The restaurant's only a few blocks away. Do you feel like walking?"

"I'd love a walk," she replied.

Meeting her had changed every plan I'd ever made, but I could manage to take her to dinner without insulting her or putting her in danger. At least I hoped I could.

When we stepped outside, the wind snapped at our faces and I stopped to wind her scarf more securely around her neck.

Our eyes met and I wanted to kiss her, but instead, I took her hand and we continued walking.

"I've been lucky, you know," she said. "I didn't mean to whine."

"Lucky?" I asked. "You know what my mother taught me? That you make your own luck."

"What do you mean?" she asked.

"Some people are so busy seeing the bad that they miss the good, even when it's right in front of them."

"I can see that," she said. "If you're looking for luck, then you're ready when you spot something worth keeping."

I said, "I don't want to miss out because I'm too busy to notice."

"Does that mean you're not going to leave?" she said.

I shrugged. "How hard can it be to find one guy?"

"You'll help me?"

"Only because you asked me to." I thought that would make her happy, but she frowned.

"Nyx, maybe you shouldn't do it after all," she said.

"Don't you want me to stay?"

"Of course!"

We'd reached the restaurant, but when she started to go in, I stopped her.

"I have something for you." I draped the bloodstone necklace around her neck and adjusted it so that the stone didn't show. She shivered when my fingers grazed the soft skin near the vee of her sweater.

"It's beautiful," she said. "What is it?"

"It's protection," I told her.

"Not exactly the kind of protection I had in mind for tonight," she said drily.

I broke into stunned laughter. I could feel the tips of my ears turn red and it wasn't from the cold. "You must be freezing. Let's go inside."

We checked our coats and sat on a hard wooden bench while we waited to be seated.

I cleared my throat. "The pizza here is supposed to be authentic Napolitano style."

"Have you ever been to Italy?" she asked.

"I was born there," I replied.

I was rescued from her expectant silence by a woman in a black dress who had arrived to show us to our table.

Elizabeth's face was full of questions, and I knew I wouldn't get away with vague answers.

"What was it like, growing up in Italy?" she asked.

The server brought out a basket of crusty rolls and I crammed one quickly into my mouth, which saved me from talking. I wasn't really ready to talk about my childhood, which had occurred several hundred years before she was even born. What would it be like to finally be able to age? Would it happen if my aunts were dead? Or was my hidden thread the only thing holding me back from a normal life? I wished I had the answer.

I thought about what it would feel like to see Elizabeth grow old while I stayed trapped in this young body. It wasn't a pretty picture.

I started to choke and Elizabeth handed me a glass of water. "Are you okay?" she asked anxiously.

I tried to chew elegantly, but the roll had turned into a lump in my mouth. I finally managed to swallow and took a big gulp of water. I pretended to be engrossed in the menu while I regained my equilibrium.

"They have a bianco pizza with shrimp," I said. "Want to share a pie?"

"I'm deathly allergic to shrimp," she said.

The thought of her being so vulnerable freaked me out. "You're careful?"

"Extremely careful," she assured me. "And I always carry an EpiPen, just in case."

"Good," I said.

She turned her attention to her menu. "How about a Margherita pizza and an order of tiramisu?"

"Sure," I said.

After we placed our order, the conversation turned to the questions I dreaded, but were part of normal social interaction. Or so I'd read.

"Where did you grow up?" Elizabeth asked.

"We moved around a lot," I said.

"Do you have any brothers or sisters?" The question was innocuous, but it made me nervous just the same.

I shook my head. "It was just Mom and me. I've been on my own for a few years now, since she died."

"But you're so young," she said. "How long have you been alone?"

"I *look* young," I corrected her. "But I don't feel it. I've had a lot of experiences."

She took a tiny bite of a roll and chewed it thoughtfully. I could tell she'd thought of something and it was bothering her.

"Have you ever been in love?"

Before her, no, but it was a little early in the relationship to tell her I was in love with her. I answered her question, though. "Not love. Lust, maybe."

"Then you've…"

"I've been around a long time," I said gently.

"I haven't," she said. "Been around, I mean."

"I know," I told her. "I can't believe it, but I don't even know how old you are."

"Twenty," she replied. "Almost twenty-one. You?"

There was no good way to answer that question. "Close," I said.

After our meal, we both ordered espressos, which gave Elizabeth major jitters. Or maybe it was the idea of spending the night with me.

"We should go," I finally said. "I'd like to get an early start in the morning, if that's okay?"

"You don't want to"—she clearly struggled to find the right words to convey what she had in mind for the evening—"sleep in?"

"Nah," I said. "I don't need much sleep."

"What do you need?" she said challengingly.

"You," I said softly. "I need you."

After dinner, we went back to her place. It was pretty clear what was going to happen, but I had second thoughts once we made it to her bedroom.

It was a textbook seduction scene. Silk sheets, candlelight, and my favorite booze on the bedside table.

I don't know why the idea that our night was preplanned pissed me off, but it did. It seemed too planned, calculating even. But before I could back out gracefully, she pushed me onto the bed and pressed against me.

Her passionate kiss was almost enough to convince me that she was motivated by honest lust and nothing else. It was enough to almost convince me she didn't have any ulterior motives. Almost.

"Elizabeth," I said, but she wasn't listening. She yanked off my shirt and then her hands were at my belt buckle. I grabbed them and held them away. "Wait."

"Wait?" she asked. She sat up and moved away from me, but not before I caught a flicker of relief on her face. It was enough for me to scoop up my clothes and make a hasty exit, like someone's Victorian auntie.

Chapter Eleven

I needed something to keep my mind and my hands off Elizabeth. I didn't want to take advantage of her. Gratitude sex was the worst.

I'd find her brother while I searched for the charms and continued to infiltrate Parsi Enterprises.

Swimming at the Y fit the bill. Their pool was clean, well kept, and, most important, empty at 5 A.M. I fell into a routine. Early-morning laps at the pool at the YMCA, a little research, and spending time with Elizabeth.

The pool was usually deserted, except for the lifeguard, when I got there. One morning, someone had gotten there before me and was already swimming furiously.

I hesitated in the doorway, unsure whether or not I wanted to share my usual solitary swim, but while I dithered, the other swimmer hauled herself out of the pool and took off her swim cap. Long red braids tumbled down.

It was the girl from Parsi Enterprises. My cousin Naomi.

"I really should cut it," she said, noticing my glance. I guessed she was in her early twenties. The older I got, the harder it was for me to judge ages.

"I was just leaving," she said. She picked up a towel but shook herself off like a puppy before throwing it around her shoulders. She left without another word, but from then on I made sure I got there early enough to give her a nod hello before she left.

A week went by before we had another conversation.

"How long have you been swimming?" I asked her after she got out of the pool. I sat on the cement and dangled my feet in the water.

"A few years," she said. "I used to come with my cousin Claire all the time."

"What happened?" I said idly. "Claire give up on swimming?"

Her face went tight. "No," she replied. "Claire just gave up."

That's what I got for trying to act normal, to have an innocuous conversation, more grief than I knew how to handle.

"That's too bad," I said.

She left without commenting on the banality of my statement.

She was always finishing her laps when I got there. We'd exchange a few words, but then she'd leave, letting me enjoy the blissful quiet.

Until one morning, when she wasn't in the pool when I arrived. I was surprised to find out that I missed her. I'd just become used to the routine, I told myself before diving into the water. Becoming attached to my cousin wasn't part of the plan.

There was no lifeguard in sight, but I dove into the water anyway. I was on my tenth lap when a flash of something dark beneath me broke my concentration and I surfaced. Treading water, I looked into the over-chlorinated depths but couldn't see anything unusual.

I resumed my laps, but something made me look down again.

Something long and dark charged me. It missed me by a fraction of an inch. I looked into the depths. A water hag stared back at me.

Water hags were older and more vicious than naiads and thrived on the sound of men screaming. Everyone thought it was an iceberg that sunk the *Titanic*, but in reality it was a few water hags in a bad mood. They feasted for days on that misery.

I wasn't going to be this hag's next meal. I swam toward the edge of the pool, but she clamped down on my heel and drew blood. I kicked out hard and connected with her jaw.

A water hag's bite could be deadly. The venom was similar to a sea snake's, which would paralyze their victims and they'd drown. I started to lose consciousness, but I forced myself to stay awake. Passing out was getting to be a habit I couldn't afford to have.

She grinned up at me, her mouth smeared red with my blood. I didn't have a chance if I tried to fight her in the water. I scrambled up onto the deck, but she followed me. She had the torso of an elderly woman, but she had a tail.

She grabbed me as I got out and I went down hard. I banged my forehead on the metal handrail. It hurt like hell, but I kept moving.

I had the advantage on dry land, but she managed to reach me and clutch me in her arms. We were both slippery from the water, but I broke her death grip.

She squeezed until I couldn't breathe, but as I looked down I saw it. Almost hidden by her trophies of men's teeth and what looked like a dried-up scalp was a coral fish on a leather string. My mother's charm.

Ignoring the sharp teeth headed my way, I closed my hand around the fish and yanked.

She gave a shriek of anger and bit into my forearm, but I held on tight.

I put up a hand and tried to summon a spark of magic, but it was as if it had been drained from my body.

I rolled over until I was on top of her, but she kept her teeth clamped onto my arm. She had the jaw of a pit bull. I needed to find something to use as a weapon. It wasn't like I had an amulet sewn into my swimming trunks. Water hags had one weakness. They hated fire. My ability to summon a flame might finally be good for something besides roasting marshmallows on camping trips.

I tried again. "*Flamma!*" A burst of flame appeared in the air in front of us and she shrieked in fear, which finally loosened her jaws from my arm.

I waved my good arm and the flame drew closer to her. She jumped into the pool and disappeared. I said thanks to Hephaestus, the god of fire.

I finally unclenched my fist, ignoring the blood dripping all over, and looked into it. The coral fish lay in the palm of my hand. I flipped it over and found what I was searching for, a miniature *F* carved on its tail. I stared at it for a long moment and returned it to its rightful place on the chain around my neck.

I grabbed a towel to stanch the bleeding and sat on the bench. I was dizzy and put my head between my knees. I heard footsteps, but didn't look up until I heard Naomi's voice.

"What happened in here?"

"I cut myself on a piece of glass," I lied.

"How did it get there?" She fired the question at me.

What was a water hag doing floating around in a Minneapolis swimming pool? They hated the taste of chlorine more than they loved the taste of human flesh. Where had the hag gone? There was a trail of water leading out of the pool area. She'd probably found the nearest manhole and traveled through the sewers back to whatever hellish lake had spawned her.

"I'll get the first-aid kit," she said. "And I'll bandage those cuts." The one on my heel wasn't bad, but I'd probably need to stitch up the cut on my forearm.

She came back and patched me up. Her hands were gentle, but when she cleaned the wound, I winced.

"Are you okay?"

"It's humiliating to cry like a little kid," I said. "Not that I'm not grateful."

"Don't worry, I won't tell anyone," she said. "Your badass loner reputation is safe with me."

"What do you know about my reputation?" I snapped.

"I was only kidding," she replied. She had the dreamy innocent expression that usually disappeared with childhood. I wasn't sure how she managed to keep her innocence, not with a family like ours. I wondered if I'd been set up somehow, but dismissed the idea. I'd tested the occulo spell on Gaston and Morta. It had held.

Had the water hag been there for my cousin instead of me?

I sat up and immediately wanted to lie back down on the cold clammy cement. I fought the impulse, but it took an effort. I leaned over and surveyed the pool.

Naomi leaned over, too. "I don't see any glass."

"I threw it out," I said.

There was about a bucket of my blood all over the concrete and she didn't even bat an eye. In the back of my mind, I wondered at such calm, but I had bigger problems to worry about.

"What did I do to bring this on?" I mused aloud. The attack

had taken me by surprise. I should have been expecting it, but I hadn't. It had been ages since I'd let my guard down like that.

"You make it sound like someone did it on purpose," she replied. "Sometimes things just happen."

That was rich, coming from the mouth of a Fate.

"What's your name?" I asked. I knew it already, but I wanted to see if she would tell me the truth.

"It's Naomi," she said impatiently.

"Thank you, Naomi, for saving me," I said. "I'm Nyx." I was still trying to wrap my head around what had just happened. "Can you keep a secret?" I asked.

"You don't know much about girls, do you?"

I grinned at her contemptuous tone. "Not a thing."

She giggled in response and held out a hand to help me up. "I can keep a secret," she said.

"I hate the sight of blood," I replied. "I would have probably fainted and pitched into the pool and drowned without you here."

"I doubt it," she said. "You seem pretty tough to me. I've got to go, but do you want me to call you a doctor or something?"

"No doctors," I said quickly. I'd been saying that a lot lately.

She stared at me for a long moment. "That's what I thought."

My cousin wasn't what I expected, I thought as I watched her walk away.

Chapter Twelve

My body ached and the smell of chlorine on my skin made me want to sneeze. I hit the showers, but I couldn't get the thought out of my mind. Had my aunts discovered my whereabouts? I rubbed the scar on my shoulder absentmindedly.

My mother had a beau once. Serge the blacksmith. We'd lived in a village where the other boys had noticed my lack of a father. Or perhaps it was my habit of constantly looking over my shoulder that set them going. Either way, they had taken to calling me names, including *bastardo*, which was pretty self-explanatory.

I'd come home battered and bruised. Serge had gently dabbed away the blood and folded my fingers into a fist. "If you take on the biggest bully, you only have to fight once. But make that battle count or you will have to guard your back for the rest of your life."

He didn't know I'd been guarding my back since birth. I took his advice anyway and the boys never bothered me again.

A week later, my aunts' harpies had found us. I'd stood in the village square, transfixed as the leader swooped in for the kill, claws extended, beak open. She let out a screech and her foul breath smelled like the opening of an ancient tomb. Serge had shoved me aside, but not before my shoulder had been sliced open by the razor-sharp beak.

My blood dripped onto the dirt and I just stood there.

"Run!" my mother had shouted. "Don't look back."

My feet carried me out of reach, but not before I glanced back and saw the harpies ripping Serge to pieces. Those razor-like claws had been meant for me, but once a harpy had tasted blood, there was no stopping it.

I rubbed the scar again as I remembered watching a kind man die, trying to protect a woman and a small boy.

I had to go through with it. I could do it. My aunts had asked for every bit of what was coming to them—and more important, my mother deserved to have her death avenged.

A face-off with my aunts would be of the last-witch-standing variety. I'd have to make sure I was the one left standing. It was the only way to make sure nobody else got hurt because of me.

After I showered away thoughts of the past, I headed to Elizabeth's. We were supposed to talk more about her brother Alex. I beat Jenny to the kitchen and made breakfast. I'd learned to cook the time I worked at a truck stop in Nebraska for a few weeks.

My specialty was perfectly fried eggs and bacon with homemade biscuits, nothing fancy, but I felt like doing something for her.

I looked in their cupboards for utensils and plates and set a couple of places at the granite kitchen counter. I made coffee and then, when she still wasn't up, put the food in the oven to keep warm and waited.

Elizabeth finally stumbled into the kitchen and I handed her a cup of coffee. She accepted with a grunt. The fact that she wasn't a morning person only made her cuter.

"Be prepared to bring your appetite," I said grandly. I set a plate in front of her. "Now eat."

"Show-off," Elizabeth teased. She took a cautious bite of a biscuit. "This is good."

"Don't look so surprised," I said. "I am a man of many talents."

For some reason, that made her blush. "It must have been fate that we met."

"Fate?"

"You say it like it's a dirty word," she replied.

"Do people believe in that stuff anymore?" I took a bite of biscuit to avoid saying anything else.

"Some people are comforted by the idea of fate lending a hand," she said.

"The hand of fate isn't necessarily a kind one."

"So you do believe," she replied.

"Do I believe that there's something out there, meddling in the business of mere mortals? Possibly. Do I believe in destiny? No."

After breakfast, I scoured the kitchen clean. I was wiping off the counter when Jenny appeared and gave me a dirty look. "What are you doing in my kitchen?"

"Nothing," I said innocently. I winked at Elizabeth, who giggled.

"What would you like for breakfast?" she asked Elizabeth.

"Nyx fixed me a delicious breakfast already," Elizabeth replied. "There's plenty left."

"No thanks," Jenny said. "I'll leave you two alone." She didn't sound happy about it.

After she left, I said, "Your roommate has all the charm of a prison warden."

She shifted uneasily in her seat. "Jenny's all right."

I raised an eyebrow. "If you say so." Time to change the subject. "Let's talk about your brother."

She had anecdotes about her brother's brilliance, tons of photographs, and tissues for when she started to tear up as she talked about him. But she didn't have any idea of who would take him or why.

"What about his friends?" I asked. "Can I talk to them?"

"No!" she said.

I frowned. "Why not?" Something wasn't right. If Alex was such a wonderful guy, why didn't he have any friends?

"He just didn't relate to anyone well, besides me," she said. "You have to understand, Alex isn't just smart, he's brilliant. That could wear on people sometimes."

"Drug problem? Gambling problem?"

She shook her head. "No vices, except this intense curiosity."

"We'll find him, I promise," I said. "Speaking of which, we should get going."

She grabbed her house keys. "I'm ready."

I led her to my baby, the purple convertible.

"And you thought the Lexus was conspicuous?"

"This is much more low-key," I told her with a laugh.

"Right," she said. "Purple Caddy. Real low-key."

"You don't like it?" I said. I pictured the guys she was used to dating. Rich boys who drove Porsches.

She gave the Caddy a long look. "It doesn't matter what I think."

She definitely didn't like it.

"You're the only one who does matter," I said. She

took a step backward and I told myself to ease up on the intensity.

"C'mon, tell me," I coaxed.

She swatted the fuzzy dice and sent them swinging. "I think it's perfect for you." I wasn't sure how to take that comment.

I opened the passenger door for her and turned the heater on full blast. I took a minute to defrost. Lately, I'd been dreaming of a white sandy beach and lots of sun. The real sun, not the anemic imitation currently making its appearance in the Twin Cities.

"Where are we going?" Elizabeth asked.

I headed to the bank. She waited in the car at the curb while I ran in and made a large withdrawal. Then we found the pawnshop and parked a couple of blocks away.

I swung her hand as we walked along.

"You're feeling chipper this morning," she said. She smiled at me.

I raised her gloved hand to my lips. "I have a good reason," I said teasingly.

But when we arrived, the front door at Eternity Road was open. Not just open, but off its hinges.

"I have a very bad feeling about this," I said. "Go back to the car."

"No way," she said.

"Don't argue with me," I said, but she was already through the door.

The place was trashed. The jewelry cases had been smashed, bookshelves shoved up against each other, and vintage gowns thrown on the floor. There was a tuba shoved partway through the ceiling.

A pungent odor hung in the air. At first I couldn't identify it, but I realized it had the stench of dark magic.

The stuffed bear now wore a trilby, a loud plaid jacket, and a happy grin, like it had just come home from an all-night rager.

Talbot stomped toward us. "What are you doing here?" he growled.

"Is the lapis lazuli ring here?"

"What do you think?"

"What happened?" I asked.

"Like you don't know," he replied. "Get out."

Elizabeth moved closer to me. I tried to see him the way she would. An angry man with strange silvery eyes.

Talbot's eyes were my only warning. He threw all his emotion my way, a magical ball of frustration, anger, and fear.

I sent a surge of protective magic back at him, which I hoped would diffuse his emotions. It did, but my magic only barely held him back. He regained his equilibrium but continued to glower at me.

Why was he so pissed off?

"You think I did all this?"

"Yes," he said impatiently.

"I didn't do it," I said flatly. "I came to *buy* the ring. A snatch and grab isn't my style."

Elizabeth kept looking around the shop like she thought she was being secretly taped for a bizarre reality show and wanted to know where the camera was.

His silvery eyes bore into me. "I believe you," he finally said.

"Do you need help cleaning up?" I offered.

He looked amused. "I've got it handled," he said. "It won't take long to clean up." *For me* was the unspoken implication. The guy had a serious superiority complex. I wondered what Mr. Arrogance would do if he knew who I was.

I nodded. "Okay." I cleared my throat. "Can you call me if the ring turns up?"

"If we find it, will you know how to use it?" He couldn't resist one last condescending remark.

I nodded but didn't turn my head to look back. I should know how to use it. It had been my mother's.

My mother had been the youngest and my grandmother's favorite. The ring was one of many gifts she had given my mother. I had recognized it the moment I saw it, but it seemed too good to be true to find it in a pawnshop in Minneapolis.

When we were without funds, which didn't happen very often since Mom was Lady Fortune and all, Mom would just pawn something. At the end, she'd parceled out her magic and kept just a little for herself, less than she should have had. When she died, she didn't have enough magic left to heal. The one thing I understood, then and now, was that she'd done it for me. I'd been tracking down her magic ever since.

A pickpocket in Verona had stolen a very valuable dagger when we were walking in the square. My mother knew the moment the dagger had been taken, of course, but she didn't even react.

"Why don't you go after her?" I asked. "You know who she is."

She gazed after the girl, who was disappearing into the crowd. "She needs it more than I do," she said.

Why would a ten-year-old girl need a dagger? I started to ask, but then I saw the tears in my mother's eyes.

I was brought back to the present when Elizabeth asked me, "Are you all right?"

"Just thinking," I replied. Was it a coincidence that the pawnshop was broken into soon after I'd been there?

"Are we done here?" she asked.

"I'm done." A hundred years done.

Chapter Thirteen

We spent another hour driving around while she pointed out the food bank where Alex volunteered, his favorite restaurants, and where he shopped for suits.

We grabbed a couple of sandwiches and ate them in the parking lot of the restaurant. I sucked down the last of my soda and then grinned at her. "Want to get out of the city?"

"Where are we going?" she asked. When I wouldn't tell her, she tried to wheedle it out of me.

"You'll see," I said. She tilted her head and gave me a little smile. In that instant, I knew my world would revolve around her smile. *Danger*, my brain told me, but I was sick of being alone.

She gave me a long considering look. "Have you ever driven on icy roads?" she asked. "Before they died, my parents taught me how to drive on these streets. Maybe I'd better take the wheel."

"How did they die?" I asked.

"Boating accident. They both drowned."

Interesting. That was the first information she'd volunteered about her parents. "I learned to drive in the Alps," I assured her.

She reclined against the seat. "Then I'll leave myself in your hands."

I started the engine and headed out of town. The heavy stone that always seemed to lie upon my chest had lifted and I whistled as I drove. I was headed for the open road and there was a gorgeous girl beside me.

"This car certainly made you happy," she said.

I knew when I bought it that the car would bring me luck. "Do you know who owned a 1956 purple Cadillac Eldorado?" I asked her.

"No, who?" she asked.

"The king," I said.

"The king of Italy?" she hazarded.

"The king of rock 'n' roll," I said. "Elvis Presley."

"And now he's dead," she said. She shivered.

"Are you cold?" I asked.

"No, a goose just walked over my grave."

I turned up the heater anyway.

When I'd headed out of Minneapolis, it had been cold and clear. But we were on a deserted country road when the sky grew black.

The wind whipped up, ferocious in its intensity, attacking the car with gust after gust. It was as if it were trying to blow us off the road.

There was so much magic in the air that I could barely breathe. I tried to take one of my hands off the steering wheel, but they were frozen there. The road curved sharply to the left up ahead.

Elizabeth shifted nervously in her seat. "Are you okay?"

"Take the wheel," I told her. She did as I asked and with effort, I managed to work one hand free. It was enough to find the lodestone in my jacket pocket. I cast a protective spell around the entire car, but the attacker was too sneaky for me.

I was completely unprepared when my foot hit the brakes and they didn't work. I fought it, but the car was gaining speed as the curve quickly approached. I threw the car into low gear, which slowed us down but didn't bring us to a halt.

"Stop it!" Elizabeth said.

"I can't," I told her, through gritted teeth. "The brakes aren't working! Pull over!"

"I'm trying!" she said. While she struggled to steer the car to the side of the road, I managed to free my other hand and dug through my inside jacket pocket for the tiny moonstone I'd bought at Eternity Road.

"Put it in park," I ordered.

"But we'll tailspin," she objected.

"Would you rather we slam into that tree?"

I gripped the moonstone and drew from the magic stored there. One touch brought my mother vividly to mind. It was during happier times, my birthday maybe. She was wrapping a present and telling me not to peek.

The memory fled as I concentrated on staying alive long enough to figure out who was behind this attack. The sky lightened back to blue and the wind died down as quickly as it had started.

Elizabeth threw the car into park and it went into a spin. I pumped the brakes hard and they finally responded. The car let out a groan before it finally slowed to a stop mere inches from the tree.

Elizabeth was shaking and I put an arm around her. "Are you all right? You didn't hit your head or anything, did you?"

She gestured to the seat belt, stretched tightly against her. "Not a scratch."

We stayed there a long time, not speaking. My hands shook on the steering wheel. For someone who was supposed to be dead, I was clinging to life with all my might.

"That was a lucky break," Elizabeth finally said, but there was a quaver in her voice.

"If we'd been in a lighter car, that wind would have blown us clean off the road," I told her.

At first I thought we'd missed the tree completely, but the front bumper had some minor damage. The weight of what I had planned to do had stayed on my shoulders like a yoke, but instead of guilt, I felt free. They had tried to hurt Elizabeth and every cell in my body screamed that it was time for the Fates to pay.

Although my life stretched in front of me to infinity, I did not take the idea of murdering my aunts lightly.

I expected Elizabeth to bombard me with questions, but she was strangely silent. Shock, I supposed.

"C'mon, let's go," I said. "It'll be okay now. Let's get something hot to drink."

Maybe something hot and sweet would bring back some color to her cheeks.

"Can you just take me home?" she asked.

The ride home was taken in silence.

Someone was trying to kill me. My aunts were the obvious suspects, but a thought occurred to me. Elizabeth had been in the car with me, and she had experienced more than her fair share of tragedy. Was it coincidence or something more sinister?

Chapter Fourteen

The next day, I hit the streets.

Besides my aunts, I couldn't think of anyone else who wanted to kill me, and they knew it would take more than a car accident to get rid of me. Maybe it wasn't me they were trying to hurt? Elizabeth. The thought sent terror through me, but I couldn't let it stop me from taking down the Fates.

It was risky, what I was planning. Infiltrating the Fates as an outsider was dangerous enough, but Morta and her tracker had made it clear they had something particularly gruesome in store for me. They'd never suspect that I'd have the balls to face them.

I spent a couple of hours at a thrift store until I found a decent-looking suit. I paid for it in cash and changed into the suit, careful to knot the tie a tad haphazardly. The suit was clean but worn. I needed to look like an upstanding young man, down on his luck, but trustworthy.

No one at the company would help me, at least not knowingly, but I knew how to help myself.

I watched the building until I saw Trevor the receptionist leave and head for the coffee shop across from Parsi Enterprises.

I followed him at a distance. He ordered, sat at a table in front of the bay window, and read the paper. I ordered a coffee and waited for my chance.

I felt a twinge of remorse about what I was planning to do to the innocent worker, but I needed to get into Parsi Enterprises and fast.

The spell wouldn't hurt him, just have him worshipping the porcelain goddess for a few days. It would work best if I touched him while I worked the spell. Otherwise, it was possible the entire café would end up sick.

He tossed the paper aside and I approached. "Are you finished with that?" I asked innocuously.

He nodded. "Help yourself." I grabbed the paper and put my hand on his shoulder and muttered, "*Vomui, vomui, vomui.*"

"What did you say?"

"Thanks," I said, but he was already bolting for the bathroom, hand to his mouth. He'd be out of commission for at least a month, which I hoped would be enough time.

I managed to sneak up the elevator to Parsi Enterprises without any hassle from security and took a seat in the waiting area. I waited to make sure that the receptionist wasn't going to miraculously show up again. The hands of the clock above the desk ticked by slowly and I was getting sick of hearing my own breathing.

I realized I hadn't even heard a phone ring. There was no one in sight so I took a quick peek at the phone system. The phones were set to go to voice mail, but I quickly deleted the programming, praying I wouldn't get caught.

The phones started to ring before I slid back into my seat.

Sawyer Polydoros walked to the front, holding a pile of documents.

"Trevor, can you make sure these get sent overnight?" he asked. A puzzled look came over his face when he saw the empty seat and the blaring phone. He glanced at his watch and frowned.

I wasn't going to be the one to tell him that Trevor would not be coming back from his break, at least not today.

He saw me and a smile lit his face. "Nyx, what are you doing back here?"

He really was a nice guy, for a necromancer.

I faked a down-on-my-luck grin. "Just checking back about a job."

His gaze took in my secondhand suit and convincingly rumpled résumé. "I see. Not having any luck?"

"Not much," I said.

"Have you been waiting long?"

The phone's shrill cry interrupted. "I can get that, if you want," I offered. "Just until he gets back."

Before he could react, I slid into the receptionist seat and picked up the phone. "Parsi Enterprises, Nyx speaking."

I put the caller on hold, or at least I hoped I did, and looked up at Sawyer hopefully. "It's for you. Mr. Sabatini from the bank."

He nodded. "You've got the job," he said. "Just until Trevor gets back. And I'll take that call in my office."

It was sink or swim. I searched for and finally found an extension list, then patched the call through. I was in.

I put the phones back on voice mail and leaned back in my seat, well satisfied with my scheme. I'd work there until I figured out how to take my aunts down and maybe even find out what happened to Elizabeth's brother.

"Are you following me?" A pair of blue eyes stared at me. I was losing my touch. I'd let Naomi sneak up on me.

"Oh, it's you. The girl from the pool," I replied. "I'm not following you. I work here."

"Since when?" she challenged.

"Since today, actually," I admitted. "Temporarily, at least."

"What happened to Trevor?" she asked.

I shrugged. "Dunno. It's Naomi, right?"

She nodded. "You remembered my name." Suspicious as any other Fate.

"Of course I did," I said. "You were my very own Good Samaritan."

"Why do you want to work here?" She crossed her arms over her chest.

I paused and tried to think of a plausible lie that a normal girl would believe. Assuming she was a normal girl.

Lies were always more believable if you kept them as simple as possible. "I need a job. Any job."

"What's your story, Nyx?" she asked. "You don't seem the day-job type."

"What's with all the questions?" I replied. "I'm exactly who I seem. A peon magician from the House of Zeus, trying to catch a break."

Her gaze was sharp. "I'll worm the real story out of you eventually," she said. "Why don't you come over for dinner tomorrow night?"

"I don't think that's a good idea," I replied. "But thanks."

"Oh, don't worry," she said. "I'm not after your bod. You just look…lonely."

"I'll pass." I didn't kid myself that the invite was motivated by concern. The girl was nosy, just like any Fate. I wasn't ready to sit down with her mom, my aunt Nona. They'd have to hide the cutlery or I'd try to gut her with a steak knife.

"What are you so afraid of?" she said. "It won't be as bad as you think. It'll just be Mom and Dad and me."

"You live with your dad?" I asked. She didn't notice my slip. It was probably fairly normal to live with your dad, but the Fates had never been much for domestic bliss. The males in the family tended to go missing.

"And my mom," Naomi replied.

"I'm not much for dinner with my bosses," I told her. "Maybe another time, though."

She grabbed her backpack and fished around for pen and paper. She scribbled down something on a slip of paper and handed it to me. "Here's my phone number in case you change your mind. The invitation is open. Come for dinner anytime."

My first day at the office had made me jittery. I checked out of the Drake within the hour, after first making sure the harpies weren't around. I'd have to hide out at the Dead House for a few days.

I left the Caddy a few blocks from the fort and headed for my makeshift home base. I was about a block away when I saw a familiar red Lexus drive by and flip a U-turn, before pulling up to the curb.

Elizabeth honked her horn and I crossed to the driver's-side window. Her eyes were red-rimmed and swollen. She looked like she'd just rolled out of bed, with unbrushed hair and a T-shirt and flannel pajama bottoms.

"I've been driving all over Minneapolis looking for you," Elizabeth said. "Don't you ever answer your cell?"

"I was at work."

She gave me a curious look but didn't ask any questions.

"How did you find me?" I asked, then realized I sounded insensitive. "Are you okay?"

"Someone left a box on the front porch last night," she said. "It was creepy."

Dread filled me. "Creepy?"

"Jenny was at her boyfriend's last night," Elizabeth said. "So I was home alone." There was reproach in her voice.

"Are you okay?"

She nodded. "They didn't take anything, but there was water all over the front porch."

"Water?" I thought of the water hag I'd fought in the pool, the troll I'd turned to stone. All from the House of Poseidon, the god of water and sea.

She held out a shoe box. "That's not the worst part. Open it."

I took off the lid. A human finger lay in the box, nestled in tissue paper like an unwanted birthday present.

"It's not Alex's," she said. "He doesn't have a tattoo." Her voice was shaky.

Why would someone send Elizabeth her brother's finger anyway? There was a lot she wasn't telling me.

I bent to take a closer look. It had been sliced off cleanly and was almost clean looking, like someone had run it under the faucet before sending it over. There was a tiny trident tattoo on the finger. Jasper. I hoped the owner of the finger was alive, but I wasn't counting on it.

Someone was sending me a message, but I didn't think it was my aunts. Nonetheless, it was a reminder there was no room in my world for happiness, for love, for Elizabeth. But I couldn't let her go back there, at least not alone.

"You'll have to stay with me tonight," I said. We'd stash

the Lexus and I'd ward her house in the morning when she was at school.

"Don't sound so excited about it," she snapped.

"You haven't seen where you'll be staying," I said. The Dead House wasn't the Ritz, but it was warm and dry and, I hoped, the last place anyone would look for us.

Chapter Fifteen

"This is where you live?" Elizabeth didn't manage to hide her look of horror at her temporary accommodations.

"Sometimes," I replied. It had occurred to me that it might not be safe to stay the night in the Dead House, in case whoever had chopped off poor Jasper's finger came looking there, but I wanted to check it out before it got too dark. The last time I saw Jasper, he was on a bus out of town. He'd come back to Minneapolis, but why?

We passed by the stone troll and Elizabeth stopped to stare at it. "That's an unusual statue for a military fortress," she commented.

I didn't want to explain what had really happened, so I shrugged. "Maybe it's a recent addition."

I helped Elizabeth climb through the window I'd used before. The Dead House looked virtually untouched. The bedrolls were behind the couch, and everything was where I'd last seen it.

In fact, the place looked eerily perfect. In the days since Jasper had left, why hadn't some other street kid stumbled upon his hideout?

Something silvery gleamed in the corner of the room. A plastic bag, full of discarded candy wrappers. Jasper had been back there, I was almost certain.

I walked over and picked it up and then spotted a bottle cap. I started to toss it away, but remembered what Jasper had told me about my aunts' little manufacturing endeavor and flipped it over to reveal the entwined *P* and *E* that made up the logo of my aunts' firm. Jasper had been here and he'd had company. But who?

"Did your brother ever mention a friend? Maybe someone named Jasper?" I asked Elizabeth.

She shook her head. "Do you think it has something to do with the finger?"

"I think it's Jasper's finger," I said baldly, not realizing how it would sound to her.

She gasped. "You think the same people who chopped off his finger might have Alex? That something happened to my brother?"

"Calm down," I said. "Jasper mentioned that he knew someone named Alex, who volunteered at a food bank sometimes. Does that sound like Alex?"

"It does," she said. "It bothered him that he had so much when other people didn't even have enough to eat."

Jasper and Alex sounded like unlikely friends. Jasper was a hustler, Alex a humanitarian.

Alex's decision to work for my aunts was even less logical. Even if you didn't know they were the three Fates, witches of the highest order, the look in Morta's eyes could turn a man's spine to mush. So why did he go to work for them?

I handed Elizabeth the cleaner of the two bedrolls, which meant I ended up with the one with dried blood all over it. We curled up together, but I couldn't sleep. I wasn't used to being so close with another person. I sat up on one elbow and watched Elizabeth. Was there anything more intimate than watching someone sleep?

I rolled over and turned my back to her. I didn't do intimacy. It only got people killed.

I woke up early and nudged Elizabeth gently until she opened her eyes.

"Are you hungry?" I asked. There hadn't been any trouble during the night, but I wanted to get out of there and get some answers.

She yawned and rubbed her eyes. "Give me five minutes."

There was one person who might be able to help me figure this out, but I didn't want Elizabeth tagging along, just in case anything went wrong. I wanted Elizabeth far, far away from it.

We headed for Hell's Belles for breakfast.

"I'm Bernie, what can I get you?" A big barrel-chested woman in her sixties stood in front of us. It was the same woman who'd sniffed the air suspiciously the morning I'd put Jasper on the bus out of town.

She told us the specials and took our order, but before she left, she said, "*Buona fortuna.*"

The phrase sent a chill down my spine, but she didn't seem especially interested in me.

After the demon waitress left, Elizabeth asked, "Why did she say that?"

I shrugged. "It's just an expression."

She gestured above my head. The wall behind me was decorated with a variety of horseshoes. "Horseshoes are lucky, and *fortuna* is another word for luck."

How had I missed it? I stared at the wall for a long moment, but none of the horseshoes were from my mother's necklace.

"I've got something to do today," I said after we'd eaten.

"What do you have to do?" Elizabeth asked. "I'll go with you."

"No!" I replied.

She stared at me.

I modified my tone. "You have class. Besides, I have a job."

"A job?"

I shrugged. "I got a job where your brother worked. It might help find him. Besides, if I'm sticking around Minneapolis, I need to work, find a place to live, and act like a normal human for a change."

Elizabeth didn't seem to pick up on what I was trying to say. Instead she focused on one word. "*If* you stay?" she asked.

"Do I have a reason to stay?"

She blushed but met my eyes. "Yes."

"Then I need a job and a place to live."

As I spoke, I realized what I was saying was true. I was tired of running, and Elizabeth was worth fighting for.

"Speaking of which, I've got to go. Duty calls."

I dropped Elizabeth off at her place and said good-bye, but before I left I put the strongest wards I knew around her house. There was no way anyone from the water world would be able to get anywhere near her now.

Chapter Sixteen

My first official morning at Parsi Enterprises was uneventful. An uninterested office drone by the name of Stan gave me a mountain of paperwork to fill out. I had no identifiable skills, at least in the civilian world. It wasn't like I could put *sorcerer* down under previous occupation, so I made up a bunch of stuff. Stan took my completed forms, gave me the ten-cent tour, and abandoned me for the doughnuts in the break room.

So far, the most ominous thing about my aunts' company was the high-calorie snack choices, but the day was young.

I waited until the hallway cleared and went in search of clues about Alex Abernathy. There were no cubicles at Parsi, just shut office doors with name after name, but no Alex Abernathy.

I found Sawyer's office and knocked. Nobody answered so I turned the handle. It was unlocked. I stepped in and shut the door behind me. His desk was bare, except for a couple of financial files and a picture of Nona and Naomi.

The whiteboard behind his desk was covered with a thick black scribble that I realized was a combination of a magical spell and scientific formula. I whipped out my cell phone and took a quick picture, then stepped back into the hallway to continue my search.

The placard had been pried off the door of the next office. I tried the handle, but it was locked.

"What are you doing back here?" a female voice challenged me. I was busted by an older woman with a bad perm and a hideously ugly House of Hades brooch on her dress.

"Looking for the copier," I said mildly. "I'm new here, just filling in for Trevor."

"This is an R and D facility," she replied. "You can't just go roaming the halls. Now get back to your desk."

"I thought Parsi Enterprises was a manufacturing company?"

"Parsi Enterprises is an international conglomerate," she replied. "And if it weren't for Sawyer Polydoros, you wouldn't have a job here. Stop asking questions and get back to work."

She marched me back to the front of the office and showed me a door immediately to the right of the reception area. "I'm the human resources manager. If you need anything else, pick up extension six-six-six-six and ask." Figures that someone in HR would have that extension.

Back at my desk, I took a quick peek at my phone. I recognized some of the scribbled symbols. The new ambrosia formula? But something was off.

The phone began ringing before I could figure it out. Answering the phones at Parsi was mind-numbingly dull. I didn't even catch a glimpse of any of the Fates until almost lunchtime, when Nona came in, along with a frail-looking Deci in a wheelchair.

Deci and I were face-to-face for the first time. We locked gazes, but I dropped my eyes first. I didn't want her to recognize me from the burning hatred in my eyes.

She was sick. I hoped it was slow and painful. I grinned widely at the thought. Nona mistook my glee for genuine friendliness.

"You must be Nyx," she said. "I've heard so much about you from my daughter and husband."

"Mrs. Polydoros," I said. "Thank you for this opportunity."

"Thank Sawyer, not me," she said, but softened it with a smile. "Now if you'll excuse me, we're late."

The rest of the day passed without incident, but I'd learned two things: My aunts didn't usually hire mortals like Alex, and they were secretive about what was going on in their research and development department.

My cell phone rang.

"Ambrose Bardoff," the caller identified himself.

"Ambrose, I was hoping to hear from you," I said.

"I think I figured out what they were looking for," Ambrose said. "Can you meet me at the store?"

"About an hour, okay?" I asked. Call me paranoid, but I wanted to make sure no one from Parsi followed me.

"I'll see you there." His tone was casual, but I caught an undercurrent of tension beneath.

When I got to Eternity Road, the door was open but the store was empty.

"Hello? Talbot? Mr. Bardoff? Anyone here?"

Something was wrong. I stopped and sniffed the air. It was full of bad magic.

"Where are you?" I checked behind the counter. He lay there, facedown, not moving. At first I thought he was dead, but I rolled him over anyway and checked his pulse. It was there, faint but steady.

There was no sign of any injury, but he was out cold.

"What the hell am I supposed to do?" I said aloud. He needed a healer. Healing magic wasn't something you learned on the streets or picked up after a couple of classes. My magical résumé was sparse: healing, an ability to manipulate the elements, and playing hell at the roulette table. None of which would help me avenge my mother's death or help Ambrose.

I was the son of Fortuna, however, and I still had a few tricks up my sleeve, but I needed my mother's lodestone.

"I'll be right back," I told the unconscious man.

On my way out, I turned the sign to CLOSED and put a ward on the door. It wouldn't be enough to keep away anyone but the tourists.

The lodestone was the most valuable item I owned, magical or not. If it couldn't fix Ambrose Bardoff, nothing would. I ran to the Caddy and dug through my duffel bag.

I started to panic, but the lodestone was there, rolled up in an old pair of my socks.

I grabbed it and raced back to Eternity Road.

The ward was in place and Ambrose was breathing.

"Ambrose, wake up," I said.

I tried to remember what my mother had told me about how to use the lodestone, but drew a blank.

"Damn it! Work!" I shouted. The stone went warm in my hand.

Minutes ticked by, but finally Ambrose groaned and sat up. "Crude but effective," he said. "I think you just saved my life."

I gave him a hand and hauled him to his feet. "Who did this to you?"

"I didn't see them," he replied. "I turned my back for a moment and then I was facedown staring at the hardwood floor. It was deadly dull until you arrived and shouted my name."

"Wait, you could hear me?" Why would anyone attack Ambrose? And ransack the store? Who was behind it?

"Yes, dear boy, it was like I was frozen, incapable of movement or speech, but aware of my surroundings," he said. "A most unpleasant experience. It was fortuitous that you arrived when you did."

"Don't you remember? You called me earlier and asked me to come down to the store," I reminded him. The blank look on his face told me the memory was gone.

"That's unfortunate," Ambrose said. "I have a feeling it was important. I didn't say anything specific?"

"Just to get down here right away," I replied.

He reached underneath the cash register cabinet and pulled out a bottle of whiskey and a glass. He offered me a swig, but I waved it away. It was a little early for me, but Ambrose had just been attacked.

"The place stunk of magic when I came in," I told him.

He looked offended. "Certainly not mine," he said.

I shook my head. "Definitely not," I said. "This reeked of black magic." The only necromancer I knew was Sawyer Polydoros, but it didn't seem like his style.

He took a long drink of his whiskey. "That narrows it down considerably. Anything else you can tell me?"

There was a trickle of blood at the back of his head. I hadn't noticed it earlier.

Talbot walked in. He saw his father bleeding and jumped to conclusions. He punched me. I wasn't expecting it and it sent me flying. I landed hard and heard the crunch of bone. He came at me again, but his father grabbed him by his collar and let him dangle in the air before sitting him down hard on a stool.

"Talbot," his father said sharply. "You have it all wrong. Nyx didn't attack me. He saved me. Apologize at once."

"I'm sorry," he said. But his eyes told me the only thing he regretted was that he hadn't hit me harder.

"Apology accepted," I said. I held out my hand, but he ignored it.

"Good, good," Ambrose said. "Now that you two are friends, I believe I'll have another drink."

"I'm watching you," Talbot hissed under his breath when he thought his father wasn't paying attention.

I grinned at him. I liked him, but he'd taken an instant dislike to me. Nothing, not even a simple friendship, came easily to me. My right leg throbbed from where I'd landed on it.

"Nyx, my boy, what brought you to our neighborhood today?" Ambrose asked with a warning glance. He obviously didn't want to talk in front of his son.

"I was job-hunting," I lied absently, my mind still on puzzling out the identity of his attacker.

"Who'd hire you?" Talbot said derisively.

"I would," his father said. "When would you like to start?"

Eternity Road would be the perfect place to search for my mother's charms. I'd found the coral fish. I would find the others.

"You saved my life," he replied. "And I could use the assistance."

I hesitated, but Talbot's glare was convincing me to take the offer.

"I have a temp job right now. I couldn't work here during the week."

"We need help on the weekends," Ambrose said. "Saturday's our busiest day."

"Our only busy day," Talbot muttered.

I shrugged. "How about this weekend? I need to find a place to live, but I can start on that tomorrow."

"I know the perfect apartment," he replied. "It's conveniently located and quite affordable. For the one who saved my life, that is."

"Dad, the apartment, too?" Talbot said. "It's been empty for ages and you promised me."

His father cut him off. "Then it's high time it was rented out."

"I'll take it," I said.

"You don't want to look at it first?"

"I can't afford to be picky."

He gave me a curious look, but didn't comment. "It's been empty for a few months, but it is furnished," he said. "Although you might want to buy a new mattress."

"You might want to ward the doors and windows," Talbot said. "If you know how."

"How would you do it?" I was messing with him. I knew how to ward off most of the things that went bump in the night. Except my aunts.

"For a sorcerer of your power?" he asked, making it clear he thought my power almost nonexistent. "Sage. Or maybe salt."

He went into full lecture mode. I found his pomposity strangely endearing.

"Which Houses use those?" I asked innocently, knowing full well that none of them did.

"The House of Zeus is known for very complex protective spells," he said. "The House of Poseidon uses the power of nature. While the House of Hades prefers the protective pentagram."

He didn't mention the House of Fates, the House of augury,

omens, and oracles. The Fates were the ones everyone needed protection from, even if they didn't know it.

I belonged to the House of Fortune, which had one member. The House of luck and lost causes.

"Or maybe I'll just hang up my antique witch ball," I said. That shut him up, but only momentarily.

"I could write down a simple spell for you to try," Talbot said.

"I think I can handle it," I said. "Pretentious little twit," I added under my breath.

Ambrose heard my comment and laughed. "My son mistakes your lack of House allegiance as a lack of knowledge."

He went to the register and took a key off a large ring. "You can move in today if you want. The power is on and it's furnished."

We shook hands and I was the proud tenant of the apartment above the pawnshop. The benefit of dealing with a sorcerer was that he didn't ask questions, every exit and entrance in the building had been warded, and the rent was cheap. Of course, the contract was a tricky one, but nothing I hadn't seen before.

I was lucky, I knew, but sometimes I was suspicious of that luck. It wasn't always good fortune when someone offered you something for close to nothing. Sometimes, there were strings attached.

Chapter Seventeen

"Ready to take a look?" I asked. I was showing Elizabeth my new apartment.

Elizabeth nodded, but she didn't look especially happy. "Hey, it's going to be great," I said. "I couldn't sponge off you forever."

"You aren't sponging off us," she said. A faint blush tinged her cheeks and she kept her eyes resolutely on the wall. "I told Jenny not to worry if I didn't make it back tonight."

My heart started to beat in triple time, then slowed to normal when she added, "I wasn't sure how long it would take."

We walked up the stairs until we came to the apartment. There were two doors, one marked 1A and the other 1B.

"Which one is yours?" she asked.

I held up the key, which had a number inscribed on it. "One-B. Let's check it out."

The apartment was small, clean, and beige. It didn't look like anyone had *ever* lived there iat least not anyone with a speck of personality.

I showed her the bedroom. It seemed presumptuous of me

to ask Elizabeth to go shopping with me for a bed for my new place, so I ordered one from a discount mattress place that Ambrose assured me wouldn't be full of lice or bedbugs and bought a king-size bed. It had already been delivered and thoughts of what I'd like to do in that bed had been buzzing around in my head ever since. But Elizabeth didn't seem to want to linger, so we headed back to the kitchen.

"At least it's clean," Elizabeth said. "But why can't you get a place closer to us? This side of town is the pits."

I raised an eyebrow. "This is the only place I can afford, and I can work at the pawnshop on the weekends to make rent." The money I had in the bank needed to stay there.

"I can help with—" Elizabeth started to say, but I shook my head before the rest of the sentence was out of her mouth.

Dating a rich girl wasn't easy, at least not for me. I had too much pride to let her support me, but apparently I did not possess many useful skills. Things were looking up now that I had a job and a place of my own, although Elizabeth didn't see it that way.

"It seems too good to be true," Elizabeth commented. "You know what my mom always said?"

"No, what?"

"That something too good to be true probably is," Elizabeth replied.

"My mother said *fortuna audax iuvat.*"

"What does that mean?" Elizabeth asked.

"Fortune favors the bold."

Elizabeth dropped her eyes, but not before I saw a flash of panic in them.

I changed the subject. "The kitchen isn't bad," I said. "Maybe I'll learn to cook."

I opened a drawer and discovered a stack of take-out menus. I handed the menus to Elizabeth. "Are you hungry?"

"Starving," she said. "This place looks good and they deliver." She held up a pink paper menu from a Chinese restaurant.

"Sounds perfect," I said.

She took out her cell phone and ordered a bunch of stuff, gave them her credit card number and the address, and hung up.

"You know, I invited you out," I said. "You don't have to try to pay for everything all the time."

"It's just habit," she said. "No big deal."

It was a big deal to me, but I decided not to press the issue. "Let me show you the rest of the place."

The tour took about ten seconds. The small dining room didn't have a table or any chairs. I'd find some furniture at a thrift store or something.

"At least the bedroom's big," Elizabeth said.

The doorbell rang, saving me from thinking anymore about beds and Elizabeth in the same sentence.

We spread out the food on the coffee table and ate sitting on the sofa.

Finally, we leaned back, replete. "Were you expecting another thirty people?" I teased her, gesturing to several untouched containers.

"Leftovers," she explained. "Besides, I didn't know what you liked."

"I like you," I said. I leaned in and touched her face. She closed her eyes.

"Make a wish," I said.

"Why?" she replied, but she kept her eyes closed.

"You had an eyelash on your cheek," I said. I held it up for inspection. "See?"

She cracked an eyelid. "Okay, I'll make a wish."

"No, you have to blow it away first."

She pursed her lips and I stole a kiss.

Minutes later, we were stretched out on the couch, kissing as if our lives depended on it. I was pretty sure mine did.

She unbuttoned my shirt, and the touch of her hands on my skin nearly drove me out of my mind. My skin went hot and all the blood left my brain and headed due south.

She traced the scar from Brad's attempt to kill me. "It must have been fate," she said.

Her words were like a bucket of ice straight to the groin. I sat up. "I don't believe in fate."

"You don't?"

"No," I said shortly. She tried to resume her exploration, but I moved away.

"What do you believe in?"

"Luck," I said. "I believe in luck. And in survival."

"That's a pretty grim outlook," she said.

"If there's anything I've learned, it's that you can't trust anyone," I said. It was a lesson my aunts had taught me well. After all, if you can't trust your family, who can you trust?

"Not even your family?" she said.

"Especially not family."

"I trust my family," she said. She looked like she was near tears, and I felt like an asshole for bringing my screwed-up family life into it.

"I'm sure you have good reason to," I said. Lame, but I didn't know what else to say. I changed the subject. "Hey, we didn't open our fortune cookies."

"They gave us a bunch." She opened one and read the fortune before pocketing it. "Hmm, interesting," she said, then popped the crunchy cookie bits in her mouth.

"You're not going to tell me what it said?"

"I'll tell you mine if you tell me yours," she teased.

I ripped open my fortune cookie. *Your fate awaits.* I stared down at the tiny writing. It was just a coincidence. "You first."

"Mine says *If you lie down with dogs, you'll get fleas*," she said.

Maybe not a coincidence. I faked a yawn. "It's getting late. I should take you home."

She gave me a puzzled look. "It's barely eleven."

"It's been a long day," I replied. "I'll drive you home."

"You didn't tell me your fortune," she said.

"I don't believe in that stuff." I wrapped my hand around the cookie and crumpled it to dust. "I'll get my keys."

"Fine," she said. That was the last thing she said to me until we reached her place.

"Elizabeth, I'm not used to relationships," I said. "I'm sorry if I upset you."

"Nyx, you just keep pushing me away," she said.

"I don't mean to," I said. "There are things you don't know about me."

"I thought that was the idea, to get to know each other."

"I know," I said. "But it would kill me if anything ever happened to you."

She leaned in and kissed me softly. "Nothing is going to happen to me." She slid out of the car and added through an open door, "I promise."

I wished I could believe it. I was putting her life in danger just by spending time with her.

Back at my apartment, I opened the rest of the fortune cookies. The same message was repeated on every slip of paper. Someone was trying to tell me something.

Chapter Eighteen

Although his father had taken a liking to me, Talbot's hostility didn't ease up once I started working at Eternity Road. If anything, it only grew worse.

He'd made it clear he didn't like me working in his father's store. Didn't like me at all, in fact.

"You're late," he said when I reported for work on Saturday morning.

"Your clock is fast," I replied.

"Is not."

"Is too."

"I expect the two of you to get along," his dad snapped.

That shut both of us up for a second. Talbot finally gave me a smile, the first I'd seen from him. "Maybe you can suggest improvements on my security system. My wards didn't hold when Dad was attacked."

I nodded. "I'll do my best." I wondered about the change in his attitude, but decided not to comment. He was prickly enough as it was.

I put triple wards on all the doors and windows and

then Talbot showed me how to use the cash register.

"We're strictly cash-and-carry," he said. "No checks, no credit cards, and for god's sakes, if a pixie shows up and wants to buy something on credit, the answer is no."

I arched an eyebrow. "You get a lot of pixies in downtown Minneapolis?"

"You'd be surprised," he said. "Now be a good little sorcerer and dust the office shelves."

I flipped him off, but did as he asked.

It was a small room with a scratched metal desk in the center. Shelves lined the wall, which contained mostly old paperbacks and useless knickknacks. I saw one lovely agate amid all the junk.

There were some cool relics of power in the office. Things I hadn't noticed my first few trips in there, like a carving of the goddess Selene. I scanned the shelves more closely and found several interesting texts. I grabbed a book about the Fates, written in ancient Greek, and a dusty hardback with a lurid cover.

I could tell that the author of the first book I found was full of crap. The one on the bottom, though, looked interesting. When I turned to the back to the author photo, I recognized a much younger Ambrose. There was a man standing next to him, his co-author I assumed, but much of the other man's face was obscured by a fedora.

Under the photo, it read *Kaelin Pavo and Dr. A. M. Green*. The bio was uninformative—like the names, a total load of crap they'd made up to sell books.

It was fiction, but to me it read like a thinly veiled family history. Ambrose knew a lot more about my family than he'd let on.

The story began at the engagement party of a young magical

couple, Luck and Chance, who were happy and in love. The man's best friend, a handsome young sorcerer, Charm, also loved his best friend's beloved.

Two men, both in love with the same woman. A familiar story, but this one had a twist.

Luck was in love with both of the young men and seemed unable to choose between the two of them.

Finally, in desperation, the young men begged her to make a decision, but Luck could or would not, so her sister proposed a contest of magic, a sort of sorcerer's duel, to decide who would win the lovely Luck's hand.

The young woman had three sisters, and the four of them just happened to be witches. *The* witches, to be specific. And the Fates, being the Fates, could not resist meddling in their little sister's affairs and so stacked the deck in favor one of the men.

I remembered I was supposed to be working, not reading, and got back to work.

I finished dusting and walked back to the front.

"Ambrose, can I borrow these?" I asked. I held up the books.

"Sure, as long as you bring them back," he said. "While you were dusting I had a brilliant idea."

That didn't sound good.

"Nyx, do you like billiards?" Ambrose asked.

"You mean pool?" I asked. "Sure."

"Good, it's settled." Ambrose's beaming smile went from his son to me.

"What's settled?" I was not following.

"You and Talbot will get to know each other over a game of billiards after work," Ambrose said.

"Dad," Talbot started to protest, but Ambrose stared him down.

I hesitated. Even if Talbot and I survived the game without one of us braining the other with a pool cue, I was leery. I hadn't had a friend in over a hundred years, and even then I hadn't revealed my true self to anyone.

I didn't want to endanger Talbot's life, but the burden of a solitary life was crushing me. He was the son of a very powerful sorcerer. A son of the House of Zeus. The most powerful witch family there was, besides my own.

The Fates would sacrifice him without a second thought if they thought it would hurt me. The three current sisters of Fate had been in power a long time. It was time to take my revenge and end their reign.

What they lacked in numbers, they made up for in concentrated power. Nobody knew how, but every five hundred years or so, the old Fates stepped down and the new ones took over. The power of all the Fates before them was transferred to the new Fates.

I wasn't concerned with nameless, faceless future Fates. These were the Wyrd Sisters I wanted. My childhood tormenters, my mother's sisters. My mother's murderers.

Why hadn't their daughters taken over already? The Fates were not immortal. They were witches, not goddesses. They aged and died, although much more slowly than mortals.

"Never mind, it was a dumb idea," Talbot said. I'd been silent much longer than the question warranted.

"No," I said. "It's a great idea. I want to."

We ended up at the Red Dragon. I gave him a wry grin. "Where your only ID is the color of your money."

"You've been here?"

"Been here, stabbed here," I told him. "In fact, it's where Elizabeth and I met."

"What was she doing in a place like this? She doesn't strike me as the usual Red Dragon clientele."

I shrugged. "Slumming, I guess." But Talbot's question hovered at the edge of my brain as I racked the table. What had Elizabeth been doing at the Red Dragon?

Talbot took a shot and missed. "Care to make it interesting?"

I knew I was being hustled, but I wasn't sure how. "Why not? Twenty bucks?"

He snorted derisively. "I said interesting, not insulting."

"What do you have in mind?"

"Loser has to dust the old man's collection," he replied.

"You're on." Ambrose had a small collection of figurines in his office.

"Everything," he said. "Even the stuff in our apartment."

"Why do I feel like I've just been scammed?"

"You know, when we first met, I thought you were an asshole," Talbot said. "And a liar."

"You were right."

We grinned at each other, in complete agreement for the first time.

I leaned in to take a shot and when I looked up, my glance fell upon the last person I expected to see at the Red Dragon. Naomi was standing there in a short black velvet mini dress and long leather boots.

I swore, loudly. "What's she doing here?"

Talbot looked up and gave a low whistle of appreciation. "You know her? Introduce me." He didn't take his eyes off her.

Naomi had already made her way to the bar in search of some refreshment.

I sighed. "C'mon," I said. He followed me through the bar. We arrived as she ordered two shots and downed them.

"You planning on driving home like that?" I asked.

Naomi shot me a dirty look. "Mind your own business, Nyx."

"Careful or I'll tell him to make it a Shirley Temple. Now give me your keys."

"You two sound like brother and sister," Talbot said.

The comment was too close to home. "Hardly."

"You're both drinking," she pointed out.

"We walked here," I told her.

Naomi grabbed Talbot's beer and took a swig, then spit it out. "This stuff is nasty."

I glanced at Talbot. "Do you mind?"

"Not at all," he said. "Nyx here seems to have forgotten his manners. I'm Talbot. And you are—?"

"Leaving," I said, firmly. "I'm taking you home."

She dug her heels in, which is when I noticed that the shots hadn't been the first drinks she'd had. More like the tenth. "You don't know where I live and I'm not going to tell you."

"You sound like a five-year-old," I told her, exasperated.

She cuddled into Talbot and looked up at him. "I guess I'll have to go home with you."

Talbot and I exchanged looks, his hopeful, mine no way in hell. "We'll have to take her to my place to sleep it off," I finally said.

The denizens of the Red Dragon didn't even blink at the sight of two guys escorting a loud, obviously intoxicated girl out of the bar.

As we walked, Naomi leaned drunkenly against Talbot. "You're cute."

I watched with interest as he blushed. Most sorcerers from the House of Zeus fancied themselves ladies' men, probably because Zeus himself never met a female, mortal or goddess, that he didn't like. But Talbot didn't know what to make of my cousin.

Naomi stumbled and went down. Talbot picked her up. "She passed out," he said. He carried her without complaint. The tender expression on his face made me nervous.

"She's a Fate," I warned him. "A mini one, anyway."

"I know," he said. "It's not the mom I have to worry about, anyway. It's her father."

"Why is that?"

"Sawyer Polydoros is more dangerous than any Fate," Talbot said. "He used to be a Hecate follower. But he double-crossed her and the next thing everyone knew, Hecate had been banished to god knows where and Sawyer was married to a Fate."

"He seems like a nice guy," I ventured.

"Nice guys don't cheat on their wives," Talbot said.

"I thought Naomi's parents were happily married."

He shrugged. "There was talk about another woman."

"Another woman? Sawyer?" I was glad my cousin had passed out and couldn't hear us.

"Yeah, but she conveniently vanished. She was young, too. A few years older than Naomi."

"Are you sure about this?" It didn't fit the picture I had of Sawyer.

"I know more about the magical community in Minneapolis than you do." He'd reverted to the snotty tone he took when he was feeling insecure, but he had a point. All the Houses kept tabs on each other. I made a mental note to pick his brain at a more convenient time.

We'd reached my apartment. I unlocked the door while Talbot hoisted Naomi up to get a better grip on her.

She lifted up her head. "Where are we?" she asked.

"My apartment," I told her. "Where you'll sleep it off and try not to puke on my floor."

"Are you feeling better?" Talbot asked gently. I rolled my eyes at him.

"Exactly how much did you have to drink?" I asked her. "You're too young to handle your booze."

"Got into Auntie's secret stash of the good stuff," she said. She swayed before she went down, but Talbot propped her up.

"You know how to have fun," she slurred. "Not like them. It's just duty this and honor that. I'm sick of it."

She threw up all over Talbot's shoes, but he didn't seem to mind that much.

"Put her in my bed," I instructed.

He bristled. "No way."

"Get your mind out of the gutter," I said. "I'll sleep on the couch. You can have the floor."

"I hadn't planned to stay," he said.

"There is no way you are leaving me alone with her," I said. "What if she gets sick again? What if I need help? What if Elizabeth walks in?"

"I'll stay," he said. I followed him into my bedroom. He tucked her in gently while I found a trash can to put beside the bed, just in case.

"What do you think she was doing in there?" I asked.

Naomi perked up for a second. "Looking for you," she said, before she snuggled deeper into the covers.

"Naomi, why were you looking for me?" I asked. But she was already fast asleep.

Chapter Nineteen

Sunday morning, Talbot's snoring woke me up. I was on the couch in my apartment. I was disoriented for a moment, but remembered that my drunk cousin was sleeping it off in my comfortable bed.

I threw a pillow at his head. "Talbot, wake up."

He finally opened his eyes. "Why are you waking me up at this ungodly hour?"

"We have to get Naomi home," I said. "Now."

He rolled over on his side. "Later."

"Not later," I said. "If you haven't noticed, she's my boss's daughter and the daughter of a Fate. She lives at home with them. Do you seriously want to piss them off?"

He sat up. "No."

"Then help me get her out of here before her parents call the police." Or their Tracker. The last thing I needed was for Gaston to come sniffing around.

"What are you guys talking about?" Naomi asked from the bedroom door.

"How to get rid of you," I said bluntly.

Now it was Talbot's turn to throw a pillow. "What Nyx means," he said, "is that we didn't want your parents to worry."

I looked at the clock and groaned. "Naomi, you have five minutes and we're taking you home."

"I have my car," she said. "It's in the Red Dragon parking lot. Or at least I think it is."

She was still drunk. I gave Talbot a meaningful look.

"I'd be happy to drive you home," he said.

After they left, I took a handful of aspirin and went back to sleep.

I had plans with Elizabeth that night, but almost as soon as I arrived at her place, a blizzard moved in.

"The roads are closed," Elizabeth said. "We're going to have to skip the movie."

That left me stranded there.

"How do you stand it?" I asked. "Does it ever stop snowing?" I yearned for the sun's hot rays or even a day where the thermostat rose above freezing.

"Spring isn't that far off," she replied.

"How am I going to get home?"

"Don't worry about it," Elizabeth said. "You can sleep over." I gave her a look.

"In the guest room, if you insist," she added, with a pout.

"It's not that I don't want—" I said.

She cut me off. "I get it. Your virtue is safe with me."

She was miffed at me. I couldn't really blame her. What guy in his right mind would turn her down?

The lake called to me, but even I wasn't foolhardy enough to go out this time. This storm made the others look tame in comparison. "What should we do instead?"

On anybody else, the look she gave me would have been a leer. On her it was plain sexy. "I have a few ideas."

Visions of those ideas swam in my brain and it was only with an extreme act of willpower that I was able to reach for the remote and click it on. "What's on television?"

She swore. "You've got to be kidding me." She walked away, but not without a parting shot. "You are completely unnatural."

If she only knew how right she was. Elizabeth avoided me the rest of the night, but Jenny didn't budge from her chair across from mine. She kept a blanket draped around her, even though the furnace was on and the room was warm.

"I'll going to bed. You can use the room you stayed in last time," Jenny finally said. The blanket slid down as she stood. Her arms were a mass of bruises.

"What happened to you?" I asked.

"It's nothing," she said.

"Did your boyfriend do that to you?"

"None of your business," she said.

There was no sense in trying to talk to her when she was in that mood, so I turned in early. Or at least I tried.

I didn't sleep much that night. I pulled open the drapes and watched the storm trying to bury all signs of life. My mind swirled as furiously as the snow. Even the storm called it a night at about 3 A.M. By dawn, city plows had already started turning the impassable roads back into safe city streets.

I was braced for trouble, which never came. I kept waiting for Gaston to reappear, or my aunts to make a house call, or some other kind of hell to break loose, but it was quiet.

I woke to the smell of strong coffee and cracked an eyelid. There was a tray on my nightstand containing two cups of coffee, along with milk and sugar.

"I knocked on the door, but you didn't answer," Elizabeth said.

I closed my eyes again and put the pillow over my head.

There was a long pause. "Nyx?"

"Yes?"

"Are you awake?" she asked in a low voice.

"No," I replied.

"Come on," she said. "Wake up."

I finally gave in, took the pillow off my face, and sat up. She was sitting on my bed, wearing a ridiculous flannel nightgown that went all the way up to her neck. Only Elizabeth would look adorable in a pink flannel nightie with ribbons and lace. It made her look like a present that I wanted to open.

Despite the urgency to get away, I wanted just one minute alone with her. I wasn't a saint. There'd been other girls, but my feelings for them were like pale ghosts compared with what I was feeling now. I knew I should leave.

I told myself I kept my distance in order to protect her, but it was really my own heart I was trying to guard.

"I thought we should get an early start today," she said. She handed me a mug of coffee.

"Oh, coffee," I said. "I could use a cup."

She patted the edge of the bed. "Come sit."

The coffee was strong and dark and had the faintest taste of something I couldn't put my finger on. It was familiar, a little bitter, but pleasing all the same.

We sipped our drinks and then I moved until I was so close that our shoulders bumped, drawn in by the need to touch her. It had been a long time since I'd been this attracted to a girl. I was immortal, but my body was that of a normal young man and Elizabeth was tempting. Her cheeks were flushed, and I thought about how easy it would be to kiss her.

I took the cup from her grasp and placed it deliberately on the nightstand. I leaned in slowly, giving her enough time to move away, but she stayed where she was, lips parted. The girl knew how to kiss, hot and sweet. Our bodies had been barely touching, but I kicked the covers off and pressed her down into the soft sheets.

Her nightgown had ridden up, which gave me access to the smooth skin of her thighs. I ran my hands along her body and she shivered. So did I, almost overcome by the sheer lust I was experiencing. It was almost...magical. I came up for air to give myself a minute to think, but tendrils of need wrapped around me and I kissed her again. As we sank back into the bed, the kiss became all tongues, spit, and teeth. Magical. Not magical, Magic. The thought came again and this time would not leave me.

I sat upright, breathing hard and pushed her away from me. "What the bloody hell is going on here?" I asked. "And tell me the truth."

There was the taste of something acidy on my tongue. It was either shame for my behavior, since I'd nearly seduced an innocent girl, or it was the remains of a spell I tasted.

She wouldn't look at me.

"I bought a little spell yesterday," she confessed.

Not so innocent after all.

"What kind of a spell?" I stared at her until she met my eyes. "And how do you know where to buy a spell anyway?"

"I thought..." Her voice trailed off.

"You thought what?" I asked. I was holding on to my temper with difficulty. I'd actually thought she'd been interested in me, but I'd been tricked. I'd been stupid, I'd let my guard down, but I wasn't going to be dumb enough to stick around to see what she had in mind for me.

I grabbed my stuff and bolted from the room, ignoring her as she begged me to wait.

Jenny poked her head out of her bedroom. "What's going on?"

"He knows," Elizabeth said. It sounded like she might be crying, but I didn't stick around long enough to find out.

"You two are something else," I shouted. I went down the stairs two at a time, but Elizabeth followed me. She was persistent, I'd give her that. I was at the door when she caught up with me.

"It was my idea," she said flatly. "Don't blame Jenny."

"It's always your idea, isn't it? Whatever stupid, dangerous stunt you two get up to, you dream it up and she follows along."

She nodded. "Yes."

I knew she would have said anything at that point in order to appease me.

"Well, I'm not a friggin' sheep to be led to the slaughter and I don't appreciate someone messing with my emotions like that," I snarled at her.

"I didn't mess with your emotions," Elizabeth said. "I messed with your libido."

I stopped and turned around. There was a faint blush on her cheeks, but I made her repeat it anyway. "What?"

"I didn't mess with your emotions. I messed with your libido. Or the potion did. It didn't make you do anything you didn't already want to do."

I was too angry to respond.

"Did it work?" she asked.

"None of your business." I should have been gone by now, but my feet hadn't moved.

"It's embarrassing, you know. The person we got it from couldn't guarantee it would, you know, get you going."

"You shouldn't be embarrassed, Elizabeth." I tried not to let my voice soften when I said her name, but it did.

"I don't have much experience," she replied.

"Is that supposed to sweeten the deal? A virgin sacrifice?"

She crossed her arms over her chest. "No, it's just I really do need your help."

I raised an eyebrow. "You have a funny way of showing it."

"Look, could we just go upstairs and talk about it? Just give us five minutes to explain."

Every bit of my survival instinct told me to run, not walk, out of that place, but I thought of Elizabeth and the way she had kissed me. It had been a spell this time, but that didn't mean I couldn't make it real.

I nodded. "Five minutes. Not upstairs. The kitchen."

In the kitchen, a stony-faced Jenny joined us. She started mixing the batter for pancakes, which seemed impossibly homey.

Elizabeth sat at the counter with her head in her hands. She didn't move from her spot even when I took a seat as far away from her as I could.

The dregs of magic wrapped around me and beckoned me to come nearer. I reached out and touched her hair, rubbing the fine strands between my fingers. It was so soft. I tilted her chin up until she met my eyes, and I cupped her face in my hands. I was lowering my face for a kiss when Jenny cleared her throat.

I looked up, disoriented for a second, until I realized where I was. Jenny glared at me.

I backed away from Elizabeth and Jenny plunked a huge stack of pancakes in front of me.

"Eat," she ordered.

"Where did you get the potion?" I asked Elizabeth.

"This darling little shop I found."

"Who sold it to you?"

"I wasn't really paying attention," she replied. "A woman."

"Think," I said. "It's important. What did she look like?" They were witches, so they were capable of changing their appearances, but it took a lot of magic to pull that off. I'd wager a glamour hadn't been necessary anyway, because Elizabeth had walked right into their trap.

"She was tall, I think."

That description didn't narrow it down much, but it could be Morta. I pushed aside my pancakes, suddenly not hungry. "Tell me exactly where you saw her."

The reluctance on her face spoke volumes.

"You have five minutes," I reminded her.

Elizabeth wouldn't look at me. She fiddled with her pancakes until I said, "You should eat something."

I wolfed down the pancakes and chugged about a gallon of water to try to flush the spell out of my system. I made Elizabeth do the same, but I could feel the effects of the magic every time I was anywhere near her.

"Did you bother to ask how long the spell would last?" I asked.

"I'm not completely stupid," she said.

I raised an eyebrow.

"Twelve hours," she added. "It lasts twelve hours. I thought that would be long enough to get the job done."

I looked at my watch and groaned. Too much time left on

the spell. If I were alone with Elizabeth for more than three seconds, I'd have her flat on her back. I was not ready for that kind of complication.

I put my fork down. "Exactly where did you meet this woman?"

She smoothed out her napkin. "This shop on Nicollet. I was desperate."

Great. The only action I'd gotten in an eon and she had been desperate. My ego might not ever recover.

"You have no idea what you're dealing with," I warned her.

She shrugged. "I was out of other options."

"You've just caught the attention of someone you don't want to notice you," I said.

She perked up at that. The girl loved trouble, you could tell. "Who?"

"Trust me, you do not want to know," I replied. "Now tell me exactly why you pulled this stunt."

She started to say something, but all I could think about was that she'd known enough to go looking for a spell. She'd deceived me and it wasn't the first time.

There wasn't a trace of magic anywhere in the house, but I had bigger problems.

Our knees bumped under the table and I sucked in my breath. I could barely think when she was around, and I wasn't sure if it was entirely the residual effects of the spell or something else. The thought didn't thrill me.

"I'm going for a walk," I said. "Can you manage to stay out of trouble while I'm gone?"

Elizabeth looked as though she might cry. I reached over and kissed her forehead. "I won't be gone long." I couldn't resist and kissed the dusting of freckles on her nose, too.

She finally smiled, which was the only thing that mattered.

I tore myself away from her before the dregs of the libido spell made me do something I'd regret. As my gaze fell on her full bottom lip, I knew it would have been worth it. Instead, I grabbed my jacket and left.

I walked around the lake several times, trying to get the spell out of my system. I finally stopped at the bench and stared at the water. It had become my favorite thinking spot.

Someone else had been there recently. I caught the gleam of a bottle cap and bent down to pick it up. Parsi Enterprises Bottling Company. I ran a fingertip over the smooth surface while I thought.

Could I forgive Elizabeth for deceiving me? I tossed the bottle cap into the air and caught it, over and over, while I thought.

I heard footsteps on the path. Elizabeth sat next to me on the bench. The potion was still in my system and I had to force myself not to reach for her. A tiny part of my brain said, *Why not? It's what you want.* But there were bigger things at stake than my love life, and I kept my hands clenched on my knees.

"There you are," she said. "I've been looking all over for you."

"We need to talk," I said finally. It was difficult for my brain to function through a fog of lust.

I turned my attention back to the lake again and pretended not to notice how great she smelled, like gardenias and freesias.

"I'm going back to the house," Elizabeth said. "It's not the smartest idea for us to be alone together until…"

"The spell wears off," I finished for her. "I'll see you back there in a few minutes."

After she left, the naiad appeared, floating on the surface of the water a few feet from where I sat. Her smooth blue skin was barely covered by her long dark hair and the thick necklaces of sailor's rope, pebbles, and old coins.

"Eavesdropping, Willow?" I asked. "I wondered when I would see you again."

"She doesn't love you, you know."

I tried to ignore the twinge her words caused.

"What do you know about love?" I asked.

"As much as anyone," she replied.

"A relationship with a naiad tends to be dangerous," I pointed out. "Not to mention short and painful."

She moved closer, until she was barely covered by the water. I felt the attraction and she wasn't even trying very hard. I was under a libido spell and it was a dangerous time to talk to the naiad. More dangerous than usual. She could suck the marrow from my bones and I'd ask for more, as worked up as I was.

"And a relationship with this Elizabeth, you do not think of it as dangerous to you?"

"Of course not," I said, but we both knew I was lying.

"Then you are a fool," she said. She flipped her hair and disappeared back into the water. I stared at the spot where she'd disappeared. She was probably right.

Chapter Twenty

Eternity Road was beginning to feel like a home, which was something I'd never had. Working there had the added benefit of helping me look for my mother's charms.

Talbot waved in the general direction of the front of the store. "The non-magical items are strictly for the civilians. Your job is to keep the civilians out of my hair."

"Civilians?"

He grimaced. "Those tourists who wander in looking for a cheap present or something to replace Aunt Edna's china, which they trashed last Christmas."

"Oh, those civilians."

"Keep them away from the good stuff," he said. "If anyone wants to sell anything interesting, you find me or Dad. No exceptions."

I nodded. "I have no interest in haggling with pixies and hags over their trinkets."

The bell above the front door jangled and we both looked up.

"Your little shadow is here again," Talbot said dismissively, but his eyes followed Naomi through the store as she tried on a cowboy hat, a flapper dress, and a motorcycle helmet.

Naomi and I had been spending a lot of time together. We'd had lunch together during the week when I was working at Parsi Enterprises. And on the weekends, she'd been dropping by Eternity Road on a regular basis. I knew I should discourage her, but I liked spending time with her.

"What does your girlfriend think of your stalker?" he asked sarcastically, but I detected a note of jealousy in his voice.

"She's not my stalker," I replied in a low voice. "She's my bosses' daughter, remember? And the girl you are obviously lusting after."

That shut him up. I left him at the cash register and walked over to where my cousin was making faces at the stuffed bear.

"What's up, Naomi?"

"You haven't been at the Y lately," she said.

I made a vague gesture. "I've been busy lately."

She looked around at the store, which was devoid of customers. "I see," she said drily.

I shrugged. "Unusually slow day." Actually, almost every weekend was like that. I wondered how Ambrose could afford to keep me on his payroll, but then I remembered how much he'd wanted for my mother's lapis lazuli ring.

"Can I help?" she asked. I couldn't shoo her away, not when Talbot was giving her that melting look when he thought no one was looking. He would make an ass of himself if I tried a blatant setup, so I'd have to be a little subtler.

I handed her a stack of vintage fabric, lace doilies, and purses. "Here, sort this."

"Have you seen much of Minneapolis since you moved here?" she asked.

I froze. "How did you know I just moved here?"

She shrugged. "Didn't you tell me that?"

I hadn't said anything to her, but I had told Sawyer I was new in town. Had they been talking about me? "What about you?"

"We moved here a few years ago, when my aunt Deci got sick."

I froze. "Deci?" I had a feeling I wasn't going to like the next words out of her mouth.

"It's short for Decima."

"That is unusual," I said. "What's the matter with her?"

"We don't know, but it's possible someone tried to poison her." Her attention was on the vintage fabrics she was folding, but her hands were shaking.

"Poison? Who would try to do that?" And who could get close enough to a Fate to try to kill her? Gaston popped into my mind, but I wasn't sure even he was that psycho.

"We're not the most popular family in Minneapolis," Naomi said. "What about you?" she continued. "What's your family like?"

"Dead," I replied. "My family is dead."

My tone convinced her not to pursue the subject.

"I still think you should have dinner at my house one night. Now go put these on the shelf." She handed me a pile of expertly folded material.

I turned around to do as she asked and almost ran into Talbot. "For god's sake," I whispered, "ask her out already."

"You think she would go out with me?"

"I'll close up tonight," I told him. "Ask her out. Right now."

I made myself look busy while they had a whispered conversation. Naomi nodded and Talbot beamed. They were perfect together, if they didn't kill each other first.

Could I really trust my cousin not to run home to Mommy Dearest and tell her where I was? Maybe I was being foolish, but I did trust her. It wouldn't be because of her that the Fates found me.

I had a cousin I truly liked, a friend I was starting to count on, and a girlfriend I might possibly even love. But if I didn't figure out where my thread of fate was before my aunts did, it would all get taken away.

Talbot and Naomi left hand in hand at around five and not one person stepped into the store after that.

I amused myself by having a one-way conversation with the stuffed bear.

It was about five minutes to closing when the bell above the door jangled loudly. I jumped and I swear the bear snickered.

He wore a tattered black trench coat, a mangy fedora pulled down low on his head, and a hand-knit scarf wound tightly around his neck. Actually, I wasn't absolutely positive that the figure was male after all. It was hard to tell by the way he or she was dressed, but something about the figure's posture suggested male to me.

The skittish way he walked around the store set my already frayed nerves on edge. I assumed that he was homeless and had come in to get warm.

"We close in five minutes," I said shortly. "Is there something I can help you with?"

He reached a hand into the voluminous pocket of his coat and placed a small object on the counter. "How much will you give me for this?"

An emerald frog gazed up at me with ruby eyes. From my mother's necklace, I was sure of it.

I resisted the urge to snatch it up immediately, but my hands shook with the effort it took to restrain myself.

"Where did you get this? Did you steal it?"

"If you're not interested…" A hand reached out to take back the item.

I gripped his forearm tightly to stop him from pocketing the frog, and to keep my mother's favorite enchantment from disappearing. "I'm interested. How much?"

He cringed and I realized he was frightened so I let him go. He tripped over an old steamer trunk in his haste to get away. His hat fell off and revealed an older man with salt-and-pepper hair. He turned his head quickly, but not before I saw what he'd been hiding.

It looked as though someone had taken a hot iron to his face, puckering the flesh on the left side but leaving the right intact. He had been a handsome man once. He smelled of cheap whiskey and long-held regret. He could have been one of any number of the ubiquitous homeless inhabiting any urban area. There was something familiar about him.

"Do I know you?"

He shook his head. "I very much doubt it."

A stranger who only looked familiar, then.

I helped him up. His hands were soft, without any calluses or rough spots that would mark him as a laborer. His clothes, although foul smelling and ragged, had the look of custom tailoring. A wealthy man fallen on hard times or simply someone who was allergic to physical work?

"I was a doctor once," he said, as if reading my mind.

I arched an eyebrow. "What happened? And how did you get this frog?"

He put his hat back on and tied the scarf more securely around the lower part of his face. "She asked me to give it to you," he muttered. "You must keep it from them."

"Who asked you to give it to me? From whom? Who should I keep it from?"

He stared at me like I was stupid. "The Fates, of course."

"What did you say?" Who was this person and how did he get my mother's favorite knickknack? Maybe it wasn't just a knick-knack. Maybe it was what I'd been looking for my whole life.

I advanced toward him and he stumbled and fell again.

I held out my hand, but he ignored it and got up slowly and painfully. "This was a mistake."

I gave him all the cash I had in my wallet. "Take this. Please."

The bell above the door rang again and I turned instinctively, but there was no one there. When I turned back around, the man was gone. The emerald frog, however, was on the counter. I picked it up and turned the emerald figure onto its back. There it was, etched into the gem. My mother's curlicue *F*. For Fortuna.

Had I found my thread of fate? I'd searched all over the world for it and then a stranger walks in the pawnshop and hands it to me? It seemed too coincidental to be believed. But he said he'd known my mother.

I added the frog to the chain around my neck. My hands shook as I returned it to its place. I waited, but I didn't feel any different. I touched the empty links where the remaining charms should be.

"Four more," I said aloud. "I'll find them."

I locked up for the night and went to my little apartment above the pawnshop. I lay in bed and tried to read, but my mind kept going back to the man and his strange behavior. I punched the pillow half the night. When I did finally fall asleep, the stranger's face followed me into my dreams.

Chapter Twenty-One

I reported back for work at Parsi on Monday. None of the Wyrd Sisters or Sawyer made an appearance, though. It seemed as though the HR manager had tattled on me or something, because the whole place was on lockdown. I was beginning to think my fake job was a waste of time, and being friendly around people I hated was wearying.

I was exhausted by the time I made it home. I'd just cracked a beer when there was a knock at the door and Ambrose's face appeared in my doorway.

"How are you settling in?" he asked.

"Not much to settle." I gestured around the room.

"I think we have a dining room table and chairs in the storage room. You can have them if you can find them," he said.

"Great," I said.

"I'll show you where we keep the furniture," he said. We headed down to the basement and he unlocked a double door. We stepped inside a room that was crammed with stuff. His storage room was a treasure trove. I scooped up a threadbare velvet Victorian fainting couch, a rickety table and chairs, and even an old record player.

"You're sure it's okay if I take all this stuff?" I asked Ambrose.

He gave me an amused look. "It's just been sitting there, gathering dust. Of course I'm sure."

"It's amazing," I said. I picked up a windup merry-go-round and turned the knob gently. Tinny music came on as the tiny horse went up and down.

"I never throw anything out," he said. "You never know when you might need it."

"How do you find anything in here?" I asked.

"Believe it or not, it's organized. This area, for instance, is where I keep the good stuff."

"Antiques?" I spotted a Victorian wheel of fortune and an old pinball machine.

He shook his head. "The fun stuff. Help yourself to whatever you'd like, but you must return it if you move out of the apartment."

"Deal," I said. I spotted a red-and-chrome table and chairs from the fifties and added them to my pile.

I noticed rows and rows of carved shelves, filled with old books.

"You have enough books to stock a library down here," I commented.

"You like to read? Take what you like," he offered.

I did like to read. I spent a lot of time alone and television, although fascinating to me from a technical standpoint, didn't hold my interest for long.

Ambrose pointed to a small bookshelf. "Take that, too."

We carried up the pinball machine, a box of books, and the Victorian wheel of fortune on the first trip, and made a second trip back for the table and chairs.

He looked around. "This place doesn't look so bad now."

"Not bad at all," I said. In fact, it felt like home. "Want a beer?"

He took out a silk handkerchief and mopped his brow. "Yes, please," he said. "Hauling furniture up three flights of stairs is thirsty work."

I opened the fridge while he peered in over my shoulder. "Not much in here."

I handed him a cold bottle.

"I'm starving," Ambrose said. "I know a place that makes a great burger. And they deliver." He took out his cell and placed an order, then popped the top off his beer and took a long swig.

"How long have you lived in Minneapolis?"

He gave me a mischievous glance. "Long enough."

"You've gone out of your way to be nice to me. Why?"

He hesitated. "I have a personal interest."

All my senses went on alert. "In me?"

He nodded. "I was like you once. Young and alone."

His words held a ring of truth, but it just made me more paranoid. I cleared my throat. "I appreciate it." I did, even if I didn't entirely trust it.

Our burgers arrived and we sat in the kitchen to eat. Ambrose barely waited to unwrap the burger before he tore into it. His teeth ripped into the meat, and I realized he reminded me of something. In Germany, I'd spied a wolf hunting in the dead of winter. Aging and battle-scarred, the animal had stood over his kill with the same ferocious stare as Ambrose's.

"Talbot is a sensitive boy and he doesn't make friends easily," he said. "I had hoped he had confided in you."

I raised an eyebrow. "About?"

"That girl," he said, spitting out the words, along with a

chunk of burger. "Naomi. She is nothing but heartbreak for my son."

I didn't comment. His stare grew in intensity. "Has he said anything to you?"

I deflected the question. "Why don't you ask him?"

His eyes narrowed. "You haven't touched your burger."

I bit into it and delicious hot cheese lava singed my tongue. "Cheese in the burger," I mumbled. "Nice."

"You're telling me you don't know anything about Talbot and a daughter of Fate?" Ambrose continued.

"I don't know anything about Talbot and some girl," I replied.

He frowned and went to the fridge for another beer. "It's reached my attention that the Fates are looking for someone," he said casually.

I nearly choked on my burger. "Someone?"

"Or something," he replied. "A Tracker came into the store last week."

I pretended a calm I didn't feel. "A Tracker?"

"He was looking for someone. Someone very special."

"And?" My meal sat heavy in my stomach and I had to fight the urge to throw up.

"Do you still claim you don't know anything of Talbot?"

"I can't tell you anything about Talbot and his love life." He was talking about Talbot's obvious crush on my cousin, but I wasn't going to be blackmailed into selling out my only friend. Or my cousin.

Ambrose harrumphed a bit, but seemed to realize he wouldn't get anywhere. His eyes weren't unkind when he looked at me and said, "I don't think the Tracker will be back. He seemed to believe me."

I released a breath I hadn't even realized I was holding.

"You can come to me if you are in trouble, Nyx," he said.

"I don't know anything about a Tracker," I lied. I needed to handle the Gaston situation on my own. "But thanks."

"Is that all you wanted to talk to me about?" I asked. "I thought you might have remembered something about your attack."

"I know who attacked me," Ambrose said casually.

"You do?" I was floored. He'd never given any indication that he knew any more than I did. "Who?"

"It is being taken care of," he said. "I want you to stay out of it. Both you and Talbot." His teeth gleamed long and white when he smiled.

I kept my mouth full so I didn't have to answer. His voice had dripped acid. There was definitely history there. Ambrose sounded like he would make whoever had attacked him pay.

"I heard the Fates were having problems. That someone tried to poison Deci."

"Interesting." His face went blank.

"What have you heard?"

He hesitated. "Nothing concrete," he finally said. "They want information about you, of course. But there seems to have been a shift of power recently. Their powers are waning as another's gains ascendancy."

"Why should I care?" I asked. I wasn't particularly attached to my aunts, but the notion that there was a faceless, nameless sorcerer or witch waiting in the wings to snatch their power didn't set right with me somehow.

"I had thought you were fond of Naomi," he replied. "Despite your unfortunate history with the Fates."

Ambrose noticed more than I had given him credit for. I was

fond of my cousin, even though it made my plans for revenge more complicated.

I gave him a sharp look, but he only smiled blandly.

"What could cause such a shift?" I asked.

He hesitated. "I've been hearing some disturbing rumors. There is talk that the Wyrd line is dying out."

"But what about Naomi? And she mentioned a cousin Claire."

"They're young. And I believe that someone may be launching an attack against the Fates."

"To what end? And what kind of power?"

"You're not going to like it," he said.

"Tell me," I said through gritted teeth.

"They took a book."

I swore. "What kind of book?"

"The Book of Fates," he replied. "It's Deci's responsibility to keep the book and it's missing. Every House has a book, but that one has information about a particular prophecy."

"What's the prophecy about?"

"In a nutshell, you." He took a swig of his beer.

"Me? What does it say?" I tried and failed to act like I had no idea what he was talking about.

"A male from the Wyrd line will bring down the Fates," he finally said. He cleared his throat. "'He, born of Fortune, shall let loose the barking dogs as the Fates fall and Hecate shall rise.'"

Ambrose knew who I really was and hadn't used the information. I might as well cop to it. "Is that why the Fates want me dead?" I'd always thought they were out to get me because my mother had outwitted them and stolen time for me, but maybe there was more to it.

"Maybe," Ambrose replied. "There are certainly others who

are betting the prophecy is true. But from what I can tell, they aren't so keen on keeping you breathing, either."

"So there are two sides, both magic, waging war? And everybody wants me dead because of this prophecy?"

"That pretty much sums it up," he said.

"And you? Which side are you on?" I asked.

"I'm Switzerland," he replied. "Not on either side."

"Why? Because I saved your life?"

He nodded. "That, and because I think the prophecy is wrong. Prophecies are tricky things. The question is, what do you intend to do about it?"

I met his eyes. "Whatever it takes."

After he left, I dug out the book I'd been reading. I stayed up for another hour, but it wasn't looking good for poor Chance. I reluctantly shut the book and turned out the light. I dreamed of bloody wizard duels.

Chapter Twenty-Two

Working at Parsi Enterprises all week and then Eternity Road on the weekends left me with little free time, but I finally got a Sunday off. It was a tantalizingly warm spring day. The weather couldn't be counted on to stay that way, though, and I had no intention of spending my only day off inside.

I also wanted to investigate the lake.

The water looked smooth and serene, but I could see dark shapes below. It reminded me of the water hag in the pool. Had Willow sent her?

"I got your little present," I called to a listening wave. There was no answer and I started to turn away when Willow appeared.

"Come closer, Nyx," she said.

"When does the lake thaw, Willow?"

"It is thawed now," she said.

"Only for water nymphs," I said. "When will the water be warm enough for me?"

"That would be foolish, even for the son of Fortuna," she warned.

I sat at the water's edge and she flopped beside me and dangled her feet into the water.

She saw me staring at her legs and gave me an icy stare. "Not all water nymphs have tails." She snaked a hand through my open jacket and unbuttoned a button on my shirt. Her cold touch should have repulsed me, but my body responded.

I captured her hand before it went into the danger zone. "Stop it."

"I am merely checking to see if you have a heart," she replied.

"I have a heart and it belongs to someone else."

"What does that mean?" she scoffed.

"It means I'm in love with someone else."

I knew she was strong, but she gripped my hands so fiercely that I winced. "The mortal? You think she will make you happy?"

"She does make me happy," I said.

"Wanting something to be true doesn't make it so," Willow replied. Her eyes held equal parts sadness and longing.

I couldn't help myself. I leaned in. I wanted just one taste of her lips. They'd taste cold and sharp. Her expression told me to come closer. There was less than a breath between us when I remembered Elizabeth and gained the strength to pull back.

"Don't try your tricks with me," I muttered.

"Tricks? I used no tricks." She seemed bewildered, but nymphs were good at pretending emotions they didn't feel, to lure men to their doom.

"But I wanted to kiss you."

Willow gave a disgusted little snort. "Men," she said. "Blaming others for their own desires."

"You mean you didn't…?"

She met my eyes. "I didn't have to," she said.

"I've got to go," I said abruptly. I'd almost kissed her, had wanted to desperately, and couldn't even blame it on magic. There was an angry splash as Willow left me.

I waited until there wasn't anyone around and then stripped down.

I dove in and swam down as far as I could. I thought my lungs would burst. Nothing. I had gone back to the surface, gulping blessed air, when a slight movement caught my eye, but before I could investigate, a naiad appeared, then another. They moved so quickly. I was surrounded.

I tried to swim away, but Willow caught me easily. "Shush, son of Fortuna," she said. "You are in my domain now."

That name on her lips startled me for a moment. It had been so long since I'd heard it, except as a curse on my aunts' lips.

"What do you want?" I asked her, but it was pretty clear. The rest of her pack eyed me with hungry gleams in their eyes. A water hag past her prime wrapped a scaly finger around her seaweed hair and twirled it flirtatiously. She smiled, which revealed teeth like razors.

Naiads were merciless, not anything like the shy water nymphs portrayed in legend. Whoever had spread that particular mythological rumor had obviously never met a naiad. They had one weakness, if you didn't count the fact that they liked to suck the marrow out of their victims, preferably male ones.

"Can't we talk about this? There must be something you want."

She shrugged. "I have everything of yours that I want. Or I will shortly." She bent to suck the breath from my lips.

"Wait!" I gurgled. "I'll grant you a boon."

Her eyes narrowed. "Swear it!"

"I swear that I, Nyx Fortuna, grant—" I looked inquiringly at her to make sure I was using the proper words.

She nodded.

"—grant Willow the Naiad a boon of her choosing," I paused for breath. I wouldn't put it past her to demand my soul just for the fun of it. "Such boon shall not require the loss of life or freedom of Nyx Fortuna or those he holds dear," I added.

She moved closer and whispered, "What you seek lies beneath, but be very sure you are willing to pay the price before you venture again into my domain. Next time, I won't be so kind."

She wrapped her arms around me and dove into the black depths. I lost consciousness. When I awoke, I was on the shore, sputtering and coughing.

I rolled over and vomited a stream of water. I gasped and filled my lungs with air. I'd had a lucky escape. That wasn't going to stop me, however, from going back down to the dark depths. But next time, I'd be better prepared.

I drove home, feet freezing in my beat-up Docs, and contemplated my next move.

Chapter Twenty-Three

A week later, I hadn't gotten up the nerve to go back to the lake. Instead, Talbot and I were hanging out at my apartment, watching the tiny secondhand TV.

"Your dad was asking about Naomi the other day."

He stopped, hand on the remote. "What did you tell him?" he asked softly, but his eyes shone silver. He was pissed.

"Nothing."

The look on his face convinced me I needed to say something. If the relationship continued, he was going to get something broken. His nose or his heart. Or maybe both, if his dad was right.

"Talbot…" My voice trailed off. What would I do if someone told me to stop seeing Elizabeth? The thought made me suck in my breath.

"Yes?" He gave me an inquiring look, but there was a hint of bravado beneath it.

"Be careful, okay?" I finally replied.

"Love is blind, Nyx," Talbot said. "And sometimes deaf and dumb as well."

What I really wanted to tell him was, to quote a sad country song, "Love's a bitch."

Talbot talked incessantly about my cousin while I rolled my eyes.

"Can we take a break from all this Naomi worship?" I asked.

He looked around at the bare walls, the pile of stuff Ambrose had given me that I still hadn't organized, and my packed duffel in the corner. "I love what you've done with the place."

"You're a funny guy," I said.

"It wouldn't take much to make it into something cool," he said.

"I'm not big on interior design," I said. I was trying to joke, but something in me resisted the idea of trying to make the apartment into anything besides a place to crash at night.

"No, I'm serious," he said. "Let's paint this place."

I gave him a friendly shove. "Better than listening to you yammer on about young love."

He finally convinced me. A trip to the hardware store later, I had picked out an ocean blue for my bedroom walls.

A couple of hours later, we had finished painting.

"It looks good," Talbot said.

I stood back to get a better look. "It reminds me of Capri." The thought sobered me. "Let's get out of here," I added. "Go do something."

Talbot surveyed at our paint-splattered clothes and grimaced. "Mind if I clean up first? I'll meet you back here in half an hour."

We spent the evening at the Red Dragon, playing pool and drinking beer. It was around midnight when Talbot sank the last shot and won. Again.

"You know what you are?" Talbot asked. "A bad influence."

"Me?" I repsonded with pretended outrage. "You just cleaned me out."

"You know what we need? Eggs and bacon. Let's go to Belle's."

"I could use some coffee," I said. "And some food. Maybe it will help me sober up."

"It's worth a shot."

Hell's Belles was empty, but there were lights on. We slid into a booth, exchanging a look. It was a twenty-four-hour joint and there was usually someone around.

Bernie finally came out of the back. "What would you like?" she asked. She fidgeted with the ties of her apron.

"He needs about a gallon of coffee," Talbot said.

Her smile was noticeably absent. "Anything else?"

"We need a few minutes," Talbot said. He didn't seem to notice Bernie's odd behavior.

She came back with two cups and a carafe of coffee and put it on the table.

"What's the deal with all the horseshoes?"

"What do ya have against horseshoes?" Bernie asked.

"Nothing," I said mildly. "Just wondering why so many."

"I like 'em," the demon in woman's clothing said. "Got a problem with that?"

The old Nyx would have been up and behind the counter, fists swinging. Instead, I shook my head. "Nope."

Her face softened. "A horseshoe is a symbol of luck. There was a time I was sorely in need of some."

"Luck? Sounds good." Was she one of the few remaining Lady Fortuna worshippers or just superstitious?

"Now, what can I get you?"

I looked at Talbot in inquiry. "What do you recommend?"

I'd been there before, but it was a habit not to reveal anything about myself.

He handed me an oversize paper menu that looked like a fifth grader had drawn the illustrations. "Work your way through the specials."

I took his advice and ordered the blue plate special and another pot of coffee.

Bernie came back with my order, which turned out to be one perfect egg, crisp bacon, and buttery toast. But the unusual part was that the egg was served in its own brightly decorated shell.

"It's too pretty to break." I marveled at the delicately painted animals, gilded with touches of gold. "It reminds me of a Russian glass egg my mother used to have. She loved that egg."

He gestured to my breakfast. "Eat your egg. It opens just there."

I spooned some of the scrambled egg onto my plate, careful not to ruin the fragile shell. I asked Talbot, "What did you want to talk to me about?"

He avoided my eyes. "Nothing."

"Are you sure? You always bring me here when you want to talk without being overheard."

He shrugged. "It's not important," he said casually. "I was just wondering about your family."

"I don't have any."

Talbot grabbed a pen and began to doodle on the paper place mat in front of him.

"Nobody? Where are you from anyway?"

Before I could answer, something lurched into the room. It was a thing of nightmares, rotting flesh, and graveyard stench. It moved swiftly for a dead thing and managed to wrap its corpse-cold hands around my neck.

Talbot broke a ketchup bottle over its skull, but it didn't even slow it down. It swatted him away and he flew across the room.

Its grip was relentless and black spots swarmed in front of me, like pesky flies. I fumbled for the knife I kept in my boot.

I took aim at its upper arms, hacking away until its arm fell away and I could breathe again.

The thing slithered away, but trailed a dark noxious liquid as it went. Corroded blood.

The only sound I heard was my own wheezing. "What the hell was that thing?" I finally got out, but I knew what it was. A wraith, called by a necromancer to do his or her dirty work.

Talbot grabbed a hold of a bar stool and pulled himself up from the floor. "Bernie!" he bellowed, but there was no sign of her. We searched the entire restaurant, including the basement and the walk-in freezers, but she'd vanished.

After we'd cleaned up the blood, I sat in the booth, willing my legs to stop shaking.

"I thought you said you knew nothing of necromancy," Talbot said.

"What are you talking about?"

"That's an athame," he said. "From the House of Hades."

"A what?"

"A necromancer's knife," he replied. "Athames are used in rituals, but yours belonged to a necromancer."

"How can you tell?"

"The obsidian handle, the engraving on the blade."

"My mother gave it to me for my thirteenth birthday," I said. "In a carved wooden box."

His gaze sharpened. "Necromancers receive their first athame on their thirteenth birthday. It's tradition."

"My mother was not a necromancer," I said.

"Do you have the box?"

"No, why do you ask?" I reached for my coffee, but it had gone cold. Some of the liquid sloshed from the cup. My mother had taught me much about magic, but she had brushed over the House of Hades and had never even mentioned necromancy. Or my father's name. She'd always said I was better off not knowing, but now I had to know.

"I need to talk to your dad," I said. I didn't want to wait until morning.

Talbot trailed behind me as I left the diner and went straight for Eternity Road. Their apartment was dark, but I pounded on the door anyway. Talbot shoved me aside and unlocked it. Ambrose was in the hallway wearing pajamas and a scowl.

"I'm going to bed," Talbot said tersely.

Ambrose was pissed off at me, but I had other things on my mind. "Do you know anything about my father?"

I watched him closely, looking for a reaction. A bland mask slipped over his face.

"Your father?"

"Yes, my father," I replied. "Do you have any idea who he was?"

There was a telling silence while he struggled to think of something to say. Something I would believe. "Why do you ask?"

"I think you know something about him."

"I know nothing," he said.

"I read the book," I said flatly. "Your novel." I didn't know who my father was. My mother had never told me his name, only that she loved him, but it wasn't meant to be. Ambrose's book told another story.

He flinched, but his face didn't reveal his thoughts. "Did you enjoy it?"

"Right up until it disappeared," I said. I'd torn the apartment apart looking for it, but it was gone. Ambrose had keys to my place, but why would he take it?

"That's unfortunate," he replied.

"Cut the bullshit," I said. "You wrote a thinly veiled story of my family. So which one were you? The dumped fiancé or the one who got her?"

He met my gaze. "The dumped fiancé," he said. "So you'll understand why I'm reluctant to discuss your father, since he betrayed me and stole the woman I loved."

"Is that why you've been so nice to me? To get your revenge?"

My question enraged him. I could see it in his eyes, but he only gave me a tight smile. "I befriended you because you are the son of the woman I loved. You look so much like her that it hurts. You remind me of all that I have lost and why."

What could I say to his controlled summary of a lifetime of pain? I should have dropped it, let him lick his wounds in private.

My throat closed, but I pressed on. "He sounds like a monster," I finally said.

Ambrose shook his head. "He wasn't," he said simply. "That made it all the worse. Didn't your mother ever speak of him?"

"Only to say that he had abandoned us," I told him.

"There is more to him than that."

"Is?" I'd never in a million years thought that my father might be alive.

"I have every reason to believe that he is in this world somewhere," he replied.

"Back up a minute," I said. "You and my dad knew my mother and you're both still alive?"

"Did you think you were the only one who has lived a long life?"

What was he getting at? "You're immortal?" I asked, stunned. I thought I was the only immortal on the planet. The Wyrd Sisters served as Fates for around five hundred years, but I knew they died. My mother was proof of that. Aunt Decima, for example, seemed to be perilously close to death, and she hadn't even finished her time as a Fate. Fates, like other magical creatures, could be killed. Who would take over for Decima if she died? Naomi had only mentioned one cousin, but shouldn't there be three of them waiting in the wings to take over the family business?

He surveyed me for a long moment. "My poor Nyx," he finally said. "I am not immortal. Only the gods are immortal. But those who are descendants of the gods, basically anyone with an ounce of magical blood, live much longer than regular mortals."

I digested the information.

"What happened after you and my mom broke up?"

"She married your father and I never heard from her again."

"Never?"

"Never." He smiled, but it didn't reach his eyes. "But I recognized you the minute you walked into my store. You have her eyes."

He was the only other person I'd ever met who had loved my mother as much as I did. I could see it in his face. But she hadn't loved him back.

Chapter Twenty-Four

Talbot and I had quickly developed a ritual. I'd walk the five blocks to Hell's Belles to get two large black coffees, which were served in Styrofoam cups. My boss would be expecting his coffee before work, no matter how poorly I'd slept the night before.

Bernie would always see me coming and have my order ready by the time I walked through the door. The coffee was so hot that it was like drinking lava.

But today, there was no sign of Bernie. Had the wraith attacked her or was Bernie in on it? A woman I'd never seen working there took my order. She brought back my coffee, but seemed slow to actually hand it over.

I took out my wallet. "Where's Bernie today?" I hoped that the thing that had tried to strangle me hadn't eaten her.

A little coffee sloshed out and splashed her hand, but she didn't even wince. "She took a vacation day."

"I'm sorry, I didn't mean to startle you," I said.

"It's nothing," she replied, but I could see her hand was red and sore looking.

I took the coffee from her and set it down. "Here, let me have a look."

The pain radiated from her eyes, but she refused to admit it. A simple spell relieved the worst of the pain and she didn't even notice that I'd done it. At least that's what I assumed.

"It feels better now," she said. "Thank you."

I paid for the coffee and left. I had dismissed the incident from my mind by the time I got to Eternity Road and handed Talbot his coffee.

He started to bring it to his lips, but his hand stopped halfway there. He sniffed it delicately and frowned. "Did you drink this?"

"Why would I drink your coffee?"

"Don't be a smart-ass," he replied. "Did you drink your coffee?" He snatched the cup out of my hand.

"No, I was kind of lost in thought and forgot," I told him. "Besides, you know how Bernie's coffee is, hotter than hell."

"Bernie was there?"

His questions were oddly specific and I realized something was up. "No," I said. "She wasn't. What's going on, Talbot?"

"The coffee has been poisoned," he replied flatly.

"You're joking," I said. I held up my cup and took a cautious sniff. "It smells okay to me."

"Careful!" The look on his face convinced me.

"Is everyone in Minneapolis trying to kill me?" I put the coffee down very carefully. "There was this new server there," I told Talbot. "She burned her hand. I'd recognize her if I saw her again."

"Let's go," he said. He carried the cups of the tainted brew to his office and then we walked to Hell's Belles.

"Nyx, we missed you this morning," Bernie greeted me. "You didn't come in at your usual time this morning."

"Bernie, you're okay!" I said.

She shot me a puzzled look. "Why wouldn't I be?"

"Nothing unusual happened to you the other night?" I pursued.

"Not a thing," she said. She didn't meet my eyes, though.

"Any new hires?" Something was definitely up.

Bernie shook her head. "I've had the same workers for years. Why do you ask?"

"No reason," I replied. "Could we get the usual to go?"

She nodded and went to get our drinks.

I scanned the waitstaff, but I didn't see the server who'd poisoned our coffee.

Talbot gave me an inquiring look. I shook my head. "No sign of her."

"How did she manage to slip the poison into the coffee?" A cute server walked by and Talbot lost his train of thought.

We took the second order and departed. As soon as we were out of sight, I held up the cup. "Do you think it's safe to drink?"

He shrugged. "Probably." He sniffed the coffee, then took a sip, so I thought it was safe.

By the time we made it back to the Eternity Road, Talbot had finished his coffee, but I hadn't touched mine. He gave me an amused glance. "Feeling a bit skittish?"

I shrugged and took a sip. "I'm living on borrowed time anyway." But it bothered me, the way I'd suddenly become so cautious. I'd always been so eager to take chances on my life, because I figured I had nothing to lose anyway.

I was scared for the first time since my mother had died. Scared of losing something. Someone. I didn't enjoy the sensation.

I unlocked the door and turned the sign from CLOSED to OPEN. "What should we do about the poisoned stuff?"

"Let's take it to Dad," Talbot replied.

I followed Talbot to his dad's office.

Talbot pushed at the corner of the bookcase and it opened with a creak to reveal another, much larger room, this one furnished exactly as one might expect from a sorcerer.

Ambrose sat at an ornately carved desk, engrossed in what looked like a grimoire, but it could just have been a really old romance novel.

"Dad, we have something to show you," he said.

I crossed to a long, low shelf full of clear beakers. I picked up the one labeled DRAGON'S BLOOD and took a cautious sniff.

Ambrose came and took the beaker away. "That is not for an untrained sorcerer."

"Untrained? I'm lucky. That's better than training."

He gave me a severe look. "You possess certain natural gifts," he said. "But I would bet that you do not use more than a tiny portion of your talents. And perhaps have forgotten much of what your mother taught you."

I stared right back. "I've forgotten nothing."

"Then you should be able to identify the poison in your cup."

It was clearly a challenge.

"Can I borrow some ingredients?" I asked, but I already knew the answer. They'd never made a secret of their curiosity about me and my abilities.

"Help yourself." He gestured to the beakers.

I took a small bowl down from the shelf. I moved slowly and methodically, not only because magic required precision, but because I was stalling.

What Ambrose had said was true. I had forgotten some of what my mother had taught me. It had been easy to tell myself that I'd never need for me to identify the rare poisons of a practiced assassin or to reverse a love spell. But I had been wrong. I needed all that knowledge and more, just to survive living in Minneapolis.

Talbot crossed his arms and leaned against the long table to watch me as I struggled to remember my mother's lessons.

"I need something to neutralize it so I can identify the poison," I finally said. "Like a clear quartz crystal."

Ambrose clapped softly. "Very good. Anything else?"

Was it a trick question? "That's it."

I stood there in silence for a few minutes. I was stuck, but I was too proud to admit it.

He handed me a lighter. "This might help."

The lighter was antique, silver, and engraved with a single peacock feather. It felt heavy in my hand.

I wasn't exactly sure how to use it, so I decided on the simple approach. "Reveal." I passed the lighter over the now cold liquid.

There was a hiss. A strange green plume rose from the coffee.

Talbot and I exchanged glances. "Poison from the golden frog," I said.

Ambrose nodded. "Someone very much wants you dead." The venom from a golden dart frog was the most toxic on earth.

"The Fates?" I suggested.

"Why would the Fates want you dead?" Talbot asked. "You work for them."

Ambrose and I exchanged glances. It was safer if Talbot didn't know my true identity.

"Who knows with the Fates?" I replied. "Ambrose, what do you think?"

"Possibly," he said. "Although from what I heard, they prefer the more direct approach. Unless they have located a certain item."

I weighed my options. Talbot was capable of taking care of himself, and even though he had a crush on my cousin, I didn't think he would betray a confidence. I hated lying to him, but it was safer for him if he didn't know my true identity.

Ambrose was alluding to my thread of fate. If the Fates found my thread of fate before I did, Morta's golden scissors would destroy it and my life would end. That wasn't going to happen, not if I could help it.

There was silence for a moment as we contemplated our near miss, but then I thought of something. "Maybe it wasn't meant for me," I said.

"What do you mean?"

"I mean, maybe someone is out to get you," I said. "Flirted with anybody's girl lately?"

Talbot shook his head. "No."

"Really?" I was just screwing with him. It was fun to see him blush.

"No," he said again, more vehemently.

"No, it's not possible, or no you're not lusting after someone?"

"The only one I'm lusting after is Naomi."

I didn't want to think about *that*. I examined the two cups carefully. At first, I didn't see anything unusual about them, just two environmentally unfriendly Styrofoam containers, but I noticed the two linked letters molded on the bottom of the cup. A *P* and an *E*, for Parsi Enterprises.

"Son of a bitch," I said. "Did you see this?"

Talbot shrugged. "Parsi Enterprises manufactures a great deal of products."

"It's also where I work."

"Who knew it would come to this?" Talbot commented. "The Fates have day jobs."

"You can be sure there's a reason for it," I said. "Probably meddling in something that doesn't concern them. Again."

Talbot shot me a curious look. "You seem to know a lot about the Fates."

I considered Talbot a friend, a good one, but knowing who I really was would put him in danger. So I lied. "Doesn't everybody?"

"I've been thinking about that athame. What do you know of your father?" he asked.

"My father?" I'd heard him, but I was stalling. It hurt to even think of the nameless, faceless person who'd been nothing more than a sperm donor.

"Do you have any idea who your father was?"

I folded my hands across my chest. "I never asked." It was a lie. I'd pestered my mother about my father's identity constantly. The last time I asked, though, was the year I turned fourteen, when she gave me an answer. Of sorts.

The Wyrd Sisters had been hot on our trail and we'd had to flee the city, but this time there was a girl I didn't want to leave, my first real crush, so I was digging in my heels.

Mother's face was drawn and white and she kept casting backward glances as we walked along. Finally, she took me by the arm and yanked me along. That was not like her. *It must be bad, very bad*, I thought.

"What about my father?" I asked. "He could help us." I had no idea what I was talking about. I had no idea who my father was, or if he was even alive.

"Your father abandoned us when we needed him the most," she snapped.

She saw the protest on my face. "Please do not have any illusions about that man. Believe me, he would kill us as soon as help us. Now move."

My mother had never been anything other than patient and gentle with me, but my questions had obviously touched a sore spot. I cooperated for the rest of the trip and we managed to evade my murderous aunties.

I tried to hand the lighter back to Ambrose, but he waved it away. "Keep it. It used to belong to a friend of mine. You remind me of him a little bit."

"You're sure?" The lighter felt right in my hand. "He won't want it back?"

"Not where he's gone." The grim tone in his voice told me not to ask any more questions.

"If someone wanted me dead..." I didn't finish the thought.

"*If*? There seems little doubt that someone is trying to kill you."

"Not necessarily," I replied. "Elizabeth was with me the first time. And the coffee could have been intended for both you and me."

"What are you saying?"

"Maybe someone assumed the other cup was for her and it was Elizabeth they were trying to kill. Her parents died under mysterious circumstances."

"Curious, but that happens in some families."

"And the person who slipped us the poison put it in both cups. Either they wanted to kill us both or they didn't mind an additional death on their hands."

"That narrows it down a bit," Talbot admitted. "There aren't many people who would kill that indiscriminately."

"Or maybe Bernie just got tired of your special orders," I said, joking.

I could tell he was getting pissed off about my lame jokes, so I wandered over to one of the shelves while he pulled himself together. There was a hex sign on the top shelf. I hadn't noticed it before so I took it down to examine it more closely.

"Careful with that!" Ambrose said.

"I've never seen one like this before," I replied. Hex signs were common in Pennsylvania, but those were mostly decorative. This hex sign was the real deal. Malevolence radiated from it.

An idea was nibbling at the back of my brain, but it slithered away before I could grasp it.

I put it back in its place, but continued to stare at the hex sign until Talbot put a hand on my shoulder. "I'm not exaggerating to say that you'd have to sell your soul to use something like that."

The image of my mother coughing up blood before her last breath flashed in my mind. "It might be worth it."

"Trust me, it's not. Revenge never is," he replied.

"How'd you get that thing anyway?" I asked.

His face darkened and I caught a glimpse of some emotion hiding beneath the surface. "I wasn't always the model citizen you see before you."

"Citizens are boring anyway," I said. "Especially model ones."

The guy had been nothing but decent to me, had been a friend, and only wanted one thing from me: for me to keep my hands out of that deadly little cookie jar. "I don't really have much of a soul left to sell anyway." Or at least I wouldn't when I was done in Minneapolis.

Talbot looked like he couldn't figure out if I was joking or not. "Did you figure out who wants to murder you?" he finally asked.

"Murder *us*," I reminded him.

"No one wanted to murder me before you came along," he replied. He smiled when he said it, though.

I grinned back at him. "No one that you knew of anyway."

Chapter Twenty-Five

The attempted poisoning had me on edge. There were already wards on the door to the apartments, the stairs, and the entrance to my place, but I added a tricky little booby-trap spell to discourage any unexpected nighttime visitors.

That night in my apartment, I couldn't sleep. Most nights, I slept like a baby despite the ever-present threat of my aunts hanging over my head—and the attempts on my life and the lives of those around me. I felt like I was missing a big piece of some cosmic puzzle.

But sometimes, no matter what I did to avoid it, I'd lie awake and wonder: If they found my thread, how would they do me in? As gruesomely as possible, I supposed.

I finally nodded off and dreamed again about the night my mother died. We'd spent most of my life traveling through Europe, but we were on our way back to Rome, where my mother was born, when it happened.

I'd turned my back for only a second. A figure in the crowd reached for her necklace. My mother resisted and was stabbed. The dagger clattered to the ground, covered in her blood. But I recognized it anyway. My mother had been stabbed by her own dagger.

She'd started coughing up blood and I carried her to an inn where we could stay the night.

"We'll stay here," I told her. "Just for the night, I promise, but you need your rest." I didn't tell her I'd given the landlord all our money to bring a doctor, but the doctor never came.

She was delirious, calling out her sisters' names, but she had a moment of clarity. She sat up and clutched at my arm. "I need to tell you something before I die."

"You're not dying," I said. "You just need to rest."

She put her hand to my face. It was so cold that I had to repress a shiver. "You know that's not true," she said. "I'm dying."

I nodded because I couldn't speak with a voice clogged with tears.

"I've hidden your thread of fate," she said. "My charms. You're a clever boy. I know you'll find it."

"But…"

"You'll know which charm. You must…" She stopped and listened. "They're here." The delirium returned and she slumped back on her pillow.

"Who did this?"

"It was Fate," she whispered. She coughed once and a spray of blood came out of her mouth and dripped onto her pillow.

Whenever I dreamed of her, I was always a wreck the next morning. I awoke cursing my aunts, my stomach in knots of hate. Maybe that's how they always found me, by the scent of my pain and anger.

I searched the fridge for something edible. I'd grown used to eating at Hell's Belles every day, but I didn't feel like being around anyone, so instead I scrambled a couple of eggs and made toast.

I remembered the book I'd borrowed from Talbot and found it under the bed.

It wasn't exactly light reading. The Greeks called Aunt Morta "the Inflexible," which seemed pretty darned accurate.

I hadn't seen much of Aunt Morta—or of Decima, for that matter. I wondered what that meant, if it meant anything. Gaston had been playing least-in-sight as well. It meant either that they'd given up, which wasn't likely, or that something else was occupying their time.

I told myself I wanted to be the one who was their downfall, but the idea that someone was trying to topple the old broads from their seat of power bothered me. My mother would have said that no matter what, they were still family and it was my responsibility to help them. But she was dead and I was bitter. I wanted to see them without friends, powerless, hunted.

My first reaction when threatened was to punch something or someone, but I didn't know how to fight an enemy I couldn't see. My best bet was to flush him out.

There was a blaring in my ears, so loud that I couldn't hear anything else.

I bolted up. I glanced at the clock and realized I'd overslept. I was supposed to meet Talbot, Naomi, and Elizabeth at Hell's Belles over an hour ago for a Sunday morning breakfast.

I spotted Talbot and Naomi sitting on one side of a booth. I slid into the opposite seat. "Sorry I'm late," I apologized. "Elizabeth here yet?"

Talbot shook his head.

Twenty minutes later, Elizabeth hadn't showed and she wasn't answering her cell.

"Maybe we should reschedule," I said.

"I could do a reading while we wait," Naomi offered.

I held out my left hand, palm up.

She took my hand and studied it carefully.

"I've never seen anyone without a life line before," Naomi said.

"That's because I'm not supposed to be alive," I said.

Naomi continued to gaze at my hand. "But your fate line doesn't seem to end," she observed. "It goes all the way to your wrist." She held up her hand. "Just like mine."

"What else do you see?" I asked.

"Death and destruction," she replied flatly. "Someone is hiding in the shadows."

"Not very specific, is it?" I asked her.

"It's not supposed to be," she said.

Why would someone—besides my relatives, that is—want to kill me? Naomi was female and a Fate, which meant she had a flair for the dramatic, but I couldn't shrug off her reading completely.

"What else do you see?" I asked.

"You're lucky in love," she replied.

I raised an eyebrow. "Not so you'd notice."

She smiled at me. "I saw the way that girl was looking at you the other day, when I stopped by Eternity Road."

"Elizabeth," I said. "And she's just a friend," I lied.

She shot me a shrewd look. "Oh-kay," she said. "If that's your story."

"Okay, maybe more than a friend," I replied. A lot more.

A shadow crossed her face "Elizabeth, huh?"

"Elizabeth? You see something about Elizabeth?" I leaned forward to look at my own hand.

"I'm still learning," Naomi said.

"Just tell me what you saw," I ordered, but Naomi shook her head and clammed up. I followed the direction of her gaze and saw Elizabeth rushing toward us.

I tugged on Naomi's braid. "Thanks for the reading."

"Sorry I'm late," Elizabeth said. "Something came up."

Something or someone?

Everyone was pleasant to each other, but the conversation was stilted. Elizabeth didn't fit in with my friends, but I wasn't sure why.

After breakfast, we took a long walk through the park. Talbot and Naomi held hands, but when I reached for Elizabeth's hand, she shied away.

"What's wrong?" I whispered, but she ignored me.

"What is that?" Elizabeth said. She pointed to a brownish red spot in the snow. There were more spots like bloody flowers in the snow.

"That's blood," I said. "Stay here." I stepped closer and sensed a trace of old magic.

"Yeah, right," she said.

In a hollow of trees, there was a deep pit, filled with congealing blood. The remains of some animal lay a little distance away. I didn't check, but I knew it would be a cow or a sheep and it would have a dark hide.

Elizabeth made a little distressed noise and turned away, gagging at the sight, but Naomi was made of stronger stuff. She walked closer to the pit and peered in until Talbot grabbed her arm. "Come away from there," he told her.

"It's just that I've read about it, but I've never seen anything like this for real," she replied. "It's fascinating."

"Fascinating?" Elizabeth said. "Who would do that to a defenseless animal?"

Naomi opened her mouth to answer the question, but I shook my head. Elizabeth didn't need to know any more than absolutely necessary. It would probably give her screaming nightmares.

I knew of the ritual, although I'd never actually seen it performed. It was used to summon revenants, ghosts—whatever you wanted to call them. The blood was for the ghosts to drink. A necromancer had done this, a night-wanderer, the one who calls the dead. Freakin' just great.

"Should we call someone?" Elizabeth asked. "We can't just leave it there."

"You look green," I said. "I'll take you home and then I'll make the calls." I would call, anonymously, of course.

"No, I'm staying," she said.

"Not even if I say please?"

"Not even then," she replied.

I stared at the scene.

Talbot dialed his dad. "Do you have a minute to take a look at something?" They had a brief conversation and Talbot hung up. "He's on his way."

Ambrose arrived and surveyed the scene silently.

"Do you know who that is?" Ambrose asked. He pointed to a photo of a young man with curly blond hair that was nailed to a tree near the pit. There was a large red *X* painted through his face. That was clear enough.

I had seen the photo before.

Ambrose moved closer to examine the photo. "Do you recognize him?"

"It's Elizabeth's brother," I told him. "Alex. He's missing."

The obvious suspect was Sawyer. He was a necromancer and knew Alex, but there was something about the scene that made me think it could be someone else. Was there another necromancer in the House of Hades? Or had Sawyer taken on an apprentice?

I handed the photo to Elizabeth. "Do you remember when this was taken?"

"I'm not sure," she said. She studied it for a long moment. "This was taken a few months ago."

Something shiny gleamed up at me from near the pit. I got down on my haunches to examine it more closely. Another Parsi Enterprises bottle cap. I started to throw it away, but pocketed it instead.

"We should get out of here," Talbot urged.

I glanced at Elizabeth. She looked like she was going to throw up. "Why is a photo of my brother here?" she asked. "Near this pit of blood? Is it some kind of a warning?"

I led her away from the gruesome scene, but the image stayed with me.

Chapter Twenty-Six

Despite her worry about her brother, Elizabeth had invited me to a black-tie event. On the big day, I washed and waxed the car until the paint shone and then headed home to get ready.

I'd borrowed a vintage tux from Ambrose's never-ending pile of rotating store merchandise. The tux had belonged to a down-on-his-luck caterer-waiter slash actor and had a cigarette burn near the left cuff but I was relieved that it fit.

I hadn't learned how to tie my own tie, though. After several frustrating minutes in which I almost strangled myself, I finally gave up and knocked on the Bardoff apartment door to see if Talbot could help me.

"Can you tie this for me?" I asked. I held up the slightly-worse-for-wear bow tie.

"You do clean up well," he said. "Hand it to me."

My tie was knotted quickly and expertly.

"Thanks," I said.

"Where are you off to?"

"Date with Elizabeth," I told him. "Some kind of fund-raiser for Blake University. We'll be dining on rubber chicken with a bunch of people I've never met."

"The perils of dating a wealthy girl," he replied.

I looked at my watch. "I'm late, gotta go. Thanks for the help."

"Have fun, Nyx," Talbot said. "But be careful."

I was already out the door. My Caddy had a parking spot of honor only a block away from the shop and I sprinted there. If I were late, Elizabeth would get pissed. She seemed to be angry at everything lately, although I couldn't blame her. Her brother's disappearance hung over our relationship like a weight.

My breath was coming fast and I slowed to a walk to calm down. Staying in one place for so long was just making me skittish, I told myself.

"Sorry I'm late," I told Elizabeth when she answered the door. I took a closer look at her.

Instead of her usual jeans and T-shirt, Elizabeth wore a long green silk dress and had her hair up. She looked every inch the debutante. She looked like a stranger. I let out a low whistle. "Who are you and what have you done with Elizabeth?"

She giggled. "I could say the same about you," she said. "You look like Rudolph Valentino or someone." I didn't tell her I'd met him.

"Rudolph Valentino?" I asked.

"He was a famous silent-movie star," she explained. "We're studying his movies in acting class."

"Acting class, huh?" She'd never mentioned an acting class before.

"Didn't I tell you? I'm majoring in acting," she said.

An actress who looked just like my dead girlfriend? That couldn't be good.

Elizabeth linked her arm with mine and dragged me over to her roommate. "Isn't he handsome?"

"He's fairly attractive," Jenny said. "After a bath." She wore an elegant gown of her own.

"Are you coming, too?" I couldn't keep the dismay from my voice.

"Don't worry," she said. "I have my own escort. You won't see me for the rest of the night." She grinned diabolically.

I counted my blessings.

"Are you warm enough?" I asked Elizabeth when we were in the car. A ball gown didn't exactly offer protection against the elements, even though she was bundled up.

"I'm fine," she said, but she was shivering as she said it.

If it wasn't the weather making her shake, what was it? I turned the heater up anyway.

The event was held at a hotel downtown. I didn't know what I was expecting, but it wasn't the luxurious scene that we found ourselves walking into. The ballroom was overflowing with people as a band tuned up in front of a small dance floor.

Elizabeth maneuvered through the crowd with ease.

Cascades of white flowers escaped from tall vases. I could feel the curious looks sent my way. My tie suddenly felt too tight. I wasn't exactly a people person, but I wanted to be the kind of guy Elizabeth could take to fancy functions. I wasn't that guy, but I wanted to be. For her.

I met people whose names I'd never remember. At dinner, I couldn't seem to keep my hands off her. I sat next to her and kept touching the spot where her dress exposed the soft skin of her back.

Despite my prediction, I was having fun. There was an open bar and the bartender was pouring generously. In fact, I was in danger of getting drunk, something that Elizabeth seemed to be actively encouraging.

"Your drink's empty," Elizabeth said. "I'll get you another one."

"I think I've had enough," I said. "I've got to drive home."

The music was from the big-band era. "Want to dance?" I asked Elizabeth. "I do a mean foxtrot."

"What's a foxtrot?" she asked.

"I'll show you." The music slowed as we reached the floor. I pulled her close and put my hands on her back, then twirled her until we were both laughing and dizzy.

Dinner was better than I had anticipated, but that could have been the champagne talking. "What did you do to get stuck at one of the cheap seats?" I asked.

"She invited you," Jenny said as she slid into the seat beside me.

"What happened to I won't see you for the rest of the night?" I asked her.

She shrugged. "My date wasn't nearly as entertaining as I'd hoped."

I looked around with an exaggerated stare. "I'm afraid I don't see your escort anywhere."

She pointed to a bewildered older man in a designer tux. He looked like he played a lot of golf. He held a drink in each hand as he scanned the crowd. He saw us, gave an enthusiastic wave, and spilled the drinks all over himself, which he'd obviously forgotten he was holding.

"Drat it, Danvers spotted me," she said. She jumped up and hurried off in the opposite direction.

"Is that Jenny's boyfriend?" I was surprised. He seemed too mild-mannered.

"No, they're having problems," Elizabeth said. "She was trying to break it off, but he can't seem to take no for an answer. Her date tonight was her solution, but now she wants to get back together with her psycho boyfriend."

"Why haven't I ever met her boyfriend?" I asked.

"To be honest," Elizabeth replied, "I can't stand him." There was an odd note in her voice, but my attention was on her plate, where I saw a lonely shrimp. I nearly threw the plate across the room.

"Don't eat that," I said.

Elizabeth was so startled that she dropped her fork. Our dining companions, an elderly man and his much younger companion, gave me a dirty look.

Elizabeth shot me an astonished look. "What are you talking about?"

"I thought you said you were allergic to shrimp?"

"I am, but I told the server I'm allergic."

I jabbed the offending crustacean with my fork and waved it in the air. "What's this, then?"

Jenny rushed up. "Elizabeth, is there a problem here?"

"No, of course not," she replied. "Luckily, Nyx spotted a stray shrimp in my salad."

Jenny obviously didn't think I was good enough for Elizabeth. I didn't know how to behave properly, she didn't know who my family was, and I liked to brawl. I wasn't anybody's idea of boyfriend material, except, perhaps, Elizabeth's.

A flash of red caught my eye and I turned to see Aunt Nona standing by the buffet. She wore a deep russet gown that exactly matched the shade of her companion's hair.

"What's she doing here?" I muttered, caught off-guard.

Elizabeth's gaze followed mine. "Mrs. Polydoros?" she said casually. The hairs on the back of my neck prickled.

Elizabeth had said she didn't know much about her brother's job, but she recognized her brother's boss at first glance. It seemed odd.

"What's the story with Mr. and Mrs. Polydoros?" I asked Elizabeth, after Jenny disappeared again.

"They're very influential in this town," she said. "Sawyer is on the board at Blake. And he's Alex's boss. Or he was until Alex disappeared." She did recognize them.

"Oh, he is, is he?" She'd called my aunt's husband by his first name. I watched my aunt and her husband as they laughed. She kept her left hand tucked in his.

All through dinner, dessert, and overlong speeches, I kept one eye on my aunt. She seemed oblivious of my presence, but I didn't buy it for one second.

While the band was tuning up, Elizabeth decided she'd had enough of my distraction.

"Nyx, what's wrong? You seem preoccupied," Elizabeth said.

My mind should have been on my date, but I couldn't take my eyes from them.

My aunt and her husband were the first ones to take the floor. He pulled her close and whispered in her ear and she responded with a laugh.

"It's nothing," I said. "Let's dance." I didn't wait for her response, but tugged on her hand until she followed me out on the dance floor.

I took Elizabeth into my arms and steered her to a spot where I hoped I was outside my aunt's line of vision, but could observe them. Something about Sawyer didn't sit right with me, and I needed to get closer to figure it out.

I watched, transfixed, until the song ended, which is when I finally got it. His trademark grin was missing. When he didn't think anyone was looking, he looked trapped.

Elizabeth said, "I'd love something to drink."

I steered her toward the bar and ordered two waters. I ended up with an ultraexpensive bottle of something that tasted like tap water. Elizabeth wasn't where I'd left her, but I finally found her staring out a window in the long hall leading to the ballroom. It was much quieter out there, and the hallway was nearly deserted. I wrapped my arms around her. "Tired?"

Elizabeth stepped out of my embrace. "Nyx, there's someone I want to say hello to." The abrupt change in mood caught me off-guard, but I followed her.

She led me to Nona and Sawyer. "Hello, Sawyer. Nona. This is my boyfriend, Nyx."

"We know Nyx well," Sawyer said jovially. "He's our newest employee."

Nona shook my hand and gave me an inscrutable smile.

"Yes, I'd almost forgotten," Elizabeth said. "He has a second job on the weekends. He barely has time for me." I stared at her. There was a hint of bitterness underneath her joking tone.

"So you're Elizabeth's beau?" Sawyer asked. "Small world."

"Yes, I am," I said. I reached over and squeezed her hand.

"Nyx is doing a wonderful job at Parsi," Sawyer told Elizabeth.

"I'm glad you think so," I replied.

Interesting, but what was more interesting was the question that popped into my mind: How did Elizabeth know a necromancer? There was magic all around us, but most people were too self-absorbed or too stupid to notice when they came up against it. Elizabeth was neither of these things.

Sawyer asked Elizabeth to dance and they left us. I knew it would have been polite to ask Nona to do the same, but I couldn't bear the thought of dancing with my murderous aunt.

"You don't like me very much, do you?" she asked, coming right to the point.

"I don't even know you," I said calmly, but underneath, I was panicking. Had I tipped my hand?

"You assume that I mean you ill," she guessed shrewdly. I guess she knew her own reputation.

"I assume that you can't believe that someone like Elizabeth would be interested in someone like me."

Her face softened and she reached out to touch my hand, but I shied away. "Of course she would be drawn to you," she said softly.

Elizabeth and Sawyer rejoined us before I could question her further.

A few minutes later, Sawyer and my aunt were called away to schmooze with some robber baron or something. Elizabeth and I were alone again.

"Why did you want me to meet them?" I asked.

She shrugged. "They seem like a nice couple." I couldn't tell if she was lying or not.

"Are you ready to leave yet?" I asked. I wasn't sure how long I'd be able to pretend that I didn't know exactly who my aunt was. Or how long I could stand to have my girlfriend lie to my face.

"What were you talking to Mrs. Polydoros about?" Elizabeth asked.

"Just being polite," I said. "Why?"

"You seemed intense," she said.

"I'm always intense," I said, trying to make it a joke.

Afterward, I took Elizabeth home.

"Want to come in?" she asked. "Jenny won't be home for hours."

I followed her into the living room, but she went straight for her bedroom. I held back, thinking she wanted to change, but she gave me an impatient look.

"Are you coming or not?"

I took her hand and started running up the stairs. She burst into laughter.

"I'm going to get all this stuff off my face," she said, gesturing to her makeup. "I'll be right back."

She slipped into the bathroom and I prowled nervously and tried not to think about what the invitation to her bedroom meant. But I was wrong. When she came back, she only wanted to talk.

"Any progress finding my brother?"

I gritted my teeth. She had a definite tone in her voice. "Some." I added, "Why do you think I can find him anyway?"

"You're smart," she said. "Street smart. And no one else had any luck. Found anything you'd like to tell me about?"

"No," I said, then amended, "Not yet. I'm working on something, but I don't want to get your hopes up."

"You seem to spend every weekend working at Eternity Road."

"I like it there," I said. "And I like the people. Talbot and I have become friends. And I haven't had a friend in a long time."

Elizabeth looked like she smelled something bad. "Do you have to jump every time he snaps his fingers?"

The statement was so patently untrue that my jaw dropped. What was wrong? She'd been on edge all night. If I didn't know better, I would swear she was trying to pick a fight.

"Talbot's my friend," I replied.

"What do you really know about him?"

I glared at her. "I know everything I need to know."

"Don't you think it's odd that he offered you a job and a place to stay just like that?"

"Why is it strange? That's exactly the same thing you did. And he didn't try to seduce me when he was doing it."

I realized how harsh my words were and glanced at Elizabeth, but she was staring at the floor. The blush in her cheeks gave her away. I felt like a heel for mentioning the libido potion.

"Not that that wasn't enjoyable," I said, trying to tease her into looking at me, but her eyes remained firmly on the floor.

"You'd better leave."

"Fine." I slammed the door as I went. Finding her brother was important, but so far, everything had led to a dead end. I couldn't lose sight of what I'd really come to Minneapolis to do, even if it meant I never found Alex.

Chapter Twenty-Seven

Elizabeth had suggested a movie. Despite having decades to adjust to the technology, I was annoyed by movie theaters, but I went along with it just to please her. She'd been snapping at me about every little thing; maybe agreeing to her suggestion would be a good olive branch.

I was on edge anyway, so it didn't take much to set me off. The movie had barely started when a couple of guys behind us started talking.

"Excuse me," Elizabeth turned around and said in a low voice, "but we're trying to watch the movie. Could you please keep it down?"

"Why don't you suck—"

I was up and over the back of the seat in an instant. The rest of his sentence was stopped by my fist in his face. Fighting was one thing I didn't need any magic for, something I was good at and had lots of practice doing.

"C'mon, pretty boy," his friend said. He made a move toward me. I took my free hand and punched him in the gut. He bent over, clutching his stomach, and I hit him in the neck.

"Nyx, stop it!" Elizabeth said. She tugged at my arm until I finally stopped using the guy as my personal punching bag. She dragged me out of the movie theater. "C'mon, let's go."

Adrenaline was pumping through my veins, but the cold night air cooled me down. I opened the Caddy door and slid in, breathing hard. I rested my head on the steering wheel until I felt calm enough to put it in drive.

"I'll take you home," I said.

"No, let's go to your place," she said shortly. "We need to talk this out and I don't want Jenny to hear us argue."

Since when? "Fine."

"Fine."

There was a chilly silence the rest of the way to my place. She waited until I'd parked the car in front of my building before she started yelling.

"What the hell was that all about?" Elizabeth was seriously pissed at me.

"What do you mean? I'm not going to let anyone talk to you like that."

"I am perfectly capable of taking care of myself," she said.

"You expect me to just sit there?"

"Yes, I do," she said.

"I can't. I won't," I said.

"I think you like it," she said accusingly.

"Like what?" I crossed my arms over my chest. I knew what she was getting at, but I wanted her to spell it out.

She glared at me. "You like to get into fights. To beat people up."

"So what if I do? It's how we met, isn't it?"

"You can't keep trying to protect me from everything."

"I want to," I said. "I just want to keep you safe." I put my forehead against hers and looked into her eyes.

She didn't say anything. We stood there, foreheads together, our lips nearly touching. Our breath mingled in the cold night air.

Finally, she looped her arm around mine and tugged me toward the stairs. "Let's go inside."

We barely made it up the stairs. I couldn't keep my hands off her. Her skin was the softest thing I'd ever touched. All the doubts that had been circling around in my brain evaporated.

"Are you sure?"

"Yes, now kiss me already," she replied.

"If you insist," I said. I backed her up against the nearest wall and kissed her deeply. She made a happy little noise and kissed me back.

"Now where is that new bed of yours?" she asked.

I was trembling as I led her to my bedroom. I rained tiny kisses along her chin, her collarbone, the sensitive hollow of her neck and breathed in her lemon-and-honey shampoo.

We were just inside the door when she started to pull off my shirt. I captured her hands in mine. "Wait," I said. "Are you sure?"

"Nyx, no matter what happens, be sure of one thing: I want this. I want you." With a quick movement, she pulled my shirt off and led me to the bed.

Later, we lay back on the pillows and she started to giggle. She gave a little bounce on the mattress. "I approve of this purchase."

I captured her in my arms and tickled her. "I intend to make good use of it."

She noticed the scar on my chest. "I am so sorry you were hurt," she whispered, then kissed the spot where the knife went in.

"It was worth it," I said.

She went still. "I hope you always think so."

Her cell phone rang with that curious ringtone I'd heard before, the one that made her go all quiet and look for someplace to talk where I couldn't overhear. This time she let it go to voice mail, but the mood was ruined.

"Go ahead and check your messages," I said. "I can tell you're dying to."

"Are you jealous?" She was trying to tease me, but it fell flat.

"Yes."

"Nyx, I would never do anything to hurt you," she said, suddenly serious.

"Don't say that."

"Why? It's true." She tried to kiss me, but I pulled away.

"Don't make promises you can't keep," I said. In a relationship, hurting the other person was almost inevitable.

She reached for me, but I avoided her embrace and got out of bed. "Go ahead and make your call. I'll get us something to eat."

I threw on a pair of sweatpants and went to the kitchen. I put sandwiches and a couple of sodas on a tray. I headed back to the bedroom, but I heard her voice through the door and lingered in the hallway. She was clearly arguing with someone, but I couldn't make out the words.

I cleared my throat and then pushed the bedroom door open with my foot. "Dinner is served."

She closed her phone with a snap. I set the tray down on the bed. "Did your phone call go all right?"

I sounded like one of those douchy guys who didn't trust his girlfriend. Wait. I *was* one of those guys. The realization was humiliating.

"Yes," she said and changed the subject, which was exactly what I deserved. "I'm starving."

"You seemed angry when I came in," I ventured.

"I was."

"Care to explain?" I tried and failed at a sympathetic tone, but Elizabeth was too pissed off at someone else to notice.

"It's just family stuff," she finally said.

"That was Jenny on the phone?" Relief coursed through me. I was giddy, unconcerned with anything but the little voice inside me that said *mine*. "What does she want you to do?" I asked idly.

She bit into her sandwich and ignored the question. "This is good."

It was clear she didn't want to talk about it. I had enough of my own family stuff to deal with, so I let it go.

"You have a bit of mustard on your cheek." I reached out to wipe it away with my thumb and when I touched her skin and she smiled at me, it hit me. I was in love with her.

"I hate to eat and run, but I've got to go," she said.

"What? I thought you would spend the night and we'd go out for breakfast."

"Another time," she said. She grabbed her clothes and dressed quickly. She dropped a quick kiss on my head, like someone kissing a child.

It was hard not to feel like a hump and dump. Elizabeth was entirely too eager to leave and I didn't like it one bit.

I caught her hand as she walked by. "No good-bye kiss?"

She laughed, but I kissed the laughter from her lips until she dropped the badass act.

"You know I don't do this all the time, any more than you do," I finally said.

"You don't?" Her surprise was somewhat unflattering.

"No, I don't."

"But you said…" Her voice trailed off.

"Too late to protect my ego now," I said. "Tell me."

"It's just you told me you'd been around. I thought you meant—"

"That I was a big old hosebag?" I frowned.

"Well, yes," she replied.

"I didn't mean it like that," I told her. I struggled to think of a way to explain it without revealing my secret. But I didn't want to lie to her, either. "I meant that I'd lived a rough life. Bar fights. That kind of thing. It's been a long time since I've been with anyone."

"How long?" she asked, trying to keep the amusement from her voice.

"It feels like a hundred years," I finally replied. Felt like because it had been that long.

She touched my cheek. "I hope it was worth the wait."

I grinned. "Definitely."

She smiled back, but then glanced at her watch and swore. "I've got to go."

The smile left my face. "I thought we'd settled all that."

"Don't pout, Nyx," she added. "It's not attractive."

I pulled her down into my lap. "Make me."

"You're such a child sometimes," she said, but she laughed before she repeated, "I've got to go."

"I'll drive you home," I said.

"Don't bother. I called a taxi," she said.

I stood and wrapped my arms around her. I whispered the words into her hair. *I love you.* I hadn't said those words to a girl in a hundred years, but I wasn't prepared for her response.

At first, I wasn't sure if she heard. "I'm glad," she finally said.

I tried to draw her back down onto the bed, but she squirmed away.

She gave me a quick kiss and then left. She was well out of the room before I realized she hadn't said she loved me back.

Chapter Twenty-Eight

Whenever I had a moment free, I took the opportunity to search for the other charms. Enough of my mother's possessions had shown up in Minneapolis to give me hope that I'd find another charm here, too.

I scoured most of the antiques stores, pawnshops, and even a couple of check-cashing places, but I didn't have any luck. I left my phone number at every spot and headed home.

I was sitting in my apartment brooding when my phone rang. "Uh, yeah, I hear you're looking for a cat carved from ebony," a woman's voice said.

"Who is this?"

"Not important," she said. "Do you want to know where you can find the charm or not?"

I was willing to take the risk. "Go ahead, I'm listening."

"There's a shop off Nicollet called Zora's," the caller continued. "The owner has a charm bracelet with a black cat on it." There was a click and a dial tone.

I stared at the phone for a minute. It was almost too good to be true. And they always said that something too good to be true would probably get you into trouble. I jumped into the Caddy and headed to Zora's. Zora's turned out to be in the Nicolett Mall area, which meant I would have to park and walk a few blocks. I passed by a bronze statue of a television character throwing her tam-o'-shanter into the air. For some reason, it reminded me of the troll I'd turned to stone.

The magic shop was next door to a Home Depot. A crescent moon on the sign above its door was my only clue that it sold magical items.

The store smelled of incense, but at least it wasn't the kind that made me want to sneeze. Candles, crystals, and basic books on witchcraft cluttered the shelves. So far, everything I saw was stocked for the tourists. A beaded curtain hung in an interior doorway. I assumed it led to a stockroom or private quarters of some kind.

"May I help you?" the clerk asked. It was Jenny, Elizabeth's roommate.

"Hi, Jenny," I said. "I didn't know you worked here."

"Nyx," she said. "It figures. What can I get you?"

"Just browsing," I said. "Do you have any charms in stock? I'm looking for something antique to give to Elizabeth."

"What kind of charm are you looking for? Love spell?"

"Not that kind of charm," I explained. "Something to go on a charm bracelet or a necklace."

She gave me a sharp look. "Nothing like that."

"I was told you might have a piece in ebony? An ebony cat?"

"Who told you that?"

"No one. Some guy." A tiny alarm went off in my brain.

She raised her hand and my gaze went to the charm bracelet on her wrist. There was a black cat hanging there, which could be the cat in question, but there were a lot of useless manufactured copies churned out in factories that mortals wore as fashion statements.

When I raised my eyes, she whipped a spell my way and I was rooted to the spot, unable to move my arms or legs. She had more than a drop of magic in her veins, after all.

"Gaston, get out here," she yelled.

Gaston? What did they say about black cats being unlucky? The search for this particular black cat wasn't turning out so well.

The Tracker strode through the curtain and grinned when he saw me rooted to the spot. "Good job, babe," he said. He held out his hand and she handed over the charm bracelet. He stuffed it into his shirt pocket. Gaston grinned when my eyes followed the motion.

"I'll take it from here. Now go get some lunch," he told her. Jenny exited through the front door. I told myself not to sweat. There was no way he could see through the occulo spell to identify me. I'd worry about what Jenny was doing with Gaston later.

"Why did you ask about the cat?" he asked.

He wasn't positive it was me. If he had been, I'd already be screaming in pain. I gulped and tried to think of what a normal, frightened mortal would say in a situation like this one. My mind went blank.

"Like I-I told her. I wanted a gift for my girlfriend."

"Cut the crap," he snarled. "You forgot one thing when you had that medicine woman craft her occulo spell."

"I don't know what you're talking about," I lied. I felt the sensation returning to my legs and I commanded them to move, but they remained stubbornly still.

"The eyes," he continued. "They always forget the eyes." He

pressed a knife against my cheek, at the tip of the eyes. "I'm going to correct that."

"What are you're talking about?" I asked. This time, my left leg moved forward a whole half step, but Gaston didn't seem to notice.

"I'm going to enjoy watching you stumble around without your big blue eyes." He pressed harder until the knife cut into the skin on my cheek.

"My eyes are brown." They'd been blue, like my mother's, but the occulo spell masked that.

"Don't lie to me."

"I'm not," I said. "My eyes are brown. See for yourself." I opened my eyes wide.

He peered into them. "It's a trick."

"No trick." My arm burned as the spell wore off. "I just came in to get my girlfriend a gift. I can buy her something else. What about that nice crystal over there?"

His gaze left mine for just a second, but it was enough. I swung out hard with my left arm, which was the only one working, and punched him hard. My fist connected with his nose and I felt a sense of satisfaction when blood spurted out. He instinctively put a hand to his face to stop the bleeding.

I kicked him hard in the balls. He dropped the knife and I dove for it. He followed me and reached it first, but his hand was slippery with blood and the knife skittered away.

He elbowed me in the face and then kicked me in the ribs, but I held on tight. He got a grip on my T-shirt, but it ripped. He dug his fingers into my side, but I grabbed his thumb and twisted until he yowled with pain.

I gained possession of the knife and waved it in front of him. He went motionless. I stood. "Stay where you are. Don't you dare even breathe." I bent over and hauled him to his feet, but kept the knife to his heart until he flinched. "Give me the cat."

He didn't hand it over, so I reached into his pocket and took it.

"You bastard," Gaston said. "You're a piece of shit, just like your father."

"Like you know anything about my father," I scoffed.

"I know more than you do," he said. The superior look on his face was all that it took for me to lose the tenuous grasp I had on my temper. I grabbed him by his hair and slammed his face into the tile floor.

I scrambled to my feet. There was blood all over me and I'd ruined another T-shirt, but I had the cat. I gave the unconscious Gaston another kick in the ribs. I grabbed a prayer scarf from the bargain bin and cleaned the worst of the blood off.

I ran all the way back to the Caddy, praying that nobody saw me. It wasn't like Gaston would call the cops. He had as much to lose as I did.

I drove in circles, hands shaking. I didn't dare go back to the apartment yet, at least not until I was sure I wasn't being followed.

The Tracker had found me. The question was, what was I going to do about it? I'd lied when I said I'd never thought about my father, but now that the topic had been broached, the thought wouldn't leave my mind. Who was he?

I watched the rearview mirror all the way to my apartment, but no one followed me. I parked the Caddy in the first parking spot I found and headed inside to clean up.

I'd stood up to the Tracker and won. More important, I had three of my mother's charms in my possession. I had bigger problems, though. Jenny obviously was involved, which meant Elizabeth was up to her cute ass in it somehow.

I stripped off my clothes and threw them into a garbage bag, then took a shower. I wiped the fog off the mirror and looked into it. There was a cut on my face near my eyelid, and I'd have a multitude of bruises in the morning.

I replayed the fight with Gaston in my mind. There had been the smell of incense—and underneath that, I realized, I'd picked up on something else, but had been too eager to find the cat to realize it. The strong smell of the grave.

Chapter Twenty-Nine

I had a feeling I was running out of time. The feeling intensified when Sawyer called me into his office on Friday. To my surprise, Naomi was there with him. Had they found out who I really was?

"We'd like to invite you to dinner tonight," Sawyer said.

"No excuses this time," Naomi added.

Sawyer was the only necromancer I knew. He was involved in this somehow. My worst fears were being realized. People I cared about were getting hurt. It was time to take fate into my own hands. I accepted the invitation.

Naomi nearly deafened me with her squeals of excitement. Was she faking it, or did the Fates still not know who I was?

"And don't be late," she told me before I left the office.

I sat outside my aunt's house for a long time. It could be a trap. Or it could be a family dinner. Or both. I contemplated attending my first family dinner, one that I might not emerge from alive.

I finally mustered up enough courage to ring the doorbell.

Sawyer answered the door.

"Nyx, glad you could finally make it," he said. He held out his hand and I shook it, faking an enthusiasm I was far from feeling.

"I never turn down a home-cooked meal," I said.

"C'mon in," he said. "I hope you're hungry. I made a heap of food." Nona appeared behind him.

Sawyer went off to do something domestic and there was no sign of Naomi, which meant my aunt and I were alone.

She led me to the living room where a baby grand piano stood at one end. I took a seat with my back to the wall, where I could see the door.

"Would you like a drink before dinner?"

I shook my head. I'd need every ounce of mental acuity to survive the night.

She took a seat opposite me. "Naomi should be down any minute. Sawyer tells me that you are an ambitious young man."

"He's being kind," I said.

"You also have a weekend job, I believe?" It wasn't really a question. I'd bet my next paycheck that she had a dossier on me already.

"At Eternity Road," I replied. "The pawnshop."

"Seems like the perfect job for you," she said.

I gave her a sharp gaze, but the look she returned me was serene. There's no way she would sit there and smile at me if she had the slightest inkling that I was the son of Fortuna. Would she?

I didn't know what to believe. At best, my aunts had reputations as meddlers, master manipulators, and liars. I couldn't tell if she was messing with me or telling me the truth. Or maybe a little bit of both.

"Speaking of which," I said, "I haven't met your other sister yet."

Nona frowned at my description of her older sister. "She's out of town on business," she said.

What kind of business would be more important than harassing me? I thought she lived for that.

Sawyer returned with a tray of stuffed mushrooms. "Dinner's almost ready," he said.

Naomi came into the room and gave me an exuberant hug. "I told you he'd come," she crowed to her mother. "I knew he wouldn't break his promise."

I pulled her braid, but gently. "You did, did you?"

Sawyer announced that dinner was ready. We took our places at the dining room table and he passed around a basket. "These biscuits are made from my mama's recipe," he said.

He piled my plate high with fried chicken, mashed potatoes, and biscuits smothered in gravy.

We made polite chitchat as we ate. I was leery of this little get-together, but the food was amazing. Sawyer was a culinary genius. A necromancer who could cook. He was a man of many talents. Too bad they included blood magic, the dark arts, and raising the dead.

Naomi went into the kitchen. A few minutes later, she came back carrying a pie in one hand and plates in the other.

She sat back down, cut a huge wedge of pecan pie, and proceeded to tear into it with gusto.

"How can you eat dessert?" Nona asked her.

"Because," Naomi said between bites, "I'll be burning it off tomorrow." Her mother shot her the kind of look that mothers give and Naomi added, "Swimming, Mom. I'll be swimming. Get your mind out of the gutter."

"That reminds me," Sawyer said. "When will we be meeting your young man?"

Naomi shrugged. "If I have anything to say about it, never," she teased.

"I expect to meet the boy who is dating my only daughter," Sawyer said firmly.

Naomi handed me a plate with a slice of the pie on it. "He's a friend of Nyx's."

"He is?" Nona looked intrigued. "Tell us about him."

To stave off answering her, I grabbed a fork and took a huge bite of pie.

"So there's a necromancer in Minneapolis," I said, after the last delicious morsel. He was sitting across the table from me, but I wanted to see their reactions.

She gave me a sharp look. "There are several witches and sorcerers in the Twin Cities, but there are no necromancers in the area. I'd know."

"Necromancers are the only ones who can raise the undead, right?" I asked.

She nodded.

"Then there's a necromancer in town," I said. "And he sent a wraith to a restaurant downtown." I didn't mention that the wraith had been after me.

I watched her reaction. Unless she was an award-winning actress, I'd swear she hadn't known.

Her husband, however, flinched. He knew something. Grave rot emanated from him.

Former necromancer, my ass. He was a practicing bone-conjurer or he wouldn't smell of the grave. It was faint, but it was there. Necromancers stank of the stuff, no matter what kind of fancy cologne they wore to mask the smell.

"A wraith?" Nona asked.

"Yeah, you know, a ghost, the undead, a spirit who has been called from his final resting place,"

"No one in Minneapolis would do that," Nona said.

She meant no one would do it without her permission.

"What if a necromancer were training an apprentice?" I asked.

Sawyer nearly choked on his pecan pie. He caught me staring. "I forgot the whipped cream," he said.

"I'll help," Nona said grimly.

"Your dad's a little jumpy," I commented after they left.

I was glad I had accepted Naomi's dinner invitation. I'd learned a lot—and maybe the most important thing was that my aunt was an excellent liar.

"There's some problem in his department," Naomi replied. "He's the VP in charge of product development."

Alex and Sawyer were both in product development. "What kind of problem?"

Naomi shrugged. "Some boring technical thing to do with the water they're using. No biggie." She pushed around the pecan pie on her plate.

"What's the matter?" I asked her. "Aren't you hungry?"

"So, you think my dad's a practicing necromancer, is that it?" she asked.

The ability to lie didn't seem to run in the family, at least not when it came to me lying to my cousin's face.

"Maybe," I told her. I didn't want to tell Naomi that I thought her dad might have something to do with Alex's disappearance.

Her parents came back, both stony-faced. It was clear they'd been fighting in the kitchen.

After dessert, Nona said, "Nyx, could you help me with the dishes?"

"Of course," I said. I wondered what she really wanted.

I followed her to her gleaming high-end kitchen. She wrapped an apron around her waist and then handed me one.

"I'm good," I said. "Did you want to talk to me about something?"

"I want you to tell me if you hear any more of a necromancer in Minneapolis," she said.

"I will," I promised. I helped her load the dishwasher in silence.

After my first family dinner, I was more bewildered than ever. I thanked them for a lovely evening and drove home. The evening wasn't what I had been expecting, but nothing in my life was lately.

In the morning, I whistled as I flipped over the OPEN sign at Eternity Road for the day.

"You're in a good mood," Talbot commented. "What the occasion?"

I'd made it through a family dinner without being recognized or tortured, reason enough for my good mood. Either Gaston believed my story or he hadn't told my aunts I was in town. I couldn't figure out why he'd do that. I ignored Talbot's sarcasm and got to work.

I was trying to sell a tourist a set of early-twentieth-century china, but she dithered about the cost. "I'll knock off another ten percent," I said.

The prospect of a bargain decided it for her and I rang up her purchase.

"*Buon fortuna*," she said.

"*Buon fortuna*," I replied, but the phrase made me uneasy. It wasn't common in the United States. Maybe it was a coincidence, but my good mood evaporated.

What if Gaston had figured out I was the son of Fortuna and decided to hurt the people close to me? He'd done it before. I grabbed my phone and called Elizabeth.

"I thought you were working today," she said.

"I am," I replied. "Everything okay?"

"Everything's fine," she said. "Why?"

"No reason," I said. "I'll see you later. Gotta get back to work."

By continuing my relationship with Elizabeth, I was putting her in danger. The aunts would not hesitate to use her to get to me, but I wasn't willing to walk away. My cash reserves were getting dangerously low and I needed money in the bank, just in case I had to run. But I was sick of running, so it was time to fight. At best, I figured I had a week before the Tracker caught up to me again.

"You know any quick ways to make money?" I asked Talbot. I wanted to buy the hex sign from Ambrose. It would take more money than I had to convince him to sell it to me.

He gave me a look. "A legal way? No. A borderline sketchy way for someone of your talents? Yes."

"How?" I asked. My friend was being suspiciously mealy-mouthed.

He hesitated. "High-stakes poker. Very hush-hush."

"A backroom poker game? Sounds perfect," I replied. I was the son of Lady Fortuna. It didn't get much luckier than that. At least where gambling was concerned.

"Nyx, I can't stress this enough. The people who run it are not nice people. They will hurt you."

I was intrigued. "Who are they? Russian mobsters?"

"Worse," Talbot replied. "Frat boys."

"Piece of cake," I told him. "I am a poker god."

He didn't seem convinced. "Ever played tarot poker?"

I shook my head.

"I'll get the cards," he replied.

The bell over the door tinkled and an elderly woman came in. She wore an ancient trench coat with worn spots on the elbows and a faded dress with thick tights and men's boots.

Talbot left to fetch the tarot deck while I helped our lone customer, who wanted to pawn something.

She opened a small silk purse and spread out a bunch of jewelry on the counter. "My husband gave it to me. He was quite generous."

I took a closer look at her stash. Her husband was a cheapskate. Every last piece was costume jewelry. From the looks of her, she hadn't had a good meal in days, but she didn't have the permanently windburned look of a street person. Not yet, at least.

"Can you give me anything for it?" she asked. Her hand trembled with the effort not to beg.

"I can give you five hundred for all of it," I said. It wasn't worth that, but maybe Naomi or Elizabeth would like the earrings.

I took some money out of my wallet and counted it out into her waiting hand. She tried not to look too eager. "I may have more at home," she said.

"I'm not sure we can use anything else—" I started, but something in her faded blue eyes stopped me. "But I'll take a look."

Her face lit up. "I'm not promising anything," I said.

"Yes, yes, of course," she said. But there was a spring in her step as she left.

I stared after her. The money wouldn't last long and then what would happen to her?

"That was a nice thing you did," Talbot said.

How long had he been standing there? "I'm already regretting it," I snapped. "And now I own five hundred dollars' worth of crap." I wanted the evidence of my folly out of my sight, so I shoved the jewelry into the pocket of my jacket.

Talbot just smiled. "Let's play cards."

Three hours later, I stretched. "I think I've got the hang of it," I said. "Now where is this game?"

"The Red Dragon," he said.

"Set it up," I said.

"Already done," he said. "Tonight at midnight."

I barked out a laugh. "How gothic of them." I added, "I'll have to stop by the bank at lunch. That old lady cleaned me out."

"Why do you do that?" he asked.

"Do what?"

"Act like you don't care," he said.

"I don't," I told him, but his expression told me he wasn't convinced.

He dealt the cards and stared at me.

"Be careful tonight," he said.

"Of a bunch of drunken frat boys?"

"I'm serious, Nyx," he said. "I know you have a death wish, but I would like to live to see another day."

"You're coming with me?"

"These guys are suspicious bastards," he replied. "Don't let their looks fool you. Besides, they won't let you in the game if I don't show up to vouch for you."

"What should we do until then?" I asked.

"Drink," he said. "You won't make it past the door if you don't have whiskey on your breath."

At five minutes to nine, we closed up Eternity Road and walked to the Red Dragon.

We slid into a hard wooden booth far away from the dance floor, but it reminded me of Elizabeth.

"You said you met here. How exactly did you meet?" Talbot asked.

"Her date stabbed me."

"Doesn't seem like a promising start to a relationship," he commented. I knew he didn't like Elizabeth. He never said anything, but I could tell.

"Tell the truth. You don't like her," I said.

He hesitated. "It's not that I don't like her," he said. "I do. I just don't trust her."

I sucked in a breath. I'd asked for the truth. It didn't mean I had to like it.

The silence stretched until the waitress brought another round of shots.

I tossed mine back. The fiery liquid burned going down. "What do you call a group of frat boys?" I asked.

"Is this a joke?"

"No, I mean the grouping. Like a murder of crows?"

Talbot thought about it and shook his head. "I don't know."

"A cluster fuck," I said. "A group of frat boys is called a cluster fuck."

"Don't be a dick," he said.

I raised an eyebrow. "I am what I am."

"And don't quote Popeye, either," he snapped.

I had expected him to laugh, but my poke at the frat boys had irritated him for some reason.

I found out why when two college boys approached our table and greeted Talbot with a complicated handshake.

"Hail, brother," the taller guy said. They were both good-looking with gleaming white teeth that pegged them as Americans and expensive clothing that told me they could afford it if I cleaned them out.

"Hail, brother," Talbot replied.

I didn't try to hide my snort of laughter. Talbot was a frat boy.

He ignored my amusement and made the introductions. "Nyx, this is Kyle and Spenser, two cardsharps you need to watch out for."

He was buttering them up before we took all their money. I shook their hands and smiled politely. "So how do you guys know each other?" I asked, just to see Talbot squirm.

"Fraternal brothers of the order," Kyle replied.

"A frat," I stated.

"Spense and I went to college together," Talbot said. "We pledged different frats, though."

I noticed that Kyle, who was a skater rat type, had an oak leaf pattern on his hand-painted shoes, but Spenser, who wore a custom-made suit, had a tie clip in the shape of a trident, which signified the House of Poseidon.

"Ready?" Spenser said. He was perfectly controlled, except a tiny twitch in his right hand that told me he was a gambling addict.

He led us through a side door that I'd assumed was a janitorial closet, but which turned out to be a back room. It was barely bigger than a supply closet, but it had a fully stocked bar, staffed by two bartenders, and an unpleasant surprise.

Brad, the guy who'd stabbed me, was sitting at a round

table, sitting atilt on his folding chair like he owned the place.

He jumped to his feet when he saw me. "You!" he said.

"I don't know why you're so pissed off," I said. "You're the one who stabbed me, not the other way around."

"You left with my girl," he accused.

I smiled at him. "She's my girl now."

His friends seemed to agree with him that this was an offense worth attempted murder.

"I can't take you anywhere," Talbot muttered. In a louder voice, he said, "Gentlemen, are we here to fight over some woman or are we here to play?"

Spenser, he of the shaky hands, lunged for the cards. "Let's play."

After a long glare at me, Brad took his seat sullenly. "Deal," he snapped at Kyle.

Talbot leaned in. "You're actually going to play a hand of poker with a guy who stabbed you?"

I grinned at him. "I'm going to clean him out," I said. "Watch." If the son of Fortuna couldn't beat a douche bag like Brad at a game of chance, I didn't deserve to call myself my mother's son.

They played with a Tarot de Marseille deck. One of the bartenders refreshed our drinks at regular intervals.

I watched the other men as I played. Kyle was there for the free drinks, but Spenser had the gambling bug bad. Brad was the one I really wanted to beat. He played cards like the cocky asshole he was, but he wasn't stupid.

We played well into the night, by candlelight. I didn't play to win, not at first. Mostly, I played to wipe the supercilious smile off Brad's face.

A stack of cash accumulated in front of me. As my stack grew bigger, Brad's stack dwindled, along with his bucktoothed smile. He stroked his cards nervously. I remembered his hands all over Elizabeth and I wanted to punch his face in.

When I'd trumped him again, he folded his hand very precisely. "How about we use a new deck?"

I glanced at Talbot. Did Brad think I was cheating? But Talbot's face didn't betray anything. He didn't even bother to frown at me, which made me think we were in dire straits.

All thoughts of danger went out of my head when I saw the new deck. It was a traditional Jeu de Tarot deck, the cards gilded and paper-thin with age. I could almost smell the faint scent of freesia that would have clung to it. My mother's lost tarot deck.

"You've seen a deck like this before?" Brad asked.

"Yes," I said. I couldn't take my eyes off it.

His eyes gleamed at my clipped reply. He knew I wanted it.

We were finally down to the last hand. Everyone else at the table had folded.

Brad's expression told me if he had anything to say about it, the night would end in my blood being spilled again.

The candles flickered. I pushed the stack of chips to the center of the table. "I'm all in," I said. "Including the deck of cards."

"It's my lucky deck," Brad protested.

I started to pull the chips back, but he stopped me. "Wait, I'll take the bet."

I smiled. Brad was desperate, which meant he was gambling with money he couldn't afford to lose.

Brad had a dead man's hand, which in traditional poker was eights and aces, but in tarot poker was the Wheel and the eight of Wands.

I flipped my cards over slowly, watching Brad's eyes as I did.

I fanned out my winning hand: Kings, Queens, Pages, and Knights.

He realized he'd lost and his eyes turned frantic. I moved a split second before he threw the knife. It hit the wall behind me with a dull thud. My head had been in that exact spot a moment before.

Then I was over the table and onto him. I smashed his head into the table before he could react.

"Talbot, get the cards and the money," I said. I gripped Brad's hair and gave him another thump for good measure.

"What cards?" he asked.

"The cards on the table," I shouted. "Make sure you get all of them."

I didn't have time to check on Talbot, because the bartenders, obviously two of Brad's friends, advanced toward me.

I'd knocked Brad unconscious, but his two friends looked bigger and smarter than he was.

"We're gonna beat that smart-ass attitude out of you," one of them muttered. When his fist connected with my ribs, I regretted the generous tip I'd given him earlier. The second man moved to hold my arms while I was doubled over from the punch.

Talbot came to my assistance and hit the second guy with a folding chair.

I looked around and noticed that Kyle had bolted at the first sign of trouble. Spenser ignored the fight; he was too occupied with stuffing my cash into his pockets.

My mouth was bashed and cut. I grinned through the blood as I hit the bartender in the stomach with rapid punches. He fell to the ground. I kicked him in the ribs until he screamed with pain.

"Let's get out of here," Talbot said. He pulled me away.

"Did you get the tarot cards?" I asked.

"Yes," he replied, but I didn't move.

"All of them?" I asked.

"Yes, all seventy-eight of the damned things. Now let's go!"

The sirens I heard in the distance clued me in about his sudden need to leave.

We ran from the bar and didn't slow down until we were a block from our building.

"That went well," Talbot said wryly. "We left most of the money." He handed me a small wad of bills and the tarot deck.

I grinned at him. "It went better than you think."

Chapter Thirty

I was going to break into Parsi Enterprises. I didn't have a key and I knew the place was warded, but it might be my last chance. There had been too many near misses lately, and in my experience that meant the aunties were closing in.

The downstairs lobby was deserted, but I didn't expect it to be that way for long. I made it to the office without detection, but the big double doors were locked up tight. I'd come prepared, though.

Not with magic, which might set off one of the wards, but with a spare key I'd swiped from Trevor's desk. It had been helpfully marked FRONT DOOR.

I turned the knob quietly. The place was about as lively as a tomb. I wanted to snoop through Alex's office.

I fished out a penlight and shone it around. I'd become familiar with the layout in the last few weeks, so I knew exactly where Alex's office was. It was locked and this time I didn't have a spare key. I examined the lock and then went back to the reception area for a paper clip.

I was sweating by the time the lock clicked and the handle opened.

I crossed to the desk and rifled through it. Then a switch was flipped on and light flooded the room. Gaston stood there, smirking at me.

"It's you, isn't it?" Gaston said. "Son of Fortuna. I've been looking all over for you and you've been right under their noses."

"I don't know what you're talking about," I said. "You attacked me at the magic shop. I was just defending myself."

I hated the guy, but I had to give him his props. He was a skilled Tracker.

He strode toward me, eyes full of premature triumph. "I knew it was you," he said. "I see I left you a little souvenir."

The cut he'd given me at Zora's had left a small scar. "I cut myself shaving."

"I finally found you," he continued to crow, so I let him go on.

I shrugged. "Think what you want."

"There's one way to know for sure," Gaston said. "Sawyer, come on out."

Sawyer appeared and his normal friendly smile had vanished.

"Sawyer, what's going on?" I told myself they couldn't prove anything.

His lips moved, but there was a roaring in my ears, which blocked out what he was saying.

He was removing the occulo spell. It felt like someone was flaying the skin from my body. The medicine woman had warned me removal would be painful, but she'd seriously undersold it.

The agony receded and I met Sawyer's eyes. He'd be able to see the real me. I'd gotten used to the spell's protection and I felt naked without it.

"He's playing you, Sawyer," I said.

"You're telling me you're not the son of Fortuna?" he asked. "You look just like her."

"I'm not saying that," I said. "I'm saying not to trust Gaston."

Gaston's grin sent a shudder through me. "Don't listen to him, Sawyer. He hates your wife, your entire family."

"I know you are behind it all," I said. "I know you've been poisoning Decima, that you tried to poison me. You're trying to take down the Fates, but what I don't understand is why."

With a quick movement, Gaston used a spell and immobilized Sawyer.

"Why was Sawyer helping you?" I asked. "Doesn't seem like his style."

"Sawyer Polydoros used to be a badass necromancer," Gaston said. "But even a badass can be made to do my bidding. I just needed the right leverage. His daughter."

"Naomi?" I had to force myself not to punch him.

Gaston grinned at me, clearly pleased to know something that I didn't know. "His *other* daughter. Wren. The one he didn't want his wife to know about."

"Who's the mother?" I asked.

Gaston laughed. "That's Sawyer's dirty little secret, isn't it? The only person in the world the Fates hate more than the son of Fortuna."

Sawyer gave me a pleading look, but I ignored it. I couldn't afford to show any weakness in front of Gaston. "So what's the plan?"

"Why should I tell you?" he snarled. "You belong to the Wyrd line."

"Let's just say we have a mutual goal," I said. "Why do you think I came to Minneapolis? I came to make the Fates suffer as much as my mother did. So what's your plan?"

The hatred in my voice must have convinced him, because he started talking.

"I want power," Gaston said. "I've been doing their bidding like a trained monkey. Do you know what that feels like?"

I had an inkling, but I shuddered. Gaston was a twisted version of me.

"I'm going to kill them," Gaston finally said. "And then I'm going to take over. You got a problem with that?"

Getting rid of the Fates was something I had to do all by myself. I raised an eyebrow. "And if I do?"

"Killing you won't work," Gaston said. "I've certainly tried enough times. But that pretty little girlfriend of yours is mortal. I'll enjoy it." Now I knew where Jenny had gotten all her bruises. Gaston was a demented bully.

"Go ahead," I lied. "I'm bored with her. Mortals can be so tiresome. Silly little fool believed every lie I told her."

"You don't care?" he asked. I'd thrown him off-guard, but despite everything I didn't want Elizabeth to become another dead person I used to know.

"Of course not," I said. "Why else did she have to slip me a libido spell?"

He gave me an oily grin. "At least you got something out of it. Maybe I'll try her out next."

"Be my guest," I said. I forced my clenched fists to relax. "Now what do you want me to do?"

"That spell didn't hold up so well, did it?" Gaston replied. "But I have plans for you."

I held up a hand. "Tracker, I have a proposition for you. Just don't kill him."

"I thought you hated the Fates."

"I do," I said. "But Sawyer doesn't have anything to do with that."

"Yes, he does," Gaston said. With a swift movement, he pulled out a knife and sliced Sawyer across the neck.

I tore off my T-shirt and applied pressure to the wound to try to stem the bleeding. My scar throbbed in sympathy. I started a healing spell, but it wasn't working. There was blood everywhere and I flashed back to how brightly the red droplets had gleamed on my mother's snowy pillow.

Sawyer was dying in a pool of his own blood. A bloody knife lay next to him. He'd been stabbed by the same knife Gaston had threatened me with. I picked it up and waved it at Gaston. "I'll kill you."

That's when my aunt and cousin decided to show up. They took in the scene at a glance.

"Do something," Naomi screamed.

"Naomi, Nona, a little help here," I snapped. "Healing spell. Now!" They recited the Latin, but it was too late. Sawyer was fading.

Naomi looked like she was going to throw up.

"I found them here," Gaston said. "Sawyer must have surprised Nyx when he broke in."

Morta appeared holding her golden shears just as she had when my mother died.

"No," Nona wailed. "Please, I'm your sister. I love him."

"She's just doing her job, darlin'," Sawyer said weakly.

Morta touched Sawyer's hand, and a glowing silver thread appeared in the air above him. She cut the thread in one quick motion and he stopped talking. Stopped breathing. His thread of fate had been severed, which had ended his life.

I saw the sheen of tears in Morta's eyes, but she didn't speak, just shook her head.

When Nona turned back to her dead husband, Morta met

my eyes and then slowly, deliberately pointed at me before she disappeared.

I stared at the spot where Morta had been. What had she been trying to tell me? And why couldn't she just spit it out already?

Nobody moved for a second. The silence seemed to stretch all the way to eternity.

Nona let out a long wrenching scream. "Why did you do it, Nyx? Tell me, damn it!"

I realized I was holding the bloody knife and dropped it.

"Revenge," Gaston said quickly. "He's the one you've been looking for. Your sister's son. Look at him closely."

Nona came so close that our noses were almost touching. It made it easy to see the hate in her eyes. "It is you," she said. "I wish I'd cut your throat in your crib."

Her pain gave me no satisfaction. The hatred I'd felt for my aunts had been washed away, replaced by pity. At least for Nona.

"Gaston did this," I said. "Not me. He's framing me."

She turned, eyes dazed with pain. "I don't believe you."

"He obviously raised a ghost for someone," I said. "It had to be someone who had a hold on him. So who? That's Gaston's knife. He tried to use it on me just the other day."

Naomi was crying so hard that she couldn't speak. "Get out," she finally said. "Don't come near me again or I swear I'll find your thread of fate and cut it myself."

"Don't be stupid," Nona said. "He's not going anywhere. Gaston, grab him."

I didn't want to leave them alone with Gaston, but I didn't have a choice. There was no way Nona would listen to me after what had just happened. I ran.

Chapter Thirty-One

I needed to talk to Talbot, to convince him to keep Naomi and her mom away from the Tracker, but when I stopped by Eternity Road it was locked up tight. Ambrose had given me a key, so I turned the lock in the door and went in.

The air smelled wrong, like mummy dust and a thick layer of decay. The smell of a necromancer.

"Talbot? Ambrose?" There was no response.

"Damn it, Talbot, where are you?" I shouted, but there wasn't any answer.

I searched everywhere but didn't find a trace of them. Something was wrong.

There was blood on the floor. I got the cleaning supplies and set to work. I didn't want Talbot to come back and have to clean it up.

As I scrubbed, questions kept popping into my mind. What had happened? After the blood was cleaned up, I opened the store. I was on edge all day and there was no word from Talbot or Ambrose.

It was nearly midnight when Talbot strolled in.

He didn't seem that surprised to see me. The real me. "Do you recognize me?" I asked. "Nyx Fortuna."

"Nyx Fortuna, wanted man," he said. "I heard." He studied me closely. "Your eyes are the same shape. And you're still good-looking. Just different. So this is the real you?"

A tiny part of me relaxed, knowing that Ambrose must be okay or Talbot would not be so calm. "Where's Ambrose? He's okay, isn't he?"

"He's recovering," Talbot said, the grin slipping from his face momentarily. "I took him to see an old…friend."

"What happened?"

"Someone tried to break into the store again, but Dad stopped them. He was injured in the process."

He was withholding a wealth of information. "But it didn't look like anything had been touched. No broken windows, no trashed door."

"Dad foiled his entry," he said. "He was shot."

"His?" I picked up on the tiny slip he'd made. "Talbot, what's going on?" I asked.

"It looks like your prediction finally came true," he said. "Someone came looking for something last night. Or someone." His glare made it clear he thought the shot was meant for me. Maybe he didn't get the memo that I couldn't be killed.

Gaston had no problem torturing or killing anyone I cared about. My throat worked as I realized how many people I'd put in danger.

"There was blood all over the floor," I said. "I cleaned it up."

"Thank you," he said politely, but the smile, which I now realized had been completely fake, was gone.

"Aren't you going to tell me what happened?"

He turned away from me, walked over to a shelf, and fussed

with a Victorian mourning locket. "If you tell me what the hell you're doing in Minneapolis. And if you've killed anyone lately."

"Naomi," I guessed. "She told you what happened to her father."

"She told me you killed Sawyer." The calm collected facade slipped for a moment and I saw pain behind his eyes.

"And you believe her?"

He didn't answer my question. "Is it true? That you're the son of Fortuna?"

I nodded. "But I didn't kill Sawyer."

Talbot cleared his throat. "My dad told me a little bit about your mother," he finally said. "I owe you an apology."

"For what?"

"For treating a son of Fortuna, the only son of the Wyrd family line, like a novice magician," he said in a low voice. "It's humiliating how attached to these little symbols I've become." He yanked off the silver ring he always wore and stared at the oak leaf engraving before tossing it on the table.

I slid it back to him. "Put it back on," I ordered.

"Will you accept my apology?" he asked.

I shrugged. "So you're proud of your lineage," I said. "That's not a crime."

"Stupidity isn't a crime, either," he replied. "But I'm full of that, too."

"Believe me, I'd rather be from the House of Zeus any day than from the House of murdering, sadistic crones I'm related to."

He tried to lighten the atmosphere. "Hey, that's my potential future mother-in-law you're talking about."

"So, it's ironic, isn't it?" I said as I poured a shot of absinthe for both of us.

"What exactly do you find ironic about your situation?" Talbot said, returning to my original comment.

I cleared my throat. "Just that I've been trying to find that damned thread for ages to finally end it."

"End it? You mean let your aunts kill you?"

"I've lived a very long time, Talbot," I said. "I've been ready to die for years. But I can't. I just have to watch everyone else die."

He was silent while he absorbed everything I was telling him.

I couldn't bear the quiet a second longer. "Will Ambrose be okay?"

"Almost certain." Almost certain made my throat clench up. It was my fault. It was all my fault.

"And now that I have something to live for, it might get taken away. It was sheer coincidence that I even met her."

"Maybe it wasn't coincidence," he said.

"If you tell me it was fate, I may have to punch you," I warned him.

He scowled. "I don't believe in fate, despite the existence of your aunts. People do things for a reason."

"What are you saying? That Elizabeth deliberately set out to meet me? Why?" He didn't answer, and I feigned a lightness I didn't feel. "Because of my gorgeous face?"

"I don't know her motivation," Talbot said.

"You think it was a setup," I said.

His expression was answer enough.

"You think she was working with my aunts."

He shrugged. "Or someone."

"And you think I'm stupid enough to fall for it?" The growing pit in my stomach told me I had been exactly that stupid.

"How much do you really know about her, Nyx?"

"More than you know about the girl you love," I said. "And are you saying I want to get caught? I don't think so."

He shook his head. "I'm saying maybe you're tired of running. Not the same thing."

I frowned. "I'll never get tired of thwarting them. My very existence is like pebbles in their shoes."

"Pebbles can get crushed," he replied.

"You didn't ask me if I killed Sawyer," I said.

"Do I need to?" Talbot seemed to think he knew me better than I knew myself. But that couldn't be true. No one knew me. Not really. Because I wouldn't let them.

"No," I told him. "Talbot, I know Naomi hates me right now, but you've got to convince her to stay away from Gaston." Ambrose and I were approximately the same height. Maybe he had been mistaken for me. A bullet wouldn't kill me, but it would put me out of commission for a day or two.

Then something dawned on me. "You said *he*. What did he look like?"

"Tall, blond guy," Talbot continued.

"Gaston," I said. "He's trying to take out the entire Wyrd family. He loves to torture and kill anyone I get close to."

Talbot clenched his fists. "If he touches her, I'll kill him." We both knew who he was talking about, but there was nothing I could say.

I changed the subject. "I thought I smelled something off," I told him. "A necromancer has been in the store."

"Impossible," he said. I'd surprised him. "I can count the number of necromancers left on two hands. Your aunts didn't take kindly to the necromancers who sided with Hecate."

"Impossible or not," I said, "someone was here. Someone who smelled of death and the dust of old bones. There's only one kind of magician who gives off that stench." Sawyer had been training Gaston in the dark arts, I was sure of it.

"Dad found out something," Talbot said. "He hesitated, but finally told me. The prophecy says that either you or the Fates must die."

"One of the Fates already died," I said. "My mother was a Fate. Only everyone has forgotten her."

"You haven't forgotten," Talbot said softly.

"But I'm not the one trying to kill them," I said. "At least not right now. Screw the prophecy."

"You're afraid to face them," Talbot accused.

"Afraid?" I repeated. "I'm not afraid. In fact, I'm going to get to the truth right now, starting with Elizabeth."

I left while his mouth was still hanging open.

Chapter Thirty-Two

Elizabeth wasn't home and she wasn't answering her cell, so I headed back to the store. I was half crazy with worry. I had to do something.

"Want to go fishing?" I asked Talbot.

"Fishing? In the middle of the night? Besides, I'm not big on killing things," he said.

"Not that kind of fishing," I told him. "I plan on diving into Lake Harriet."

"Nyx, that lake is full of naiads."

"I'm aware," I replied. I hesitated before asking my next question. I didn't want him to discourage me from going, but I wanted to know what I was up against. "Anything else I need to worry about?"

"Besides hypothermia and naiads? Good lord, isn't that enough?"

I shook my head. "Something is calling to me. I have to know what's down there."

"I'm in," he said. "I have something you should take with you." He left and came back a second later with a wet suit.

His eyes turned the silver of moonlight in the rain. He said a couple of words over the suit then handed it back to me.

"It'll keep you warm enough, but I can't guarantee it will keep the naiads away."

"Not much will," I said. "Thanks, Talbot."

We took the Caddy and parked a few blocks from the lake.

"There's something there, I can feel it," I told him.

A bright moon was reflected on the smooth surface. "Like what? Besides some seriously scary naiads?"

"I don't know, but I'm going to find out."

"You'll freeze to death," he said.

"I have a badass sorcerer as a best friend," I said. "I'm sure he can think of something."

Talbot gave me a playful shove on the shoulder. "Best friend, huh?"

"The best." I shoved him back.

A dark shadow appeared above the clouds. Was it a flock of migrating birds? The rush of heavy wings sent ice down my spine, and then I heard a harsh sound, something between a caw and human speech. Harpies.

I stood rooted to the spot, unable to move, barely able to breathe.

"Run," I said through numb lips. "Talbot, run now. Head for cover."

"I'm not leaving you," he said. The harpies were getting closer.

"For once, could you do what I ask you to do and get the hell out of here?"

I shoved him, hard, and he finally took off, but it was already too late. The lead harpy, her black hair streaming behind her, had gone into a sharp dive, headed straight for Talbot. Swift

Wing was the most vicious of the bunch, but her sisters Shadow and Fleet Foot were no walk in the park, either.

He was lost from view in a whirling mass of beating wings and screeching voices.

"Not this time, Swift Wing," I said. I took out my athame and stabbed at the flurry of wings until they parted. Talbot was alive, but Swift Wing had bloodied him. She was playing with him, like a cat plays with a rat. She grinned when she saw me and raked his cheek with her talons and slashed his chest, just to let me know the game was almost over.

I ran for her and hacked at her leathery wing so she couldn't fly. The other harpies were gaining on me, their hot breath at my neck. I stabbed Swift Wing in her right eye.

She shrieked with pain and dropped Talbot's limp body. I made a grab for him and dove into the lake. I hoped the cold water would slow the bleeding.

The remaining harpies were enraged at the death of their sister. They dive-bombed us repeatedly. I stayed underwater until my lungs were bursting and then returned to the surface to gulp air.

The harpies' cries of mourning were awakening things in the lake I'd rather have sleeping.

"Willow, where are you? I need your help," I shouted desperately.

Her head broke the surface of the water. "You called, bane of Fate?" I noticed I was no longer son of Fortuna, but the decidedly less friendly bane of Fate.

I didn't have a lot of options. "Take him somewhere safe," I said. I thrust Talbot's unconscious form at her.

She took him from me gently.

"Somewhere he can breathe!" I called after her, but her only response was a quiet splash.

Once Talbot was relatively secure, I turned my attention back to the keening, bloodthirsty harpies, who were cursing me and my descendants in their strange garbled tongue.

I reached for my knife, only to realize I'd left it in Swift Wing's body, which was lying near the shoreline. I'd have to risk it.

I swam to the shallows and waited. I scooped up a couple of decent-size rocks and waited until Shadow made another dive. She came close enough for me to see the color of her eyes, which were a muddy brown, before I threw the rock right between them. It stunned her and she went into a tailspin. Her sister rushed to assist her and I ran for it.

I managed to free my knife, but not before I felt the tip of Fleet Foot's claw at my back. I turned and slashed, expecting to wound her slightly, but her entire foot came off. She squawked in pain. She scooped her dazed sister up in her beak and then took to the skies, trailing blood as she flew.

I lay on the cold ground and gasped for air. Talbot? Where was Talbot?

I called Willow's name, but she never came. I lay back exhausted until I heard a splash. I looked up to see Willow propelling Talbot along the surface of the water.

I waded in to meet them. He was conscious, thankfully, and she'd managed to bandage his wounds.

"Thank you," I told Willow gravely. "Thank you so much." I kissed her cheek and she blushed.

"Be well, son of Fortuna," she said before diving into the lake.

I helped Talbot to shore, and we sat shivering in the moonlight.

"Those were the Fates' harpies," he said grimly.

"They were after me." The silence stretched out until it became unbearable. "Well?" I asked at last.

"Well what?"

"Are we still friends, even though you almost got killed and will have a scar for life?"

He stared at me, his eyes unreadable. "We're still friends."

It was more than I deserved. I nodded because my throat was too tight to speak.

I took him back to his apartment, where I had to explain everything to his dad, who didn't look in much better shape than Talbot.

"I'm sorry," I told Ambrose. "I didn't mean for either of you to get hurt."

"I know you didn't," he replied.

There was a knock on the door and I went to answer it.

"What are you doing here?" Naomi asked. She slapped me before I could get a word out.

I stepped into the hallway and shut the door behind me. "I probably deserved that."

"Where's Talbot?"

"He's asleep. What are you doing here?" I asked. She made a run for the apartment door, but I blocked her way.

"I could ask you the same thing. I can't believe you had the nerve to show your face after what you did," she said. "You murdered my dad."

"Your mother and aunts murdered my mother."

"So we're playing tit for tat now?"

"I didn't kill Sawyer," I said. "Gaston did."

"I don't believe you."

"Don't," I said. "Let him finish off the Fates. He's already poisoned Deci and killed your dad. Don't listen to me and you'll die. I don't give a fuck about the aunties, but I do care what happens to you."

The anger in my voice seemed to convince her when nothing else did.

"Nyx, what's the matter with you?" She sounded like we were best buddies. Like her mother and her sisters hadn't almost killed my best friend.

"What's the matter with *you*?" I threw her words back at her. "How could you?"

"How could I what?" she asked. She flipped one braid over her shoulder. The gesture incensed me.

"Quit playing dumb, Fate," I spit out contemptuously. "How could you let the harpies attack Talbot? My friend. Your boyfriend."

She gripped my arm so tightly that it hurt. "A harpy attacked Talbot?"

I knocked her hand away. "Harpies. Plural. As if you didn't know."

There were tears in her eyes. "I didn't, I swear. Is he—?"

"Alive? Yes, no thanks to you," I told her. "What's a kid like you doing in a family like ours?"

"The aunties aren't so bad," she said. "And my mom's great."

"So was my mom," I said.

"I'm sure she was."

"And they killed her. Their own sister."

"It was her time," she said.

"How would you feel?" I asked. "If it were your mother? One day she's fine, and the next she's spitting up blood. A week later, she was gone and I was alone." I realized I was shouting and lowered my voice.

"I would feel awful if something happened to Mom," she said. "But I would understand that it was meant to be. Being a Fate isn't a job, it's a responsibility. There are rules."

"Don't kid yourself that they always follow the rules," I told her. "They mess around in people's lives all the time."

"It's not messing around," she protested.

I glared at her. "Then what is it?"

"It's a sacred trust," she said.

I snorted.

"I want to see him." Her voice was high and frightened.

"I'm not convinced you didn't have anything to do with it. You know what they say: Like mother, like daughter."

She flinched, but met my eyes. "Gaston has the harpies, not the Fates. Deci gave them to him ages ago."

"Why would she give a psycho like Gaston her deadly little pets?"

She bit her lip, but then told me. "She needed him to find someone, and he wouldn't do it without a bribe."

"Me?"

She shook her head. "Someone else. He wasn't successful, but she let him keep the harpies."

"Interesting," I said.

She walked past me into the apartment. Just like a full-fledged Fate.

Ambrose was pacing like a caged wolf, but when he saw my cousin he stomped into the other room. All the good stuff was at Ambrose's place. A cushy but faded Oriental rug was spread out in front of the sofa, and a silver tray filled with drinks and snacks sat on the coffee table.

Talbot was lounging on the red velvet sofa, looking like Lord Byron in an old smoking jacket from the shop. She knelt in front of him and caressed the good side of his bandaged face.

"Nyx told me what happened," she said. "Are you okay?" If I had any doubt that Naomi cared about Talbot, it was dispelled when I saw her touch his face.

He pulled her onto the sofa and whispered something in her ear that made her blush.

I turned away to give them some privacy. When seconds stretched into minutes, I cleared my throat.

They broke apart, wearing matching blushes.

"How did Gaston manage to convince Deci to give him the harpies?" I asked Naomi.

"I can't tell you," she said.

"You have to tell me, you little idiot," I growled.

"I don't have to tell you anything," she snapped.

"I can't believe you can't see what he's after," I said.

"What is he after?" Her expression didn't give anything away.

"He's after the Fates," I said. "He's been your little errand boy for so long. The aunts couldn't even see it when he started to turn on them."

"Do you have any proof?" she asked.

"Naomi, just get your mom to go somewhere safe," I told her. "The farther away from Gaston, the better." Part of me wanted to leave the Fates to Gaston, but Gaston got his kicks from hurting women. There was no way I'd let him win.

"Why should I believe you?" She was in a snit, but I couldn't really blame her. I'd handled it badly.

"Trust me," I said. "You don't want to turn your back on Gaston." I rubbed the scar on my wrist.

She stared at me for a long second. "I do believe you are serious. But you're still an asshole."

"I might be an asshole, but you know I'm right," I said.

"Don't be mad at Nyx," Talbot said. "He saved me."

"You were lucky," I heard Naomi murmur.

"We all need a little luck," Talbot said.

It was going to take every bit of luck we could find to get through this.

Chapter Thirty-Three

The next day, the harpies hadn't returned, but I couldn't shake off the sense that there was a whole lot of bad juju headed my way. And I still hadn't heard from Elizabeth.

I decided to look for Elizabeth after her last class. I parked the Caddy in front of the imposing brick building where she took her acting class and got out and sat on the hood. College kids streamed through its doors, but I didn't see Elizabeth in the throng.

Why were snooty colleges always made of brick or stone or something equally hard and unmoving? Perhaps to impress prospective students and their families even more, it was named after some forgotten Romantic poet.

I waited until I spied a likely-looking coed and sauntered up to her.

"Hi there," I said.

Her eyes did a full inventory of me before she cracked a smile.

"Well, he-llo," she replied, drawing the word out.

"I'm looking for Elizabeth Abernathy. Have you seen her?"

"I don't know an Elizabeth," she replied. "And I know everyone. Except you."

"Tall, blond, gorgeous? Green eyes?"

"You can check the commons," she said. "I saw a girl matching that description there just now. With her boyfriend. But I think her name is Beth."

Beth? Elizabeth wasn't a Beth. Beth was the saintly, sickly girl from *Little Women*, which I'd been forced to read when I'd been holed up like a rat in a London attic one winter. Elizabeth was my daring, bold, funny girlfriend. Wasn't she?

The flirty coed had the boyfriend thing wrong, too. People got stuff wrong all the time, I told myself, but a cold creeping dread filled my heart.

I assumed a nonchalance I didn't feel. "Point me in the right direction?"

After the coed offered directions and her phone number, I took the first and declined the second, but took my time to find Elizabeth. Time I needed to unclench my spine, ungrit my teeth, and return my heartbeat to a normal rate.

The commons, which was just another word for an interior courtyard, kept out most of the wind, but ice and snow had found their way in just the same. Long icicles hung from the rim of the roof and stabbed at the air like frozen daggers.

At first, I thought the courtyard was empty, but then I noticed two figures huddled together at a cheap industrial picnic table, the kind that was bolted down. As if anyone would want to steal a scarred metal table.

There she was, in the wool coat that brought out the green in her eyes. And sitting next to her, staring into those green eyes, was the Tracker. I'd never seen him like this, all gooey-eyed, instead of lit with animosity.

Gaston was sitting too close to her, but Elizabeth didn't move away. The fog of lust I'd been walking around in had cleared and I saw her with dreadful clarity. Her too-pale face looked ruthless in the pale afternoon light.

My only satisfaction came from the fact that they were arguing.

I had the foresight to mutter "*obscura*" before I was spotted, but that was my last clear thought. They wouldn't be able to see me, but I would still be able to see them.

And I didn't like what I saw.

"That isn't what I agreed to do, Gaston," she said.

"Tell me where he is," he said.

There was a stubborn set to her lips that I recognized. "No."

He grabbed her wrist and twisted it until she winced. She yanked her hand away. "Don't touch me," she said. "You may be able to get away with that with Jenny, but I'm not your punching bag. I wish Jenny had never met you."

"You're already in it this far," he said. "And there's your brother to think of."

"Is that a threat? I agreed to get to know Nyx, that's all."

"You agreed to get him to fall in love with you and you agreed to break his heart." The words sent a spike of pain to my heart, but I told myself to be cold, to be still, to wait.

"You promised they'd let Alex go," she burst out.

Excuses, rationalizations, and bargains all swam up from my heart to my brain until the thought coalesced. I'd been conned. There was no other explanation. There were no coincidences. Gaston worked for my aunts and apparently, so did Elizabeth. The girl upon whom I had pinned so many hopes was a liar.

My brain was boiling with ideas, how to hurt them, how to make them pay. I'd been a willing victim to Elizabeth's seduction. I'd been a sucker, a fool. But all that was over now. I would remind them that I was one of the Wyrd family. And my reminder would hurt.

I passed the coed on my way out but didn't return her smile. I was afraid showing my teeth would scare her.

I slammed into Eternity Road.

"Talbot, can I borrow your laptop?" I hollered.

"Help yourself. It's on the counter," he shouted back. His voice came from the office, which is where his father brought him since the harpy attack. Talbot was on serious lockdown. The wound on his face had started to heal, but whenever I looked at him I was reminded of how I'd put him in danger.

"Thanks!" I sat at the cash register and fired up the laptop. The Internet had to have been created by a true sorcerer. It was amazing the stuff you could find out with one click of a mouse. Especially when you knew the girl who claimed to love you was a liar. I typed in "Elizabeth Abernathy" and got a hit almost immediately.

A younger Elizabeth, hair in pigtails, standing next to her brother at a local science fair. The headline read "Boy Genius Finishes in First Place."

Then her parents' obituary. At least she hadn't lied about that. I tried her brother Alex and found everything I needed to know.

The article was a puff piece. At sixteen, boy genius Alex Abernathy graduated summa cum laude from an Ivy League university and then went to work at a local Minneapolis business in research and development. It didn't mention the business by name, but in the photo, Alex held a bottle of that atrocious nectar of the gods that Gaston was always sucking down.

That was the link. I'd found bottle caps all over the city. All with the Parsi logo and smelling of nectar of the gods. Gaston was double-crossing my aunts, but why? What did he get out of it? He'd been their loyal dog for a good long time and they kept him supplied with the orange liquid that rotted his brain, but extended his life. What had changed?

There might still be time to stop him, if the aunts would listen to me.

I'm not proud, but I waited until everyone was out and searched Elizabeth's house. I went there looking for answers, but what I found surprised me.

I crossed to the desk, only to find the drawers locked. I used a trick a retired thief had taught me instead of magic and after a few tries, the drawer slid open. It looked like a typical home office filing system, everything neatly arranged and labeled, except for one folder in the back.

I took it out and opened it. I spied a reproduction of an oil painting of me as a baby. It had been painted by a starving artist in London. The original hung in the Louvre.

There was a black-and-white photo of me, in uniform right after the war ended, kissing a girl I didn't even know. Another of me at my friend Marco's funeral. He'd been fifteen when we met and had died an old man. I'd passed myself off as his old friend's grandson.

The third photo was taken sometimes in the early eighties. I wore Doc Martens, tight black pants, and no shirt under the same leather jacket I carried with me everywhere. The punk scene had appealed to me. The angry music and angrier people who loved it. I had fit right in.

Where had she managed to get these?

"What are you doing in here?" Elizabeth's voice came from the doorway.

"Why do you have all these pictures of me?"

"Nyx, come sit down and we'll talk," she said. Of course she recognized me right away without the occulo spell. She'd known what I really looked like the entire time.

"Let's talk now. I think you have some explaining to do," I told her. I threw the photos and they landed in a pile at her feet.

"Nyx, I wanted to tell you," Elizabeth said.

"Tell me what, exactly? That you've been playing me this whole time? Yeah, I finally figured that out," I said.

She didn't know what to say. What could she tell me that would ease the ache in my stomach?

She ran from the room and I followed close at her heels, straight to the kitchen, where Jenny sat.

"He knows." Elizabeth burst into tears.

I knew everything I needed to know. I'd been betrayed by the girl I loved.

"We've looked for you for a long time," Elizabeth said.

"So our meeting wasn't a coincidence?" I asked. I kept my voice carefully even, but inside I was raging. She'd waited until there was someone else around before telling me the truth. If I was honest, it was lucky she did. I don't know what I would have done if Jenny hadn't been there to witness my humiliation. Beg, plead, cry. Or all of the above.

"Morta," Elizabeth said. "It was her idea."

The words were razor blades to my heart. "Go on," I managed to say.

"Your aunts asked me to find you," she said. "So the entire time, you knew." My aunts had asked for a cease-fire, while all the time they were planning on ripping out my heart, one way or another.

"Knew what?" she asked.

"That I was cursed with eternal life. That my aunts want my thread of fate."

"Hardly a curse," Elizabeth said. "It's a gift."

"A gift? To watch everyone you love die? To be alone in the world? To know it's safer that way because if you do love someone, you'll have to watch them die and you'll be alone again? Does that sound like a gift to you?"

Elizabeth put a hand on my shoulder, but I shrugged it off. I couldn't bear for her to touch me, to know I'd been played like a trout on a fishing line.

"You make me sick," I said.

Elizabeth flinched, but continued anyway. "They want to know where it is."

"Where what is?" I stalled, but I knew right away what she meant. "If I knew, I'd give it to them. Don't you understand? I have nothing left to live for." It had been a cleverly crafted illusion. "You couldn't see them for what they are?"

"I've never met them," she insisted. "We communicated through Gaston." An elusive thought niggled at my brain, but I was too angry to pursue it.

"You deliberately slipped me the libido spell to get me to sleep with you," I accused.

"That was his idea," she said. "He said your aunts were getting impatient."

I stayed stone-faced, but I was gasping for breath on the inside.

"So your boyfriend Gaston was giving you tips on how to seduce me, is that it?"

"It wasn't like that," Elizabeth burst out. "And he's not my boyfriend, he's Jenny's."

"Was my boyfriend," Jenny objected. "He's a psycho."

"So you believe in all that fate stuff?" I asked her.

"I don't know," she said. "But I was desperate."

"Our meeting at the Red Dragon wasn't coincidental?" My tone was even. "And here I thought I was just a lucky guy." The whole thing—our meeting, our relationship, everything—was fake.

Elizabeth threw me a quick, panicked look. "I had no choice."

"You went out with me because of my aunts?" The hot rage I'd felt had turned to ice in my veins.

"Please, Nyx, I would give you anything," Elizabeth said.

"Apparently," I replied.

She flinched, but recovered quickly and glared at me. "You make it sound so sordid."

"Isn't it?" I hadn't even noticed when my hands had clenched into fists. I flexed my fingers until they unlocked.

"Nyx, don't you love me? Why can't you tell me?" Elizabeth cried.

"My death is far from here and hard to find," I replied. I wondered if she would understand the quote.

"*The Golden Bough*," Jenny said. "I do appreciate a well-read individual."

I gave her a look that I hoped clearly indicated how little I gave a shit what she appreciated.

"Look, you're wasting your time," I replied. "I could take what you're offering, but you'll never be free of them."

"I need to try," Elizabeth said.

"What was the plan, exactly?" I asked her.

She wouldn't look me in the eyes. "I was supposed to…befriend you."

My fists clenched again, but I forced my hands to relax. "And then?"

"Get you to tell me where your thread of fate is and I would be free."

"So they hired you to break my heart? Congratulations on a job well done." Lying, treacherous bitch.

"They have Alex," she said flatly. "They are holding him somewhere. Until I do what they want."

"So now you decide to tell me the truth?" I asked.

"Nyx, I love—"

"Don't say it!" I screamed the words. "Don't you ever say that to me."

"Alex is—" She gulped, and then continued. "He's my brother. I'm his only hope."

"Why should I believe you?" God, how I hated her, but even with everything I now knew, I wanted her to say something, anything to let me love her again.

"You have no reason to believe me," she said. "But everything I'm telling you is true."

"Only one person in the history of the world has managed to steal a thread of life, and she's dead now."

"That's what you have to do?" she asked. "Just give them a thread?"

"I have to give them *my* thread. The thing that keeps me alive. They killed my mother and they want to kill me." They'd offered another option, but it wasn't one I was going to consider, not now. The burning need for revenge had been reignited.

"She didn't take her own thread when she took yours?"

"No, she didn't think she had to. The Fates live a very long time. Not forever, but close enough. My mother never dreamed her own sisters would cut her thread."

Her face softened, but she was smart enough not to try to touch me. "So you'll do it?"

"I haven't agreed to do anything," I replied. I'd told her too much. "What's in it for me?"

"Please help me," she begged. "Just think about it before you give me your answer."

What would Gaston do to Alex and Elizabeth if I just walked away? It wouldn't be pretty. I couldn't have another death on my conscience. But that didn't mean I would be her dumb lovesick puppy ever again.

I met her eyes and nodded slowly.

She threw her arms around me, but for the first time I felt nothing when she touched me. Betrayal made me numb.

"Why'd they choose you?"

"Does it matter?" she replied.

"It matters to me."

She wouldn't meet my eyes. "Convenience," she said. "Gaston and Alex hung out after work sometimes and I guess Alex talked about me and…"

"And what?"

"Gaston said I looked like your ex-girlfriend."

"He should know," I said bitterly. "Since he's the one who killed her." I went on, "Why did they think it would work?" It had worked, all too well, but I didn't want to think about that now.

"I fancied myself quite the actress," she said bitterly. "Alex was so proud of me. He—" She gulped and then continued. "—he used to say that I was so good at becoming someone else that I could fool anybody."

My mind was whirling. "Tell me again why you agreed to do it," I said.

"I told you," Elizabeth said. "They have my brother."

I cleared my throat, hoping to dispel the nausea. "Where?"

"I don't know," she said. "Do you think I'd agree to something like this if I knew? I'm not a bad person."

"How did you get involved with them anyway?"

"After my brother disappeared," she said, "Gaston showed up at school. He told me they had my brother and what they wanted."

"So you never talked to Nona Polydoros about this? Or her husband?"

"Why would school trustees have anything to do with this?"

She didn't know who they really were.

"Gaston never mentioned anything about Parsi Enterprises? Or his bosses?"

She shook her head.

"You're sure?" Murderous rage overwhelmed me for a moment. Either my aunts were covering their tracks or Gaston had gone rogue.

"They're really dangerous?" she asked.

"Ever read Shakespeare?" I asked.

"Certainly," she said.

"He didn't get everything wrong," I told her. "In the normal course of things, a witch isn't someone you'd want to mess with."

"And double-crossing one is even worse?" she hazarded.

"Yes," I said. "Remember, I am the son of a witch."

Elizabeth asked me, "What happens if your aunts find your thread of fate?"

I thought about lying, but I'd made a vow to be truthful. "I die, I suppose. I'm living on borrowed time."

My mother had trained me from birth to sense a lie, and I knew I'd been handed a big fat steaming pile of them on a silver platter.

"Tell me again exactly what my aunts promised you," I went on. There was no way my aunts were going to let Elizabeth and her brother go after this.

"I was to befriend you and they'd let my brother go," she said flatly.

"And you believe them?"

"I have money," Elizabeth said. "I can pay you."

"So you lied about not having any money, too," I said. "Was anything you told me true?"

She met my eyes without flinching. "The important things were."

I was going to break something if she said she loved me.

"I need to go," I said.

She started to cry. "What am I going to do?"

I knew what I had to do, but still I hesitated. There are always consequences for magic, and I knew there would definitely be consequences for challenging my aunts. But my lips still moved, saying the words I'd almost forgotten in the endless years since my mother had first taught me the spell.

"What's in it for me?" I said. "Seems to me that I'd be the one taking all the risks."

"True," Jenny said. "We are prepared to offer you more-than-adequate compensation."

"How adequate?" I asked. I didn't really care about the money.

She named a figure that made my jaw drop. "It's been a long day for you, I'm sure," she added. "Why don't you sleep on it?"

"I'll help you," I said. But if my plan didn't work, I'd be looking over my shoulder for a long time. I was determined to live. Not because of some make-believe happily ever after, but to make Gaston pay.

Chapter Thirty-Four

Eternity Road had everything you needed, if you only knew where to look. I knew where to look.

I searched the shelves until I found what I wanted. I intended to get stinking drunk and brood about my faithless girlfriend. Make that ex-girlfriend.

I grabbed the ornate bottle and marched up to the counter with it. "How much for the wormwood?" I asked.

Talbot took one look at my face and said, "It's yours. But I must warn you that you'll have a devil of a headache in the morning."

"It won't be the first time," I replied.

"Do you want to talk about it?" he asked.

I hesitated. It wouldn't change anything, but I could feel myself wanting to confide in him. "Got a couple of hours?"

He walked to the door and flipped the sign to CLOSED. "I do."

I started to crack open the bottle, but he shook his head. "In your apartment," he said. "It will be much easier to put you to bed when you pass out. Besides, we are not drinking two-hundred-year-old verde absinthe straight from the bottle. We will do this properly. Otherwise, it will be too bitter."

Bitter fit my mood exactly, but I didn't argue. Talbot grabbed two crystal glasses, etched with a fine line of silver, and a spoon. "Do you have ice?"

I nodded.

"And sugar cubes?"

"That's doubtful," I replied.

"I'll be right back," he said. He headed for the office and returned a few minutes later with a silver tray on which he'd placed what I assumed was the appropriate paraphernalia to mix up some of the green fairy.

We walked the three flights to my apartment without speaking. Once inside, Talbot busied himself with making our drinks while I sat on my couch and commenced with the brooding.

Talbot handed me a glass of the cloudy green liquid and I chugged it. This world was too much for me. It hurt to be in it.

"Easy, Nyx," he said. "It's not that swill you're used to drinking. Now let's discuss your situation."

"My situation?" I repeated. "My situation is that I am well and truly screwed."

"Elizabeth finally showed her hand, I take it."

"You knew?" I said. "Now I feel like an even bigger jackass."

"Don't," he said. "I only had my suspicions."

"I don't want to talk about it." I handed him my glass. "Let the pity party begin."

He gave me the drink without comment, for which I was grateful. I couldn't take a lecture at this point.

"Make this one a double, please." I handed him the glass. I swallowed the next drink without tasting it. The alcohol hit my bloodstream and suddenly, my tiny apartment seemed too confining. "Let's go out," I said.

"You're not in any condition to drive," Talbot said.

"That's okay." I noticed I'd already begun to slur my words, but I ignored it. "We can walk. The Red Dragon isn't far."

The crisp night air sobered me up a bit, but I planned on taking care of that when we got to the bar.

The Red Dragon was crowded, but we found a table without any problem.

I gestured to the seats. "It's my lucky night, but then again it always is."

"Maybe it isn't luck," Talbot suggested. "Your air of sullenness combined with that rather sizable chip on your shoulder is scaring away the other patrons."

He took out a handkerchief with a flourish and used it to wipe the bar stool seat. Talbot liked to act like he wouldn't caught dead in the Red Dragon if it weren't for me, but I thought that secretly, he loved hanging out there.

I glowered at him, but he ignored me. The rest of the bar stool occupants made a mass exodus, however, and seats on either side of us quickly became available.

"Someone will fill these seats again sooner or later."

And my prediction was correct. No sooner had I ordered my first round of shots than a pretty little brunette sat beside me.

"See?" I looked over at Talbot triumphantly, but he was busy inspecting his shot glass for cleanliness.

"See what?" the brunette asked.

"I was explaining to my friend Talbot here that I am incredibly lucky and then you sit next to me."

"You're cute," she said.

Some sixth sense made me turn around, just in time to see

Jasper stroll into the bar. The night was just getting better and better.

"What's the matter?" Talbot asked, noticing the look on my face.

"I need to talk to that guy," I said. I swayed when I got to my feet. Talbot held out a steadying hand. "Where?"

"Skinny guy in the ratty trench coat," I slurred.

The moment Jasper saw me, his face paled and he ran out of the bar. Talbot, whose motor skills were functioning better than mine, ran after him.

I staggered through the door and cursed the impulse to drink my problems away. Jasper had answers and I'd let him slip away.

Talbot, however, saved my ass. He had Jasper collared and was holding him as far away as possible without losing his grip.

"Why do you want to talk to *this*?" Talbot asked.

Jasper was skinnier and dirtier than ever.

"I released him from a troll," I replied. "And he repaid me by leaving his severed finger at Elizabeth's house. I want to know why."

"Let's go inside," Jasper said. He glanced around uneasily.

"Afraid to be seen talking to me?" I asked. "I'm hurt."

We found the least noisy corner table, and I waited for Jasper to speak.

"Well?"

His throat worked, but no sound came out. "They'll kill me if I tell you," he finally said.

"I'll kill you if you don't." I meant every word.

Jasper's fingers drummed on the table nervously. The end of his missing finger had been cauterized, but the wound was jagged. Like a water hag's teeth.

Talbot couldn't take his eyes away from Jasper's missing finger. "How'd that happen?" he asked him.

"Water hag," Jasper said.

"Why did you come back to Minneapolis?" I said. "After I told you to leave town. After you begged to go home."

"I forgot something," Jasper said. His gaze shifted away from mine.

"What did you forget?" I said. I wanted to reach over and slam his head against the table until he started to talk. I restrained myself, but it hurt.

"I had some information that I knew would be valuable to certain parties," he said.

I glared at him. "You stole the recipe for the nectar of the gods from Alex."

He nodded. "A few months ago. He didn't even notice it was missing."

"But the Fates did," I said. "You were dumb enough to try to blackmail them?"

"No," he said. "Not the Fates. The Tracker."

"That's how you lost your finger," Talbot said. "Gaston."

He looked at his feet. "It wasn't the original recipe," he said. "New and improved. By Alex."

"Why did they want to improve it? Magical people have been drinking it for hundreds of years." Not to mention their Tracker.

"They wanted to sell it to mortals," Jasper said.

"Nectar is toxic to mortals," I said. "One sip would make a human go insane."

"Not Alex's version. He fixed it. Only minor side effects."

"They think he took the formula for nectar of the gods," I said. "That's why he went missing."

I was regretting the last few shots. It made it hard for me to think, to process what Jasper had told me.

I was drunk, but not so drunk that I didn't notice when Elizabeth and Jenny walked in.

They didn't see me, but I watched them as they found a table. I wasn't the only one paying attention to the two women who were obviously slumming.

A guy dressed in black watched them, too. In fact, he made a beeline for their table. There was something familiar about him, but I didn't realize what it was until he had nearly reached them. It was the douche bag who'd put a knife in me the night I'd met Elizabeth. Brad. Talbot's frat buddy. The guy I'd owned at the poker table.

Alcohol and adrenaline mixed in my veins until they combined to form a red-hot rage. Talbot noticed my death stare and laid a hand on my shoulder. "It's best to leave it alone," he said.

"Leave it alone? That asshat gutted me like a fish and now he's making a move on my girl? Hell no!"

I tapped Brad on the shoulder and hit him the second he turned around. My knuckle snagged on some of his man jewelry, but he went down like a brick. I picked him up by the collar and smacked him again.

"Stop it!" Elizabeth said.

I kept pounding on him until Talbot grabbed my arm. "Calm down," he said. "It's time we went home. Before someone calls the cops."

I shrugged him off and stalked outside, fuming. My hands clenched with the effort it took for me not to go back into the bar and beat Brad into a pulp.

"Nyx, wait up," Elizabeth called out, but I kept walking.

"Leave me alone," I said.

"I wanted to tell you," she said.

I whirled around. "Don't ever lie to me again," I said.

"I won't, I promise," she said. A glimmer of hope lit her face, and I felt like a heel for what I was about to say.

"Don't worry, I'll do the job for you," I said.

She gave me a relieved smile. "That's great, Nyx. You won't regret it."

I would, more than she would ever know. "And then I never want to see you again."

The light went out of her eyes. "Whatever you want," she said in a monotone.

I crossed my arms over my chest to stop myself from taking her into my arms. "That's what I want."

Without another word, she walked away.

Lucky in cards, unlucky in love, that was me. I sat down hard on the curb. I noticed the cut on my hand and put my knuckles to my lips, tasting the sharp tang of my own blood. Even while I was beating the shit out of him, Brad had managed to make me bleed.

Worse, Jasper had taken advantage of my distraction and disappeared.

There was probably a lesson in there somewhere, but I was too tired to look for it. I put my head in my hands, ignoring the fact that I'd sat in a portion of suspiciously slimy sidewalk.

Chapter Thirty-Five

Talbot passed out at around three in the morning, but not even the massive amount of alcohol I'd consumed could stop the humming in my brain.

I called a taxi, which dropped me off in Elizabeth's neighborhood. I staggered down to the lake. "Willow, come out, come out, wherever you are."

I plopped down at the shore's edge. A minute later, she was next to me. She smelled sandy, but warm, like a day spent at the lake. Not like winter at all.

She stared at me for a moment, and clapped her hands. "She's broken your heart, just as I said she would."

"You don't have to sound so happy about it."

"But I am," she admitted. "Very happy. There is something about you that is pleasing to my eyes."

"You smell good," I said.

"Spring," she whispered.

I leaned in to kiss her, but she pushed me away. "Not like this."

I almost tipped over. Drunk, I realized. "Like what?" I asked, but my words slurred, so it sounded more like, "Lick wah?"

"You are broken," she said. "Weak. Not the son of Fortuna."

That was the last thing I remembered before I passed out.

I woke up, dehydrated and unsure where I was. It was dark, except for a single wavering candle near me. I was lying in a cave, on a pile of fur, naked. There was a warm female body next to me, also naked. Willow. Alcohol-blurred images flashed in my mind. My head throbbed in time, as if someone was using my skull as a drum. I had an even bigger headache than the one pounding my temples. Willow. Naiads were legendary for their sexual appetites, but they were also legendary for their vengeance if scorned.

I'd slept with someone I didn't love before, but never while I was in love with someone else. I'd never been in love before, so I didn't know the proper etiquette. Even though Elizabeth had taken a sledgehammer to my heart, I loved her.

I wanted to reach for my pants and sneak out of there, but instead I put a hand on Willow's bare shoulder. "Willow, I'm sorry, but I have to leave." I hoped my hand wouldn't come away a blood stump.

She sat up and gave me a sleepy smile. "Good-bye, son of Fortuna."

"Last night, it was…" I began awkwardly.

"Two friends giving each other comfort," she said. "That is all."

I tried to mask the relief I felt, but I wasn't entirely successful. She tossed me my pants with a little more force than necessary. I shrugged into my clothes, but swayed on my feet.

She didn't stir from her fur and left me to find my own way out of the cave.

I had to stop once to throw up, but I finally found my way home. The next time I woke up, I was in my own bed and Talbot stood over me. "There's a bucket over there," he said. Right before I heaved. Repeatedly.

My throbbing head only emphasized how stupid I'd been. Images of my night with Willow kept resurfacing, no matter how hard I tried to block them out, which made other parts of me throb.

What kind of man loves one woman and sleeps with another? Elizabeth had betrayed me, but that didn't erase how I felt about her, no matter how much I wanted it to. I hadn't been able to drink, fight, or fuck her out of my system. Instead, I'd made things worse.

My stomach lurched and I rolled over to heave again. Maybe having the marrow sucked out of me by an irate naiad was what I deserved. Once my stomach was empty, I closed my eyes and slept.

When I woke up again, my mouth felt like I'd been sucking on felt. I staggered into the living room. Talbot was sleeping on the couch. I threw a blanket over him.

I nursed my hangover with some aspirin and a Sprite. I'd slept most of the morning away. I made a pot of strong coffee as quietly as I could, but Talbot stirred and stretched.

"What time is it?" he said with a yawn.

"Almost noon," I told him.

"What happened to you last night?" he asked.

"I spent the night at Willow's."

There was a long silence.

"What were you doing? Trying death by naiad?" Talbot commented.

"There are worst ways to die." I said.

"I thought you'd grown out of your death wish," he said.

"Things change," I said.

He walked to the coffeepot and poured a cup. "What about Willow? How does she feel about the whole thing?"

"She was fine with it."

"A naiad who was seduced and abandoned is fine with it? Yeah, that sounds right." His voice was overflowing with sarcasm.

"Willow's my friend," I said defensively.

"Elizabeth's not worth throwing your life away," he said.

"Don't blame Elizabeth for my desire to end my life," I said. "I made those plans long before I met her."

"It seemed like you were making new plans," he said.

"Don't say it," I said. "Don't tell me that I'll meet someone new. I won't."

"You never know what will happen," he said.

"But I do," I replied. "It's my life. Someone I love always dies, eventually, and I'm alone again."

"It happens to everyone, mortal or not," Talbot said. "You can't stop it."

"It's not going to happen to me, not again," I said. I'd been fooling myself, living in a dream world. It was time to finish it. Before that, I needed to apologize to Willow. "I'll go talk to Willow," I said, which seemed to satisfy Talbot because he finally shut up. I drove the Caddy, but left it about half a mile away from the house. I hiked to the lake.

I was over my head and I knew it, but that didn't stop me. When I entered the woods, the wind rustled through the trees, sounding like a shuddering sigh.

I ignored the warning and forged ahead. As I got closer,

cold gray fog rose up out of nowhere and I remembered an old proverb that my mother always liked: "If it does not get cloudy, it will not get clear."

The fog formed into hands, which is when I realized that it wasn't ordinary fog. Gaston had become extraordinarily good at controlling the weather. And trying to kill me. The foggy hands wrapped around my throat and pressed down on my windpipe, effectively cutting off my breath and my ability to cast a spell.

I'd walked into this battle fully loaded, though. I didn't have to speak to make magic work for me. I'd fastened the lodestone to the silver chain around my neck. If I could only reach it. I stretched out my hand and my fingertips made contact.

I was losing consciousness, but I summoned enough strength to evaporate the fog, and my breathing returned to normal. The magical attack was over, at least for the moment, and I finally relaxed.

I made a right and another right and the temperature dropped. It felt as though I was breathing in icicles, but I'd made it to the lake.

There was a large dark blot in the water a few feet from the shore, but I couldn't make out what it was in the dark.

"Willow, is that you?"

No answer.

The object bobbed in the water and drifted closer until it was almost within arm's reach.

"Nyx." My name was a harsh croak, and it came from the dark blob in front of me.

"*Flamma*," I said. The magic illuminated the shallows. I swore when I saw it wasn't a blob at all. It was what was left of Jasper.

I waded out and pulled him to shore. I laid him gently on the ground. His arm hung at an impossible angle and something, possibly a water hag, had gnawed on his chin until she'd reached bone.

I took off my jacket to cover him, but he lifted his good hand weakly. "Too late for me," he rasped.

His voice was fading so I bent to hear him.

"Need…to tell…you," he said. "Alex…the water…Don't…" But whatever he wanted to tell me was lost as Jasper died.

Chapter Thirty-Six

Jasper was gone. I closed his eyes and moved him under a copse of trees. There was nothing else I could do for him. But he'd said something about the water. A warning, but there was more.

"I know where they're stashing Alex," I said to myself. The sound of my own voice made my head throb, and I nearly lost the idea in the pounding of my brain.

I kicked off my Docs, socks, and jeans. Anything that would weigh me down was gone. My teeth clattered, and I shook with the effort to make it stop.

I'd reached the water's edge, but I couldn't bring myself to go in.

Willow appeared, almost as if she'd been expecting me.

"I am glad to see you," I said. It was a ridiculous statement, considering I was naked, shriveled, and blue with cold.

She didn't look enthusiastic. "I warned you before, Nyx Fortuna. It is not safe for you in my domain."

"Just take me down there," I said. "I know he's there. What are you afraid of?"

She met my gaze and I realized her eyes were a lovely green-ish blue. "Not everyone is indestructible."

"Please," I said. "It's important." I could go it alone, but the other naiads would be on me within seconds.

Her face went pale and I felt like a jerk. "Never mind," I said. "I'll go down there on my own."

"You'd never make it," she said. She gestured to me. "Come to me. Quickly!"

I waded into the water and was clasped in her strong slender arms. I had asked, but suddenly I wasn't sure I'd made the right decision. Now I owed her not one, but two favors. As if reading my thoughts, she said, "In return, I ask that you tell no one that I've helped you."

I started to say something but got a mouthful of water as she plummeted to the icy depths of the lake. I opened my eyes underwater. At first I couldn't see anything, but as my sight adjusted, I spotted a murky glow. I soon lost track of how long I'd been in the water, and which way I'd turned the last few times.

At last, just as I thought my head would explode, our heads broke through the surface of the water. I gasped great lungfuls of air as I looked around.

"Where are we?"

"In the Driftless," Willow said simply.

A subterranean river ran through the cave. The sound of water dripping down the walls of the cave was the only sound I heard. In the middle of the river, a stone structure rose out of the water.

The walls of the cave were decorated with bits of glass, painted figures, and other items embedded in the limestone, which I realized were fossils. I ran my hand along the wall.

The water was clear and I could see dark shapes, sleek and

dangerous as sharks, swimming below. There was no way to get to the island in the middle unless I swam for it.

"I must leave you here," Willow said. She trembled against me and I knew she was afraid of what was ahead.

I squeezed her hand. "Thank you."

She swam away without looking back. I wondered how I would make it out without a bunch of naiads trying to eat me, but I'd worry about that later. I needed to find Elizabeth's brother and then get both of them out of my life for good.

My feet touched the bottom and a thick mud squished between my toes. The water suddenly grew deeper and I began to swim.

When I came to the entrance of the labyrinth, I examined the carved letters above the archway more closely. It was definitely a magic spell, but not one I was familiar with. I put out a finger and traced the letters and a jolt went through my hand, up my arm, and to my heart.

I entered and found that the interior of the labyrinth was free of any water. The air seemed safe enough, although it was so cold I could see my breath.

I summoned a small flame for warmth and continued through the maze. There was a faint chuckle and then a voice whispered something, repeating the same word over and over. I strained to make out the word, but was unable to hear what the voice was saying. The cold became an icy tiger that sank its fangs into me and I waved my hands, trying to remember how to command the flame to grow, but I couldn't.

I stared at the carved words above the archway. It either read ABANDON HOPE, ALL YE WHO ENTER HERE or BABY, I'M A FOOL FOR LOVE. Which might actually be the same thing.

I tried again, but couldn't figure it out. My Latin sucked. A memory of my mother rushed into my head. We were sitting in a meadow somewhere. I must have been around seven or eight. I held a slate and a piece of chalk and was laboriously copying out letters as Mom watched. When I finished, she'd swept me into her arms and danced me around. She'd been so beautiful that even the butterflies had stopped to watch her. I missed her, missed being part of a family.

I dismissed the memory reluctantly. I couldn't be distracted when I entered the labyrinth. As soon as I took the first step, I could smell the magic. It smelled wrong, though. Not fresh and lemony and part of the natural world.

Magic was always there, always with us, at least according to my mother, but this magic was different. This magic smelled old and dark, like someone's seldom-used basement. I stopped and sniffed again. Someone's basement, that is, if they regularly stored something dead there. This magic smelled of blood, of fear, of pain.

I pushed it a little with my mind, testing the boundaries. It pushed back, hard. The dark magic was all around me, so thick that it was like a wall. I murmured a few words and punched a way through, but it was heavy going.

Was Alex there? I knew the answer lay somewhere in the labyrinth.

I pressed on, disoriented by the dark magic. I could taste it on my tongue whenever I breathed in.

The heavy stone walls closed in on me and then I heard a laugh. " 'Come into my parlor,' said the spider to the fly," a voice whispered.

This was bad, very bad and I suddenly doubted that I would find my way to the heart of the labyrinth without any help.

From behind me came the faint sound of someone calling

my name. I stopped in my tracks. There was definite peril ahead, but if I turned back now, I might not get another chance at the labyrinth. I was woefully unprepared, though. The voice called out again. Willow. The note of worry in her voice decided it for me. I'd go back.

I had a phenomenal sense of direction, but I was dizzy with magic and didn't know which way to turn. I needed to get the magic out of me before I exploded.

I knew it was time to get out, but my mind was blurry and I fought the urge to lie down and close my eyes. My legs had grown as heavy as stone and it took an enormous effort to kick one foot in front of the other.

Had I been there for minutes or hours, listening to that voice? I stumbled and fell. I lay there and a part of me knew I should get up, but I didn't. I was no longer able to see clearly in front of me as my eyelids grew heavy. Finally, I gave in and listened to the voice. Sleep, it said. Sleep now. So I lay down on the cold stone floor and slept.

Just before everything went black, a familiar face appeared.

Chapter Thirty-Seven

When I came to, I was sprawled on a narrow cot in a candlelit room.

"Wake up, wake up, why won't he wake up? Maybe I'm dreaming again."

I cracked open bleary eyes to see a blond guy pacing. He was rake-thin, dressed in a threadbare pair of jeans and a holey sweater. The sleeves were pushed up to reveal a nasty scar that ran up his left arm. I recognized him from the photo, though.

He stopped to stare at me.

I stared back. "Where am I? What happened?" I asked. I felt as if I'd been beaten with a sock full of quarters or something. My ears and hands stung and I realized if he hadn't found me, I'd have hypothermia. But something about it didn't feel right. Was the whispering voice just a hallucination or the spell of a tricky magician?

"Questions, questions, he's full of questions," he replied.

"Alex, is that you?"

He reacted to his name, but not in the way I expected. He looked over his shoulder fearfully. "Did she send you?"

"No one sent me," I said. "But obviously, someone didn't want me to find you. Why?"

"Why? Why? Why?" he echoed. Was I dealing with a lunatic?

I sat up and the covers slipped down to my waist and I realized I was still naked. I looked around and saw clothes draped over a makeshift rack near the fire. We were in a room of about ten feet by ten feet.

"Can I borrow some pants?"

He nodded.

"Alex, how long have you been here?"

"School, school, I'm late for school," he said in a singsong voice. He was batshit crazy, but who could blame him? He'd experienced more of the magical world than many mortals could take.

I tried again. "Alex, do you remember your sister Elizabeth? She sent me."

He put a finger to his lips and went completely still, listening to something no one else could hear.

"She hunts," he whispered. "But she won't find me. Not here."

Was he talking about a naiad or one of the Fates? I strained to hear. For a moment, nothing, and then came the sound of footsteps.

I motioned Alex to be quiet. I held my breath, but the footsteps receded and finally stopped.

I wrapped a blanket around me and checked to make sure my necklace was still around my neck. Just having it near me helped me regain a little strength.

"She's a leech, sucking out all the good," Alex said.

"Who are you talking about?"

"Don't tell me that she's fooled you, too," he replied.

Bile rose in my throat. "You're talking about a naiad?"

"Who else?" Alex had been raving earlier, but seemed more and more lucid as we spoke.

"How do you survive in here?"

He shrugged. "They bring me food sometimes. I try not to eat it, but sometimes I'm so hungry." He gripped my arm. "Don't eat or drink anything here."

"Alex, we need to get out of here," I said. "Can you make it?" How was I going to fight off the naiads and haul Alex back to the surface? He didn't have the strength to swim on his own.

"Just watch your back," he said.

"Do you know a way out, Alex?"

He ignored my questions. His face twisted with rage and pain. "I killed them."

"Who?" I asked. "Who did you kill?"

He stared at me for a long moment. I assumed he was trying to make up his mind about me.

"My whole family. Car accident," he said. "I was driving. I lost control."

"I was nearly killed just the other day," I told him casually. "In a car accident. But it wasn't an accident at all. It was magic."

He started to rock back and forth. "No one left. No one left. No one left."

"Elizabeth is alive," I said.

It took him a minute, but he snapped out of it.

"Elizabeth is dead," he said. "They're all dead."

I shook my head. "No, she's alive and well. I promise."

"He told me they'd died. That they'd all died. That it was just him. Why would he leave me here?"

"I don't know, Alex," I replied. "I don't know."

I knew Elizabeth, didn't I? She was a good person. Was it possible that she had been collaborating with Gaston in her brother's kidnapping?

No, only a monster would leave anyone here. Gaston had been working alone, at least in that. My anger at her treachery lessened.

"Why did he trap you here?"

He gave me a look of cunning. "Don't you know?"

I held on to my patience with difficulty. I was running out of time, and his vagueness wasn't helping.

I shook my head. There were only a few reasons that someone would kill—jealousy, greed, or power.

"It's a secret," he said slyly. "Mother told me not to tell."

"Your mother is dead," I reminded him.

His eyes lost focus for a moment. "She still walks in the labyrinth," he said. "She visits me. This is where she drowned, you know."

"No, I didn't know." Another detail Elizabeth neglected to mention.

"He wants her to get me to tell the secret, but I won't."

"What secret?"

He stopped, listening for something only he could hear. "Shh," he said. "She's coming." He grabbed my arm and led me to the entrance. "You have to go."

"Come with me," I urged.

"I can't," he said.

"Why not?"

"I can't find the way out," he replied. "I've tried. I made it to the water once, but then…" His body shook with fear.

"I'll get you out of here," I promised.

He gave me a smile that didn't reach his eyes. "Others

have said the same," he said. "And now they are all dead."

"I'll let you in on a little secret," I said. "I can't be killed no matter how hard they try."

How could Gaston have done this? Fury went through me at the thought.

"I can't leave," he said. "I'm trapped. The naiads won't let me pass."

"Let me worry about the naiads," I said. "Let's get out of here."

He nodded and a glimmer of rationality appeared, but it was gone as quickly as it had come.

"*Illuminate*," I said. I really didn't remember my Latin, but a straightforward command worked just as well and would help discharge some of the magic.

A blue light appeared on the smooth marble wall and began to move in the direction I'd come from. I followed it.

I grabbed Alex and threw him over my shoulder. He was so thin that it wasn't difficult to carry him.

As I walked, the smooth marble walls shifted and moved. A straight passage out became a dead end. Instead of reaching the exit, we headed deeper and deeper into the labyrinth. My heart rate accelerated as I thought of the possibility of wandering the halls forever, slowly going mad right along with Alex.

Then the whispering began.

"Don't listen, Alex," I commanded. I put him down, tore a strip of fabric off the bottom my shirt, and then shredded it into small pieces. I stuffed the small wad of cotton fabric into my ears and made Alex do the same. The whispering became a shout, but the fabric muffled the sound. My head cleared, but as we continued the walls and ceiling pressed closer and closer, narrowing until there was barely room for me to walk upright.

Then the passageway opened up into an enormous chamber with four doors.

Which way should I go now? The faint blue light I'd summoned cast a shadow on the stone walls. I put Alex down to catch my bearings. There were rows of pillars, and a statue stood watch in the center. The god Poseidon clutched his trident in one hand. I looked at the statue carefully and noticed that the trident pointed to one of the doors.

When we left the labyrinth, a sea hag waited in the shallows. We reached the stone steps that led to the water. She let out a wail of rage and Alex flailed wildly. I had a hard time keeping my grip on him.

She waggled a finger at me to tell me I'd been a naughty boy, and then smiled at me, showing her razor-sharp teeth. She gestured to Alex, making a motion to give him to her.

I shook my head and she howled again, a ferocious primal scream that scared me all the way to the marrow of my bones. She wasn't messing around this time. I could never outswim a sea hag. My best bet was to stand and fight.

She lunged for me. She came close enough for me to see each individual glistening scale on her tough skin. I caught a whiff of her breath, which was like the odor of the slime that grew in trapped water.

Alex's weight slowed me down enough that her next swipe with her long fingernails took a gash out of my leg. I sent her sprawling, and her head connected with a stone column. I heard a crack, but didn't wait around to see if she was still alive. I swam.

I was already winded by the time I broke the surface of the water. Alex chose that moment to start shrieking, which would let every naiad within five miles know where we were.

I clapped a hand over his mouth. "Alex, cut it out. Now." He continued to flail and shriek, and I was growing weaker.

"If you want to see your sister again, shut the hell up!"

He went silent and still. I could barely see the shore. A heavy fog had rolled in, concealing more than it revealed. The shore looked a long way off, but I got Alex in a firefighter's hold and swam awkwardly to shore.

I threw Alex onto the beach and then collapsed there next to him. I was so tired, but I couldn't rest yet. I had to get Alex to safety.

I walked to Elizabeth's house, still half carrying Alex, but the house was dark. I could have broken in, but it would be safer back at my apartment. And Talbot would be there for reinforcements. I hiked to my car. It was after 1 A.M. and the temperatures had dropped. We wouldn't last long out there in that weather. Alex was shivering and blue by the time we made it back to the car.

I helped him into the passenger seat of the Caddy and then turned the heater on full blast. He rocked back and forth, mumbling to himself. Every few minutes, he stopped and cocked his head, listening. "They know," he said. "They know."

He was freaking me out. The sooner I got him to Elizabeth, the better. I parked in front of her house and waited, but she never showed. Alex finally fell asleep and I started the car and cruised through the quiet Minneapolis streets.

Where was she? I wanted to tell her that Alex was safe, that he was finally free, but I couldn't even find her.

I didn't want her gratitude. I wanted to reunite her with Alex and get her out of my life for good. But Elizabeth never came home.

Chapter Thirty-Eight

I woke when the sun hit my closed eyelids. I stretched and smacked my elbow on the steering wheel. I was disoriented for a moment, unsure where I was. I stared bleary-eyed out the windshield, but it was frosted over.

When I swore, my breath fogged in the air. I wiped it clear and stared out. I was parked about a block down from Elizabeth's house. Alex was curled up in the passenger seat. At first I thought he was dead, but then I saw his shoulder rise. He was breathing.

I turned the key and prayed that the Caddy would start. It rumbled to life and I headed to Talbot's. I needed to have it out with my aunt and I didn't want Alex to get caught in the crossfire.

After depositing Alex at Talbot's for safekeeping, I drove to Aunt Nona's house and pounded furiously at the door until she answered.

"Come in before one of the neighbors call the cops." Her hair looked like it hadn't been washed in days, and she was wearing a black sack of a dress. There was little trace of the fashionable, confident woman who had been my aunt just a few days before.

I shouldered my way past her. "Why are you still even here? You're in danger."

She tried to act like she didn't know what I was talking about.

"Calm down, Nyx," she said. "Now, why don't you come in and tell us what this is all about?"

I followed her into the kitchen. "How can you continue to trust that guy?" I asked. "Hate me if you want, but since when do the Fates operate on blind trust?"

"We don't," she said.

"Did you talk to Naomi? Did she tell you that I didn't kill Sawyer?"

She gazed at me with her ferocious mother eyes. "Leave my daughter out of this. Naomi has never harmed a soul."

There was a *yet* hovering on my tongue, but I didn't say it. "I happen to *like* Naomi," I replied. "And believe me, I've tried to tell her that it's not the smartest idea to hang around me."

"Try harder," she commanded.

"Someone has tried to kill me," I said. "At least twice."

She shrugged. "It happens."

"It happened to Sawyer." Her icy calm cracked for a second at my comment, but she recovered quickly.

"I'm one of the Fates," she said. "We're not exactly the most popular people on the planet."

So the rumors Ambrose had heard were true. Someone was gunning for the Fates.

"Then you admit it's possible that someone else killed Sawyer?"

"You can never hide who you truly are, Nyx," she said. "At least not for long."

"Who am I?"

She shrugged. "That's up to you. But you are not a killer."

"Not yet."

"You are your mother's son," she said, as if that explained everything. Maybe it did.

"Who do you think killed Sawyer, then?"

Her silence was my answer. She didn't know. It wasn't unheard of. The Fates didn't know everything, but when they did know something, they couldn't resist meddling.

"Did you know that your necromancer husband was training Gaston?"

She looked as though she might deny it, but finally said, "Former practitioner. He stopped before we got married. He was a civilian when he died."

"Sawyer is the one who taught Gaston how to call a revenant," I said. "Your husband trained Gaston in the dark arts."

Nona sat down hard on a chair. "He would never do that."

"I'm sorry, but he did," I said. "Sawyer's the one who broke the occulo spell that concealed my identity—and after he did, Gaston stabbed him."

Her eyes darkened, and I caught a glimpse of the ruthlessness necessary for a Fate. "Then he will die."

"How did Gaston manage to fool you for so long?"

"We are not all-knowing," she said. "I saw him as he used to be, not who he had become."

I wondered if Gaston had been telling the truth about Sawyer having a secret daughter. And if it was true, did Nona know about Wren?

My aunt didn't look like she could handle any more bad news. I didn't know how to help her, so I made some tea. I searched the cupboards until I found the bourbon and poured a liberal dose into Nona's tea.

"Nona, I know you're hurting, but you have to believe me," I said. "You and Naomi are in danger. Are you going to just let him get away with it?" I paced the length of her kitchen. "Gaston killed your husband. He tried to destroy the House of Fates."

"Who are you really angry with?"

I met her eyes. "I'm angry with whoever trapped Alex Abernathy in that labyrinth."

"You think that I had something to do with it?"

"I'm not accusing you of anything," I said. "But it happened right under your eyes."

"You didn't have to accuse me," she said. "I can see it all in your eyes."

"Elizabeth told me everything," I said. "How Morta kidnapped Alex, made a deal with Elizabeth to get her to break my heart."

She took a calm sip of her coffee, but her hand shook. "I didn't know anything about it."

"You let that monster terrify an innocent girl right under your nose."

"Innocent? Elizabeth Abernathy?" My aunt's tone said it all. She had a point.

"You should not make decisions when you are angry."

"Are you trying to help me or hurt me?"

"I have always wanted the best for you," she replied.

"Yeah, right," I said. "That is, when you didn't want me dead."

"You are your mother's son—sensitive, kind, and with her good looks."

"But?"

"There is no but," she said. "Despite our…estrangement, I wish you no harm. Others, perhaps, do not feel the same." I had a lifetime of proof that the Fates wanted me dead and now she wanted to be friends? It didn't make sense unless she'd finally found someone she hated more than me. Gaston.

"I've been considering your cease-fire," I said. "And I accept. At least until we trap Gaston."

"Done," she said.

"Why now?" I asked.

Her shoulders went tense, but she answered without a hitch. "Don't you think it's time? You are our only nephew."

"And Morta agreed to this?"

She turned her back to me as she loaded a plate into the dishwasher. "She sees the benefits. We want to bring you into the business."

Was she talking about the fate business or Parsi Enterprises?

"Morta's figured something out," she said. "A way to end it for you, even without a thread. Don't make her do it, Nyx."

"I'll think about it," I finally said. "But in the meantime, you'll work with me to trap Gaston?"

She nodded. "He will regret taking on the Fates."

"Weren't you kind of breaking the rules?" I asked. "Being married and all."

She looked startled. "There aren't any rules about marriage," she said. "Only…" She paused.

"Only no sons," I finished for her.

"That's because of the prophecy," she said and then clapped a hand over her mouth.

I didn't put any faith in prophecies about destiny. "Do you mean to tell me that my own family wanted to kill me just because some seer needed to make a quick buck?"

She shrugged. "We overreacted."

"What kind of prophecy?" I certainly wasn't going to share what Talbot had learned.

"I don't know," she said. "Morta's the eldest. She's the one…" Her voice trailed off uncertainly.

"I get it," I said. "Morta's the boss. Do you think she'd go along with tricking Gaston?"

I spent a restless night on their couch.

In the morning, I jumped up when I heard a noise in the kitchen. Nona was sitting at her kitchen counter with an untouched cup of coffee in front of her. She didn't even glance up when I came in. "Don't you want to punish Sawyer's killer?" I asked, trying to shake her from her lethargy. "You've been sitting around when you should be kicking ass."

"Nyx, you know that I can't interfere," Nona said.

I snorted. "What are you talking about? You always interfere. You live for it."

She shook her head. "Not anymore."

"Sawyer deserves better. Naomi deserves vengeance on the man who killed her father. Your husband."

Her head snapped up. "Things are not always as they seem," she said, finally meeting my eyes.

"That's bullshit and you know it," I told her. "You didn't think twice about ruining my life."

"Elizabeth was supposed to bring you back into the family," Nona said. "She wasn't supposed to break your heart."

"Well, she did," I said. I ignored the whole family-reunion thing.

"Forgive her, Nyx," she said. "Forgive yourself."

I knew we weren't talking about Elizabeth any longer. "I

don't blame my mother for dying," I said. "I blame you."

"It was her time."

"This is what I think we should do," I said. "We're going to stop Gaston from hurting anyone else ever again."

She gave me the first smile I'd seen since Sawyer died. "I'd like that. Very much."

"I need to see Elizabeth," I said. "But I won't tell her anything about what we're planning."

"That's a wise decision," Nona said. "She loves her brother. She'll do anything for him."

"She loves me, too," I said, but the words rang hollow, even to my own ears.

"Are you sure?" Nona replied. "Does she love you enough?"

I didn't know the answer to that question, but I knew I had to find out.

First, I had to put the plan in motion. It killed me to pick up the phone and call Gaston, but I was out of options.

"I have a proposition for you," I said. "But I have a few conditions."

"I'm listening," Gaston said shortly. I could tell that he didn't like the fact that I was finally showing some balls, but too bad.

He'd used Elizabeth to get to me. I'd been played and I didn't appreciate it. It was time to get a little of my own back.

The bastard was going to go down. He deserved to suffer as much as I had.

Maybe all that ambrosia they'd been giving him to keep him alive had finally rotted his brain.

"You said you had plans for the aunts," I told him. "How can I help?"

"I want you to steal something for me."

"What?"

"Snip, snip," he said.

"You want Morta's scissors?" I asked. "It'll take me a few days."

"Call me when you get it," Gaston said.

After I hung up with him, I said, "He bought it."

There was a short pause. "Good," said Nona.

I went to Eternity Road to talk to Talbot. He was with a customer, but he took one look at my face and shooed the guy out the door.

The door was barely locked before I spilled. "I am totally screwed," I told him.

"What has happened?"

I told him everything I'd learned. "I'm missing something," I concluded.

"Gaston knows more about your family's business than most," Talbot commented. "Do you think Sawyer was the one who raised the revenant?"

"I think so," I said. "But I don't know why. He seemed like he was in love with my aunt and she with him. She was devastated when he was killed. But I did wonder…"

"Wonder what?" Talbot prompted me.

"Why would he have a necromancer on his payroll?" The answer to my own question entered my brain.

"You've thought of something," he said.

"Maybe," I admitted. "But if it's true, it's pretty horrible."

"Tell me," he demanded.

"Alex mentioned that his mother talked to him. I thought he was just…unbalanced, but what if it's true? What if Gaston threatened Sawyer, got him to summon Alex's mother to drive Alex crazy? And then used the spirit to do his dirty work?"

"Why would he do that?" Talbot said. "That's monstrous."

"I have no idea," I replied. "But I'm going to find out."

Chapter Thirty-Nine

The next few days were spent drinking at the Red Dragon and waiting to hear from Gaston.

Talbot had Alex stashed somewhere safe, with wards surrounding him. I wasn't ready to reunite the siblings, not until I was sure it was safe.

I didn't like the idea that someone else was trying to kill my aunts. The prophecy said that was my job.

He finally called. I drove to the Mall of America, headed straight to the food court, ordered lemonade, and then took a seat. Gaston wouldn't do anything in public, not in the world of YouTube and viral videos.

"Did you get them yet?" He took a long sip of his orange soda.

"Not yet," I said. "I'm sure they're jittery because of Sawyer's death." I kept my voice cool, unconcerned, even though I wanted to punch him.

"I already nabbed the Book of Fates, but Morta is a little less trusting than Deci."

"I want it all," he said. "And when I get it, I promise you I'll help find your thread of fate and cut it for you. That's what you want, isn't it?"

"That's what I want," I said. I'd wanted to die for a long time. Why was I so uneasy about the idea now?

"Then we're in agreement?"

I crossed my arms. "Why do you think I can get the scissors when you couldn't?"

"Because you're from the Wyrd family line," he said.

"You can't touch them yourself," I guessed.

He frowned. "I've tried," he finally admitted. "It didn't go well."

"If you can't touch them, what good are they?" I asked.

He grinned at me. "That's where you come in. You steal them and hand them over to me. I'll be able to use them if they're freely given to me by someone with Wyrd blood."

"I'll do it, but the deal has changed," I told him.

"What do you want?" He didn't seem surprised. Probably because it was something he would do.

I named a sum that would make a Saudi prince gasp.

"You want that kind of money and you don't even know where to get what you need to acquire?"

"You mean steal," I corrected him.

"Semantics," he said. "I want you to steal Morta's golden scissors," he continued. "And then I'm going to cut her thread of fate."

"How am I supposed to find her scissors?" I said. "Or her thread of fate?"

"That's the easy part," he said. "I'll tell you where to look."

Gaston had been my aunts' pet monkey for a long time. He was most likely planning a double cross, but I didn't have a choice.

Morta lived in an elegant high-rise apartment downtown. No suburbia for her.

It didn't take much to slip inside behind a chatty couple and head up the stairs. The alarm would have been tricky, but Gaston very cooperatively gave me the code.

She kept her golden shears in, of all places, the sewing room. The thought of my aunt placidly cutting out patterns with the same scissors she used to end lives seemed ludicrous, but the evidence was right in front of me.

Rows of bright fabrics were neatly folded neatly on built-in shelving and an elaborate antique quilt hung on the opposite wall. The scissors were lying on a table covered by a partially finished quilt.

I reached for the scissors, but before I touched them my skin started to tingle.

I wrapped the scissors in a bit of fabric and slipped the bundle inside my leather jacket.

Then I saw it hanging above the fireplace mantel, where Morta would have to look at it every day.

A portrait of my mother. She wore a bright red dress and layers of charms around her throat. It was so like her, it was as if my mother were in the room with me. I touched the fine chain I always wore around my neck. She'd been wearing it when she died.

My throat closed up as I stared up at her.

"She was beautiful," someone said.

I froze and prayed that it wouldn't be my aunt Morta standing there when I turned around, but I knew it was. I was completely screwed, but I tried to play it cool.

"It looks nothing like her," I lied.

Morta scowled. "You don't remember her as I do." I thought I actually detected a note of regret in her voice.

I wasn't going to trade fond memories of my mother with the person who'd murdered her. "Did you hear about your little errand boy Gaston?" I asked.

"He hasn't proven himself unfaithful yet," Morta snapped.

"No, but you haven't seen him in days, have you?" I'd bluff my way out of this.

She ignored my taunting. "Tell us where your thread is."

"I don't know," I replied. "I hear you've found a way to get what you want without my thread of fate. So why haven't you done it already?"

"I wanted you to consider coming to work for us instead," she said. "I thought it would be a more palatable solution."

"I don't care what you think," I snarled. "Did it ever occur to you that I've never known where it is? That I'd cut the damned thing myself if I could find it?"

"You would deny yourself eternal life?"

"Everyone I've ever loved is dead," I said. "I'm alone. There's nothing here for me in this life. Find it and cut it. You'd be doing me a favor." I knew better than to let on how much Elizabeth meant to me, although from the gleam in her eyes she had a pretty good idea.

"We've looked everywhere," she admitted. I gave her a surprised look, but Morta ignored it.

"I thought maybe she'd hid it in plain sight," I lied. "Right under your noses." But as the words came out of my mouth, I realized it might be true.

Morta snorted. "She'd never leave it with us. It would be the first place we would look."

"But did you?" Her silence gave me my answer. I scanned the

rows and rows of threads hanging in neat rows, but I didn't find what I was looking for.

My aunt's gaze suddenly sharpened. "Tell us what you really seek."

I hesitated. "You won't believe me," I finally said.

"Try me," she replied.

I told her part of my theory, and to my surprise she didn't dismiss it. "Decima has been gravely ill," she said. "But we haven't been able to discover the cause."

"I think she may have been poisoned," I said. "Someone tried to slip me the venom of a golden frog in my coffee. I thought it was you."

"It was not," she replied. Her gaze sharpened. "You know who it was."

I nodded.

"Tell me," she commanded.

"You're not going to like it," I warned her.

"I do not like many of the things that come out of your mouth, Nyx Fortuna," she said. "But you are not a liar."

"How do you know?" I asked.

"Know thy enemy," she said. "I know everything about you. Or I thought I did. You managed to surprise me by coming to Minneapolis. Now speak."

So I did.

Morta gave me a smile that sent a chill down my back. "He will be dealt with, and you are going to help me do it."

I thought of the way the Tracker had bruised Jenny and man-handled Elizabeth. He liked to hurt women. I hated Gaston only slightly more than I hated my aunts, but I agreed to do it anyway.

We arranged to meet at the lake house. Elizabeth was already there when I arrived in my purple Caddy.

She met me at the front door. "I thought you'd never get here. Come in out of the cold," she said. She gave me a stiff little hug, but didn't even notice when I didn't hug her back.

Even though my back was turned, I knew the second Gaston arrived, still swilling his bottle of nectar of the gods. I hoped it choked him.

"Did you bring it?" Gaston said. He stared at the object in my hands. "Is that it?"

I nodded.

"Let's go into the kitchen," he said. "I'll make you some hot cocoa. My specialty."

He was playing the jovial devoted servant, but I could see a trace of panic behind his eyes. There was no way I was going to drink anything he served me.

"Where's the money?" I asked.

"Did you bring what I asked for?" he replied.

I handed it over and he opened the container. As I expected, he didn't bother to look closely at it.

I put the bottle cap on the table and sent it spinning toward him. "You foul traitor," I said. "You did it. You did it all."

"Nyx, what are you talking about?" Elizabeth said.

"I know you raised a ghost, attacked Talbot, tried to kill me, but what I don't know is why," I said.

"Why?" Gaston roared the question, and the genial mask he'd shown my aunts was stripped away to reveal his true nature. "Immortality, that's why. It took me years, but I finally got this." He held up a thread of fate.

"You wanted revenge and used me to get it."

"All those years of slaving for them," he said bitterly. "But have I been rewarded with immortality? No." The logic of a crazy man. Eventually, I'd have to track down the nectar-of-the-gods soda and destroy the formula, but right now I had bigger problems.

"You've lived longer than the average mortal. It seems to me you had a sweet deal," I said. "So why the sudden desire to take out the aunties?"

"Power," he said. "I want power. And they're in my way."

"You're willing to kill for it?" I asked.

"Your aunts wanted to kill you," Gaston responded. "But I liked you, Nyx."

"Weren't you the one who tried to blow my car off the road?" I asked. "And tried to serve me up as a water hag snack? Sent the harpies after me?"

"That doesn't mean I don't like you."

Liked me so much he'd tried to kill me, several times. He was still trying to con me, even after everything I'd learned. Why did he think I was going to fall for it? The nectar of the gods had obviously rotted his brain. Or he had a double cross planned. Or maybe both.

"And you also needed me to get what you wanted," I guessed.

"There was that," he said, apparently deciding that I was a lost cause.

"Did you know?" Elizabeth asked me.

I shook my head. "Not right away," I said. "I thought it might have been my aunts. It was Gaston the whole time."

"Why? Why would you do all this?" Elizabeth asked.

Gaston ignored her, picked up the container, and opened it. He held up a pair of golden shears.

I held my breath, waiting, but he stopped to gloat. "I had them fooled," he said. "They trusted me. With their lives."

"Gaston," I said flatly. "You are a traitor."

"You're a fine one to talk," Gaston said. "That's why I knew you'd do it. You hate them as much as I do."

"You've got me there," I admitted. I waited to see what he would do. If my theory was correct, he would be using those scissors very shortly. "But I never trusted my aunts and they never trusted me." At least not until now. Had Morta believed me?

He opened the canister and held the thread up.

"No, stop," I said, but without emphasis.

He took the golden shears, snipped the thread neatly in two, and threw the scissors at me. "I don't need these anymore." He picked up his bag and left.

Seconds later I heard a thud, the sound of something heavy dropping to the floor. I expected to feel relieved, but I wasn't prepared for the melancholy that enveloped me.

Nona and Naomi appeared. "Did you hear it?" I asked.

Nona nodded. "I heard everything," she said.

"I can't believe it was Gaston," Naomi said. "He taught me my first spell."

"You did well, Nyx," Nona asked. "My husband's death has been avenged."

"What happened?" Elizabeth asked. "I thought you were going to give him a thread of fate."

I put the shears in my back pocket. "I did," I said. "I gave him a thread of fate. Just not the one he wanted."

"Whose thread was it?" Elizabeth asked.

"Gaston's," I said.

"You mean…" She couldn't finish the words.

"He's dead," I said. "By his own hand."

"This sounds like a goddamned Greek tragedy," Elizabeth said. She glanced at me. "No offense."

"None taken," I replied. "I'm Roman."

Elizabeth plonked down on the couch and put her head in her hands. "You tricked him."

"He was a killer," I reminded her.

Naomi broke into great noisy sobs. I sat next to her and held her while she cried it all out.

"Can I see Alex now?" Elizabeth asked. "I have so much to tell him, so much to apologize for."

"First we need to call someone," I said. I hesitated and then added, "To take care of things."

"You mean to make sure that evil man is dead, don't you?" Naomi asked.

"That, too."

"I'll call," Elizabeth said. She picked up the phone and dialed. "My name is Elizabeth Abernathy. There's been a death. Could you come to the house right away?"

When she put the phone back down, her hands were shaking.

"I'll make you some tea," I said. I was getting to be an expert at serving tea to grieving women. I had no doubt that my aunts would grieve for Gaston, despite learning that he was not the person they thought he was.

"When can I see Alex?" Elizabeth persisted.

"As soon as we get things taken care of here," I promised her.

We waited in silence until we heard the ambulance pull into the driveway. The verdict was that Gaston had suffered a heart attack.

"He was so young," one of the EMTs commented. "And he had so much to live for."

"Not really," I said, in a voice, too low for them to hear. Gaston didn't have anything to live for, because he was consumed by hate.

Chapter Forty

After the ambulance had come and gone and taken the body with it, the Wyrd Sisters sat and stared at each other in some sort of silent communication. I paced back and forth. It's not every day that you end a life. I didn't know how my aunts could stand it.

"I'll be right back," I told them, although neither of them seemed to hear me.

I jogged out to the car to get my cell. I needed to call Talbot to let him know what had happened.

As I put it in my pocket, there was a cold trickle down my back. Someone was watching me. When I turned around, my aunt Morta stood before me.

"Why did you let me take your scissors?" I asked without preliminaries.

Her eyes were full of winter. She raised an eyebrow. "Take? Nobody takes from the Fates."

"You let me have them," I said.

"You did well, son of Fortuna," she said. "You have potential." Her long silver hair glittered like ice in the sun.

I crossed my arms. "Potential? Is that what you call it?"

"You dealt with Gaston with a ruthlessness to be admired."

"I didn't want to do it," I said. "I had to. There's a difference."

"Is there?" she asked, as if we were debating the merits of red wine versus white or something.

"Killing someone?" I responded. "It wasn't easy."

"It's not meant to be," she told me. "Still, I was impressed. I would like you to work with us."

"No," I said flatly.

"You don't wish to think about it?"

"No," I repeated.

Her face didn't change expression, yet suddenly there was an overwhelming air of menace in everything she said. "You will."

She left without another word.

I stared after her for a long time before I called Talbot.

"How's Alex doing?" I asked.

"He's recovering," Talbot said. "He and Dad have hit it off. But he's been dosed with bad magic for a long time. He has long screaming nightmares."

"That bastard," I said. We both knew I wasn't taking about Alex.

"How'd it go at your end?"

"He did exactly what I predicted," I replied.

"So it's all over?"

"I guess so."

But I kept waiting for the other shoe to drop.

Two days later, Alex came home. To be honest, I hadn't wanted Elizabeth to see him until he'd become a little more coherent.

He was skinny and shaky and squinted at the bright light of

day. Tough girl Elizabeth wept when she saw him walk through the door.

They holed up in the study, but I couldn't hear what they said. Alex and Elizabeth emerged hours later. Alex looked drawn and pale, but they both were smiling.

Alex was shaking so badly he could hardly stand. Elizabeth helped him to the sofa and he sank back against the cushions, as if exhausted. "It wasn't even about me," he said. "It was all about you." He pointed to me.

"Alex, it's not Nyx's fault," Elizabeth said. She gulped. "You don't know what he's done for you. That's why, that's why he…"

I didn't blame her for not wanting to put the horrible act into words. "It's okay," I said. I couldn't bear to touch her, even though I knew she hadn't had much choice. The whole experience had reminded me what a bad idea it had been to get involved. With her. With anybody.

And as if the world needed to remind me of that fact, the next day Elizabeth simply disappeared.

By nightfall, Jenny called, frantic. "Have you seen her?" she asked without preliminaries.

"Since when do you care?" I asked. "You let Gaston get his hooks into her without thinking twice."

"I was trying to help her find Alex," she said. "And things just got out of hand."

I didn't trust her, but there was real panic in her voice.

"Do you know where Elizabeth is?" Jenny asked.

"We're not exactly talking," I said. "Why?"

"Goddamn it," she replied. "I had hoped Elizabeth was with you."

A surge of adrenaline hit me and that's when I knew something was wrong. "When did you see her last?"

"This morning," she replied. "But she was supposed to meet Alex and me for lunch and she didn't show up."

"Why would you think she would be with me? She doesn't need me anymore, remember?"

"Oh, get over yourself, Nyx," Jenny said, with a familiar note of exasperation in her voice. "The girl loves you. They were holding her brother hostage. When are you going to forgive her?"

"I don't know." Forgiveness. It was a foreign concept. Hard to wrap my mind around. Could I forgive Elizabeth? Did I even want to try?

Jenny was still talking. "Alex is not taking it well."

"Tell him I'll find her," I said. "No matter what. And Gaston is gone. He can't hurt her."

"You tell him," she said. There was a pause and I heard Alex's quavering voice. "Nyx?"

I repeated what I'd said to Jenny and it, surprisingly, seemed to calm him.

I was sure my aunt Morta was behind it. Her face had been like stone when I'd refused to join the family business.

Even though I'd tricked Gaston into cutting his own thread of fate and saved their asses, it wasn't enough.

I hadn't enjoyed it. In fact, it made me sick. I was not cut out to be part of the Wyrd family.

I drove to Nona's and didn't bother to knock before I strode in. The three sisters were sitting motionless in the living room, as if they had been waiting for me. Deci looked emaciated. The poison was still in her system.

"You look like hell," I said.

She snarled at me, but it was a halfhearted effort. I had other things on my mind.

"So I guess the cease-fire is over?" I asked. The aunts knew what I'd ignored about myself. I would do anything for the one I love. I hadn't thought I was capable of love, at least not since my mother had died.

"What do you want from me? To beg?" I got down on my knees. "I'm begging. Let her go."

"A bargain, my boy?" Morta asked. "Your life for hers?"

I started to nod, willing to do anything to save Elizabeth, but my mother's voice rang in my head. "Never take the first deal you're offered."

"No," I said. "We need to set terms first."

Bargaining put a gleam into Morta's eyes. "Good."

"We need you to find someone for us," Nona said. I'd heard that one before.

"How long will it take?" I asked.

"That's entirely up to you," Morta said.

"Who am I supposed to find?"

Nona opened her mouth to speak, but Morta forestalled her. "Not until the terms are set."

"You set Elizabeth free before I leave," I said. "And she goes back to her old life without any more interference from you. You don't touch her or her brother. In fact, you forget they even exist."

"How do we know you'll keep your side of the bargain if we free our little bargaining chip?" Morta asked.

"Because I know what you'll do to her if I renege on my promise," I replied.

Morta let out a cackle. "Smart boy."

"Anything else?" Nona asked, clearly impatient for it to be done.

I almost didn't dare to say it. "When I find this thing

you're looking for, I'm done. I get to walk away. No repercussions."

"There are always repercussions," Nona said. She looked at her sister, who nodded. "But there will be none from us."

"Then we're agreed?" I asked.

"Agreed," Morta said. She spit on her hand and held it out to me. I copied her gesture.

I had a pretty good idea what my aunts would ask me to do. After all, they'd been hounding me about my hidden thread of fate for the last few centuries. I bet Morta couldn't wait to snap that sucker in half. She'd probably use her teeth.

But to my surprise, that wasn't the task they set before me.

"My daughter Claire is missing," Morta said shortly. "I expect you to find her."

"Missing?" I stared at her stupidly. "And what kind of witch is named Claire?"

"She's not a witch yet," Morta said. "Her training was…interrupted."

"What happened?" I asked. The thought of Morta reproducing made me slightly sick to my stomach, but I was curious about her daughter Claire. Did Decima have a daughter, too? Where were my other cousins?

Morta stared at me, her face expressionless.

"Oh, for god's sake, tell him," Nona said.

Morta remained mute but gave her sister a little nod.

"She ran away," Nona said bluntly. "Almost a month ago. We haven't been able to get a glimpse of her or where she is."

"The Tracker couldn't find her?" I'd assumed that he would have been the first person they sent.

I was right. "He was not successful," Morta said flatly. Of course, he might have had a reason to lie."

"What? Gaston couldn't find a trace?" If the Tracker hadn't been able to find her, I didn't stand a chance. There was something they weren't telling me.

I hesitated, glanced at Morta, and blurted it out. "Could she be dead?"

"No!" Morta shrieked at me. "She's not dead."

Nona laid a calming hand on her shoulder and Morta subsided. "We're sure she's alive," Nona said. "Something is obscuring our vision where she's concerned."

"You have one month," Morta croaked.

"A month? You have no idea where your daughter is and you're only giving me a month?"

I met Nona's gaze. "So much for trusting someone in the name of family."

She turned away. "There are extenuating circumstances."

"The circumstances are that you're a treacherous hag," I snarled, but my insults only seemed to make her sadder. If that was even possible.

"We need you to go somewhere that others are not able to travel," Nona said.

Morta handed me a photo. "This is her most recent picture. We are hoping that you will be luckier than the Tracker."

Luck? Is that what this was all about? I was the son of Fortuna, the luckiest person alive. They must be desperate if they were relying on me.

I glanced down at an attractive, sunny blonde of about twenty-three. She looked nothing like her mother or anyone else in the family. "Was she adopted?"

Nona and Morta exchanged glances. "She resembles her father," Morta finally said.

"Who is…?"

My question remained unanswered. I guess my family wasn't big on the issue of revealing paternity. We weren't ever going to be a normal family, but I didn't think they were out to kill me. At least not right now.

"All you need to know is that you were destined to take your place as a Fate," Morta said. "Not fall in love with a mortal and live a normal life."

"I don't believe in destiny," I replied. My aunts hadn't mentioned the prophecy. I found the omission very interesting. There'd never been a male Fate in the history of the world. Why were they suddenly talking up the job to me?

Morta left the room and returned with Elizabeth.

"Remember what I said," Morta reminded me.

"Like I could forget," I replied.

Elizabeth's hair was mussed and her eyes were red-rimmed, but she had pasted on a big smile. "You weren't kidding about your family," she said wryly.

I touched her face, trying to reassure myself that she was really there. "Are you okay? They didn't hurt you, did they?"

She let out a shaky laugh. "Nona baked me chocolate chip cookies."

Chocolate chip cookies couldn't take away the fear I sensed in her voice.

"I want to talk to her alone," I said to Morta. She gave me a long look and motioned to Nona and Deci, who followed her out of the room.

"They'll leave you alone from now on, I promise," I said.

"How do you know?" She'd put on a good front, but her voice shook as she asked the question. I hated my aunts for that.

"You're safe," I said. "My aunts will leave you alone as long as I cooperate."

"What happens now?"

"I have to find someone," I told her. "But you're out of it from now on."

"Do you have to go?" Her question ended on a sob.

"What do you think?"

She gave me a tiny smile. "I'm sorry, you know."

"For what?"

"Sorry I hurt you, sorry for everything."

Willow's face flashed in my mind. Not as sorry as I was.

"Do you still…care about me?" she asked. "Just a little?"

I took her in my arms. "I'll be back." I whispered against her hair. I would fight for her, even though, in my secret heart, I knew she didn't love me. In the history of the world, men had done much worse for a woman.

I wanted to ask her to wait for me, to tell her I loved her, but words failed me. Instead, I put into my kiss all the things I wanted to say but couldn't. I'd saved her brother. She was grateful to me for rescuing Alex and confusing that emotion with love. It wasn't love, but it was something. Maybe it could be enough.

Then I walked away, determined to make destiny my bitch.

Acknowledgments

I'm lucky to have so many great friends! Stacia Deutsch, Debby Garfinkle, & Alyson Noel—for the good coffee & advice and even better friendship. Collyn Justus—because she kept asking why. Mary Pearson and Melissa Wyatt for their emails chock-full of advice and support. Jessica Rothenberg for the brilliant feedback. My agent Stephen Barbara for his great sense of humor even when I lose mine. My editor Devi for her tough love. My family for understanding deadlines and still talking to me afterward.

extras

orbit

meet the author

Marlene Perez is the author of paranormal and urban fantasy books, including the bestselling DEAD IS series for teens. The first book in the series, *Dead Is the New Black*, was named an ALA Quick Pick for Reluctant Young Adult Readers as well as an ALA Popular Paperback. *Dead Is Just a Rumor* was on VOYA's 2011 Best Science Fiction, Horror, & Fantasy List. Her novels have been featured in *Girls' Life*, *Seventeen*, and *Cosmopolitan*, and Disney Television has optioned the rights to the first three books in the DEAD IS series.

She grew up in Story City, Iowa and is the youngest of twelve children. She lives in Orange County, California with her husband and children. Visit Marlene at www.marleneperez.com or at the Welcome to Nightshade Facebook Community Page at http://www.facebook.com/pages/Welcome-to-Nightshade-DEAD-IS.

introducing

If you enjoyed
STRANGE FATES,
look out for

DARK DESCENT

Nyx Fortuna: Book Two

by Marlene Perez

Nyx Fortuna is still reeling from Elizabeth's betrayal, but Nyx's cousin Claire has run away and he has to find her and bring her back or Elizabeth will suffer at the hands of his aunts, the three Fates. Claire has gone into the underworld of Minneapolis, where no one, not even the Fates, can follow. But Nyx must journey to a place where Hecate's dark magic has Claire in her thrall. Saving his cousin means releasing Hecate from her underworld prison and perhaps fulfilling the prophecy foretelling the Fates' downfall.

Chapter 1

"If I cannot deflect the will of Heaven,
I shall move Hell."

The whispering woke me up.

"Nyx, wake up, you're in danger." I recognized the speaker as Sawyer Polydoros, but that was impossible. I was on the couch, TV blaring, with a tower of empties on the coffee table beside me, but all I could hear was the sound of Sawyer's panicked voice.

It had to be a dream. How else could I be hearing my dead uncle's voice?

But I was the only son born to a Fate and stranger things had happened.

I inched up into a sitting position and listened, but the whispering had stopped.

There was someone in my apartment. Whoever or whatever it was barely drew breath, but a strange odor enveloped the room. Less pungent than a troll, but stinking of death nonetheless. A thin stream of moonlight lit the room enough for me to make out a long shadowy figure.

A wraith. I'd tangled with one a few months ago, managing to hack off its arms. I was guessing it was back for round two.

The thing was blocking the door between me and my bedroom, which is where my athame was. I'd need my knife if I had any hope of making it out alive.

There was another shadow by the front door. He'd brought a friend. Fantastic.

Sawyer's warning had given me a few precious seconds. The wraiths didn't know I was awake.

Wraiths used to be human and still retained a certain humanlike appearance, until you got close enough to look into their cold dead eyes and then you realized they weren't human in the least. By then it was too late. The trick was not to let them get too close or they'd rip out your heart and have it for a snack.

I needed to get to my athame. I jumped over the coffee table, but my foot caught on the cans and sent them falling. The noise distracted my guests for a split second while I made a run for the bedroom.

I charged the wraith blocking my way. As I had suspected, it was the same wraith who'd attacked me at Hell's Belles a few months ago. Its arm was missing, which meant it wasn't there to invite me to tea. I needed to finish the job this time or it would finish me.

Only a necromancer could summon and control a wraith, but Sawyer had been the only necromancer in Minneapolis, and he was dead. It was finally occurring to me that Sawyer might not have been the only necromancer in town, just the only one I knew about.

The wraith saw me coming, but I kicked its legs out from under it and charged into the bedroom. I headed for my athame, grabbed the handle, and pivoted, but the thing was already upon me.

The wraith opened its mouth and the smell of rotting flesh filled the room. I threw a lamp at it, but it kept coming. I choked back vomit and lunged for it. The knife went in with a wet noise and the wraith fell to the floor, gushing dark noxious blood all over my floor.

I'd momentarily forgotten about the other wraith. Until it came up behind me and bit me on the back of my neck.

My body went numb immediately. I fought to hold on to the knife as an icy sickness traveled down my spine.

"Nyx Fortuna, you will die this evening," it hissed.

It knew my name, but not that I couldn't die? Interesting.

"I can't die, you rotting piece of filth," I said. Or that's what I wanted to say, but my tongue was swollen.

It seemed to get the point of what I was trying to say, though.

"Not yet," it replied. "But soon." It clawed at my neck. I thought it was trying to rip out my throat, but it latched onto the thin silver chain around my neck and yanked.

There was no way he was getting the only thing I had left of my mother. I gathered my remaining strength and stabbed it in the eye. It shrieked with pain.

The knife clattered to the floor and then I fell beside it.